HOPE

Novel-in-Stories

Sommer Schafer

To John and Damyanti
Thank you

"The people dreamed and fought and slept as much as ever. And by habit they shortened their thoughts so that they would not wander out into the darkness beyond tomorrow."

- *The Heart is a Lonely Hunter* by Carson McCullers

HOPE

-1-

A Final Affair

In the middle of downtown Hope (described in the tour books as a "quaint and historical island paradise in Southeast Alaska") is a patch of fenced-in muskeg from which three licheny log posts peek, the remnants of a pioneer's cabin that started sinking into the muskeg the months following the 1954 earthquake and officially succumbed to the ground around the same time that the runway was built in '67. Wild blueberries and salmonberries grow there as do dwarf trees covered in lichen, wild roses, and a very hardy Swiss Chard that went rogue after an avid public-lands gardener planted twenty seeds of it in 1970. Long-timers and local historians believe that the cabin belonged to an un-named man who came up around 1905 to look for gold. Accounts from that time mention a white man, "hairy as a bear," who frequented the brothel, often sang "uproariously in the road exhibiting no shame" after visiting the bar, and, once he discovered that there was no gold on the island, put all his efforts into building a log cabin "about which he appears to know nothing." No one knows what happened to him, though by some accounts he went crazy and disappeared into the mountains.

In 1969, the Hope General Assembly agreed to officially designate the spot "a place of historical significance," and erected the fence and a placard with an artist's rendition of what the cabin might have looked like. And even though the cabin might as well not even be there, there are, after all, those three licheny posts, which lend a certain historical and mystery-tinged aura to the place.

Whenever old-timer Maggie Whitehall passes the sunken cabin on her walk from the library, she likes to imagine what Hope would have been like then: the one dirt road imperfectly hacked by the Russian missionaries into the muskeg and ash spewn from the eruption of Mt. Agnes 5000 years ago, sitting dormant one mile from Hope's shores. The crazy white man piecing together his cabin from felled spruce trees; working away at it and looking sexy while doing it. He'd be fit and muscular. He'd exude sweat and alcohol, tobacco and fire smoke. It would be dark and smoky in the cabin; it wouldn't keep the ocean wind or cold, rain or snow out at all. And beyond it would be a great wild humming quietness full of grizzlies, deer, bald eagles, ghosts.

Maggie was one of the first to come up as a nurse in 1945 when several hundred troops were stationed in Hope to defend the country from a possible Japanese infiltration from the Pacific. She still has fond memories of making out with Jim Johnson in one of the bunkers by the runway. He was the first one she let touch her breast, which soon became all too common with other men. She discovered how lucrative and satisfying it was to work evenings and nights in the "gentlemen's trade," which filled a gaping niche in Hope for all those sex-hungry men up for the war or fishing or hunting or business-starting. They were a varied bunch. Some hated the rain and boredom of island life; couldn't wait to get back to Oklahoma or California or Pennsylvania. Others had left behind acts of crime or unfortunate family names that would have destined them to lives of averageness or poverty. In Hope they started over again, pretended they were somebodies who took what they wanted and went on to open restaurants and Hope's first stores and became powerful and rich. Maggie called the shots, learned that she was good at it, and the men respected her seeming expertise, not for once taking into consideration that she simply had one of those fantastic imaginations and was in fact living the clandestine life she had always imagined for herself. Free, wild, unapologetic.

She is now seventy-nine and wears her black hair in a bulbously bisected beehive so that it rather looks like she's carrying a large, decapitated ant on her head. She has never once left Hope since 1945, not even the year her best friend got married back home in Philly or after the 1954 earthquake or the year her mother died or the summer of 1985 when it rained without stopping from April to mid-May and then again from September through November. There had been more suicides that year than any other, which is why Hope's two drug stores now stock lights especially designed to combat seasonal depression, which are available year-round. She volunteers at the library and is often seen walking slowly to and from there in her red polyester jacket, hands around stacks of books.

Somewhere along the way she also became known as Hope's sole witch, though many of the Tlingits know that that's just not true; that she's simply the only white witch in town and they can't account for her powers at all.

Maggie is one of those good witches, people say, but Holly, head barista at Lucy's Café, hopes, *hopes,* that she also works those less-than-good spells.

"She probably charges good money for those," Holly tells her Puerto Rican mother over the phone.

Holly likes to think of herself as a hardened hipster who dyes her hair black to hide the gray because who wants to see gray on a 28-year-old. Definitely not her. And then on top of that she favors streaks of barely visible purple to give herself the feeling of "purpleness," which is an aura that has always spoken to her in ways she can't quite define. But the hardened part is something she can't put her finger on, whether it's because of her run-away father or her high-strung mother or her aunt who always had a comment for her during her (horrible) teen years: *Vas a salir así? Dios mío!*

Hope had been that dream place for Holly, far from Portland and the big city, a place where you could know everyone if you chose to and not if you didn't; a place where you could really be free. You could also make a name for yourself, if you wanted, which is why she liked acting in the local plays where she favored loud, brazen roles and loved the make-up and costumes and the fact that people in town would recognize her afterward and say how great she was. The local radio station, KROAR, would let anyone have their own show, even if you had a stutter, spoke with the whisperings of a moth, or had a tendency toward uncontrollable laughter when nervous. It fucking didn't matter! But especially, Hope was a place where you didn't have to face the white face all the time and all that mainstream shit. You could just sort of be, but better yet, be exactly who'd you'd always *hoped* to be.

Holly met Maggie over coffee during her break one morning, having phoned Maggie two nights before expressing the need for "consultation." *Consultation!* Maggie had laughed loudly into the phone, which was one high-pitched burst. *Wherever could you be going with this, child?*

It was just to get a sense of her, Holly told herself, not being one to rush head long into things. Was Maggie sane or just some crazy old woman who liked to walk around with her hair all up? Holly knew of her and knew what people said. She was one of Hope's "originals." She volunteered at the library and the animal shelter. She ate every Thanksgiving in the community dinner at the Alaska Native Brotherhood Hall because she had no family. She had been a call girl back in the day when every Alaskan town had them. Some said she still was. She mostly kept to herself though everyone revered her.

And finally, here Maggie was, a small coffee table between them, drinking a mug of black coffee, shoulders slightly hunched as if she were trying to capture the heat from the coffee and direct it within. Holly noticed how smooth and pale her face was, only a fan of wrinkles extending from the corner of her eyes, skin hanging loose from her jawline. Her nose was long and thin, the bridge high but distinctly feminine; "lady-like," if there was such a thing. And what hair! Piled on and black as coal. But more than anything, it was Maggie's smallness that surprised Holly; the way her tiny body barely filled the space of the wooden chair; the way her wrist bones rotated like dials whenever she drank from her mug. And yet, Holly felt that there was something distinctly robust about her, whether it was because of the way she kept watching Holly, focused, even when people passed by, or the way she threw back the last mouthful of coffee in one quick, surprising motion, setting the mug back down without a sound.

Holly lowered her voice and bent her head over the remnants of brown milk foam sticking to the sides of her mug. "I'm having man, *husband* troubles. I may need some, well, assistance." And then lowered her voice more. "Spells and such."

From the beginning, Hope had provided Holly with so many delightful distractions. The white men, for one, who were tall and bearded and built, but only in that humble sort of way where you had to see them naked to really see. But then the effort of having to see them order their espressos from her even when they were already over or she was planning on telling them that they were going to be over that night, that afternoon, that moment. "It's over," she had told Ben over the foam in his latte, into which she nevertheless couldn't resist swirling a coffee-tinged heart because he was so sweet. Some hadn't taken it so nicely. Some had even been put off Lucy's Café for a time, instead going to Hope's second café, The Kingfisher, down by the docks.

Matt, however, had been different, and though he was fifteen years older, she had married him in a small wedding on a boat in the harbor. They had circled into the bay and followed an Orca and her two babies because seeing them was remarkable; a good token, people had said.

At first it was a dream life. The fact that they could drive down to the docks in the night and find his little skiff; that they could make that thing rock and roll, the wool blanket laid down, the metal ridges of the skiff's floor cutting into her back, one time seeing the lid-less eye of a salmon caught, staring at her from against the side, forgotten. The games of Scrabble in his rented wood-smoked cabin that let in the weather yet shared the esteem of the other sea-stung houses that hunkered against each other like barnacles, an enviable line on the small peninsula that jutted out into the harbor from downtown. You had to know someone to get into one of those places. And then José was born and time passed and he was a 2-year-old, and Matt would take him to the café so that Holly and the others could play with him, bring him bits of hot bagel or blueberry pie or smoked salmon quiche. Those were memories she still had, despite it all. Matt's other lovers soon came to encompass their little family like fringes around a quilt, sewn on tight. In the pure, blissful innocent early years, she could let it pass her over, assume the best, find fortitude in the immense love she thought she had for him.

Now, Holly cautiously raised her eyes to gauge Maggie's reaction. Maggie, however, was suddenly deep in the throes of deep and phlegmy laughter. The person at the next table turned to look. "I'm sure we can make something happen, dear," she said just as loudly, wiping away a tear.

Holly felt her face grow hot, something she was not at all accustomed to. She brought one hand to her forehead. Then she grabbed her elbows and gave them an imperceptible squeeze as if combating a growing cold.

"I wouldn't call them 'spells,' however dear," Maggie said quietly. Her eyes were little balls of black and the wrinkles around them seemed to quiver with joy, as if her eyes were silently laughing. Maggie continued talking quietly, and Holly suddenly realized that she felt violently indebted to her for the discretion, for who in her right mind considered spells by which to rid herself of a cheating husband?

And yet, why not? It was a different frontier here, after all. Anything could happen and anything did! Everyday, people in Hope learned to return to the sacred earth; to live off the land and forage like their ancestors; to build cabins with their own hands and commune with animals as if they were brothers and sisters. And witches, they were among the oldest, most sacred professions, of the earth and the heavens and Mother Nature. It is simply a returning, Holly thought, a returning to the way things have always been.

Maggie continued to talk slowly, quietly. She had the habit of sticking her tongue out, periodically, and swiping it across her lower lip. Holly watched her lips move. She knew then that Maggie's mind and will and personal power were of the highest variety. She couldn't help thinking that she and Maggie, they actually probably had a lot in common. They were women who had done and would do what they wanted. They could feel the magic of the natural world around them. They had been freed by it. Nothing like decorum would ever define them.

"They're more like *workings*," Maggie smiled, revealing browned teeth.

"Yes?" Holly stared into Maggie's eyes, feeling no more trepidation; feeling free and elated. We could be long lost relatives, really, couldn't we? she thought.

"But let's not talk of these things here." Maggie began to collect her things from the table and floor, her sweater and red jacket, her large bag, three books. Her gaze fell to the task as her little hands moved quickly. "I'll mail you a contract. Thus, I'll need your address." Then she stopped and looked at Holly again with laughing eyes. "No, I don't just know it, in case you were wondering. And, hon," she looked instantly grave, "I'll need to know just what exactly you intend. Whether you want your husband out of the picture or *out*, if you understand what I'm saying. The world is a complicated place, yes?"

On her walk home, Holly thought about Maggie's question. She had *never* wanted anyone dead, not her father for leaving them or her mother for forbidding dating or even that jackass fisherman Billy Wuthers who had smacked her a good one when she had dumped him, after which she had kicked him solidly in the balls and left him moaning and hunched over on the dock with the gulls screaming overhead. No matter how bad someone had been or could be, she just couldn't ever see them dying because of it. That's my one weakness, she acknowledged. I'm not badass enough. I couldn't, for instance, torture someone for information. But on second thought, she knew that if anyone ever tried to harm José, she could kill. Or at least severely maim.

She crossed the street at the four-way stop, walked past the Presbyterian church, and was soon in her neighborhood—the "old" Hope where she and Matt had bought a small single-story slat house with peeling shutters, lopsided cement steps a previous owner had added, and a rotting shed to the side in front of which she parked her fifteen-year-old Corolla and Matt stored his kayaks. Matt, however, hadn't lived there in 6 months. He had moved back into the little cabin on the jutty they had rented when they'd first married, though Holly knew he spent most of his nights with his latest girlfriend, Florentina, a visiting marine biologist from Switzerland.

Holly was thinking about the ways of killing and could see herself in every scene, a veritable Uma Thurman. In one, shooting Matt in the head. In the next, using expert martial arts to beat him, broken and hemorrhaging, to the ground. By the time she was home, she felt fierce and powerful; hot to the touch.

José, now eight, was sitting at the dining room table, which she and Matt had excitedly bought for $2 at the Hungry Hippo thrift store ten years ago, doing his homework. He was such a good boy. He didn't deserve any of this. She pulled out one of the chairs, sat down, and heaved an enormous sigh. She touched José's cheek and ran her hand through his thick black hair; thick like Matt's, black like hers.

When José's homework was finished they had dinner, washed up and went to bed at the same time because she was always so exhausted at the end of the day. But in bed, she couldn't help it. Couldn't help wondering about the reality of things, how some people stayed in love while others didn't. Some needed to roam; others could be happy, satisfied with things just the way they damn were.

Why had he married her? Matt began to muse moments after their ceremony was over and the Orca and her two babes had descended for good. His parents had gotten a divorce when he was a sophomore in college, though it hadn't come as a surprise. Afterward, when he visited his dad in the sleek silver condo his dad had bought before the divorce was final, he watched him field two, three girlfriends at once, incredulous and amused by his dad's sudden Don Juan-ness. His dad's happiness seemed frenetic, as if a dog long leashed suddenly released to the streets.

Matt was picky, and the sex was never right away. But it was almost always releasing, and not simply in the biological sense. In the psychical sense. He loved himself this way, and he loved every single woman he had been with. By the time he met Holly, he had slept with dozens of women but knew them all like the sparse freckles scattered down the length of his arms, or the constellations he could name when star gazing. When, at 35, one freckle looked like it was turning cancerous, he went in to have it looked at and thought again of Tiff, how he had heard just a week before that she had drowned herself in the river near her parents' house. She had been shy and timid at first, still a virgin at 27, but he had helped her come out of herself, even convinced her to take a trip with him to Costa Rica where they had watched the sea turtles lay and bury their eggs and then walk across the sand back into the ocean, leaving their eggs utterly behind, exhibiting too much blind faith in nature, he remembered thinking.

Matt had decided as a teenager that married life would never be for him. It probably shouldn't be for anyone. The matrilineal Maso in southeastern China, he had read in his Women and Anthropology class in college, accepted multiple men as lovers. No one married there; it was considered unnatural and impractical. It was a freer society, it seemed to Matt. Love and lust were given free agency, and people could be with each other in earnest without succumbing to the bullshit of pretense.

And so at his wedding ten years ago, with his and Holly's happy friends around them, and the orca family slumping their way into the bay, and Holly before him in her short white dress and off-white veil fashioned from old curtains found at the Hungry Hippo, he assumed he had married her because it would be different for him than it had been for his dad and, well, than it was for everyone else. He could take it to another, truer level in Hope, whatever that might be. He'd certainly have it figured out by then, he thought.

Yet there he was, having just said "I do," a gold band snug around his finger, and having absolutely no idea to what level his moments-old marriage had arisen.

Today he sees that, despite the uniqueness of life in Hope, he had foolishly fallen for it all. The wife, the house, the kid. The sex with Holly had always been good, even when he was with another; even when they were fighting. It was when she stopped talking to him in those moments of passing, the close encounters in the tight kitchen just before leaving for work, the intimate teeth-brushing in their small bathroom, the chatter of determining chores and other domestic-ness that were the true tokens of their love, that he knew it was coming to an end—had already been over for a while. Also, when they ate together on those rare occasions toward the end, trying to preserve the peace for José's sake, Holly would slam down the dishes of food on the linoleum table so that in between the silence, Matt smiling at José and José watching Holly bring his hoped-for favorites, there were great big spasms of sound, hardness coming into hardness. Sometimes, a handful of green beans would slide off onto the table; once, a slick piece of chicken landed in Matt's lap.

He believes he knew Holly wanted him out before she knew it herself, and so he simply left her a note one morning while she was sleeping, *I think it's time I move out.*

When Holly found the note on the kitchen counter, she couldn't control herself. She ripped the paper into a hundred pieces, squeezed them in her palm, and dumped them into the stainless-steel saucepan Matt liked to cook his omelets in, and set fire to the pile, watching the pieces curl and turn to ash.

The next day, they both sat down with José between them on the couch and told him how mommy and daddy were just taking a little break, kind of like the time he had to take a break from his best friend, Justin, who kept biting him when they were three. For an eight-year-old, he seemed especially mature, but Holly hoped this wasn't just to compensate for what she and Matt lacked. Shouldn't he be a bit more eight-year-old like, whatever that might be?

Maggie's contract came three days later in a used manila envelope with a piece of white paper taped across the front to cover the old address. There was no return address, but Holly knew. Inside was one lined paper. Handwritten in pencil, the letters were small and square-ish and perfectly proportioned.

September 24, 2005

Holly Lopez agrees to pay Maggie Whitehall $250 cash, plus two fresh king salmon for services rendered as follows:

1. Professional assessment of situation at hand, which is the desire to make Matt Adler disappear at the request of Holly Lopez, the aforementioned's wife. Such assessment may include research into Matt's whereabouts at all times of day, and an in-depth study of his routines and patterns of behavior. I reserve the right to follow him with discretion, gather pertinent information, and contact Holly with any questions that may arise.

2. The establishment of Matt's permanent residence outside Hope; that is, I will cultivate in him the desire to leave Hope, Holly, and José. Such "cultivations" will remain at my discretion.

At the bottom of the page was written:

Please be discreet. Holly, your word will act as acknowledgment and agreement. Call me upon receipt. 974-8854.

At the bottom, in elegantly sloping cursive, her signed name.

Maggie Whitehall.

Holly read it several times while perched on the seat of the couch, thighs tense, arm muscles clenched as she held the paper. Finally, she breathed, and then laughed once into the quiet room. That was her voice! That was she in the contract, about to take action!

She picked up the phone. Maggie answered immediately. She must have known I was going to call, Holly thought, and felt sparks of self-congratulation at having made her exemplary decision.

"And to be clear, dear," Maggie said, "you just want him out of Hope."

For a moment Holly couldn't imagine what she was talking about, and then she replied loudly, "Oh! Yes, yes, yes. Yes, just out of Hope. Really, I, I can't imagine . . . the other. It's not necessary. I think, I think José should have him in his life a bit. "

"Very good," Maggie answered and hung up.

Eight days later, Maggie had established what she felt was a satisfying, accurate, and in-depth assessment of Matt. She had never noticed him before, and now that she knew so much about him, she was beginning to feel somewhat warm towards him. He was just another human being, after all, and, despite Holly's feelings, not the devil. In her work, she always strived to remain both objective and driven.

First the obvious. He was of above average height, though Maggie herself would have classified him as "short" compared to the type she usually went for. He had a small-ish face with close-set eyes and a pointy chin, attractive cheekbones, dark eyes, long lashes, and the most incredible curly dark hair. He seemed at once aware of his most attractive features and indifferent to them.

He was a naturalist and spent his days working for the Department of Fish and Game. He had an office (the walls covered in topographical maps and a stunning photo of the Baranov Range, framed, above his desk) and spent some time in it, but spent most of his days in the field, taking boats or small planes out into the wilderness. He listened to classical music with a proclivity towards the Romantics, but also to Dave Matthews Band, the Beatles, and, often when cooking, jazz. He listened to New Age when he did yoga, which was almost every evening. He spent the majority of his nights with Florentina in her apartment out by the ferry. On Mondays he took José out to eat at the Three Amigos Mexican restaurant downtown where he always ordered the chicken chimichanga and José ordered nachos with beef, no onions. Maggie always followed, hovered, and sat at an unremarkable distance. She was good at this.

He had many friends who liked visiting when he was in his office. He always offered them coffee or tea from a little plug-in he kept on top of a file cabinet. They would sit and talk and laugh. When he walked around town, people crossed the street to talk to him. He seemed well-liked and loved. He liked to laugh but was never overbearing. Listened but always had something to add. The way he held himself reminded Maggie of some of the men she'd known in her day; leaning slightly on one leg with his hands in his pockets, chin down but eyes on the person talking; every so often taking his hand out of his perfectly-fit jeans and running it through the curls near his right temple, sometimes rubbing his fingers across the faint stubble at his chin. He doesn't even realize he's admired, watched, she thought to herself one afternoon while watching him from around the corner of the Russian Orthodox Church downtown. He doesn't care, and yet. He knows that this, this uncaring, is also precisely what makes him attractive! Afterwards, she rewarded herself for all her hard work by treating herself to a martini at the Seafarer's Bar. Men are such lovely playthings, she eyed herself appreciatively in the mirror across the bar.

When Matt wasn't with Florentina or José, he liked to visit an old girlfriend who worked as bank manager at Hope First Bank. She was married, so it didn't appear that either one was taking things too seriously. She lived in a mansion on the hill above the animal shelter in the new development. Her husband led hunting expeditions all summer and wasn't around. Matt often visited her Saturday nights. Maggie watched them in the hot tub until the cold of the night drove her back into her little Honda and home again where she could compose her notes.

Occasionally, she called Holly to keep her informed. She wasn't sure she liked Holly, who seemed just a tad too *something*—naive, hot-headed, so very young. And Holly tended to get just a bit too chatty whenever Maggie called. But checking in, Maggie knew, was part of the job, and doing a half-assed job was not her style.

"Well, now you know he's kind of a skank," Holly said during their first chat.

"Dear, *all* men are skanks," Maggie replied, already bored and regretting her decision to call that night.

"Oh dear," Holly was laughing. "You may be right! How right you *are*!"

Maggie sighed and felt suddenly and surprisingly sympathetic. Holly, the sweet girl, did have such passion. And, yes, she had been dealt a tough hand for the time being.

"He should have never cheated on you," Maggie found herself saying. "He's a nice man, love, and he should have known better."

Holly burst into tears. Hearing it said out loud like that, at long last, and from none other than Maggie, unleashed something in her, and because José was with Matt for the night, she could cry as loud and as hard as she wanted. "Fuck that Matt!" She screamed to the ceiling in between her sobs. Maggie pulled the phone from her ear and let Holly have her cry, though it was quite taxing and Maggie was having to muster up every last ounce of her patience. Should she charge more for this? Yet on the other hand, every girl needed a good cry every once in a while. She knew that. When Holly let it go on just a smidge too long, Maggie put the phone back to her ear and said loudly, "Yes, yes. But all is well. All is going well," and quickly hung up.

After two weeks had passed, a riotous thought came to Maggie one night at midnight as she roamed the low tide in the full moon, collecting bull kelp and mussels. There was something about Matt that was exceptionally unpredictable and manly. Unbearably sexy. She would have him herself! Of course–what a perfect way to kill two birds with one stone! She wanted him–desperately–and, of course, there was the matter of her contract with Holly. Had it really taken her two weeks to come to this conclusion? Two weeks of watching him order Americanos and rosemary bagels with sun dried tomato schmear at Lucy's? Two weeks of his hair washing and teeth brushing; of toweling off in front of the foggy mirror? Of his lean, muscular nakedness? Of his making love in ways that were athletic, admirable, spirited? Here was a man who was loved, admired. But he was also a man who spent many evenings of his returned bachelorhood alone, eating sandwiches with pickles and drinking beer. Who ate Doritos when he watched movies and read from a Kindle in bed. Who seemed to prefer kayaking at sunset, alone. What a delightful conundrum he was. One of her greatest pleasures was watching him sleep as she sat near his bedroom window, never once hearing a wayward snore or fitful mumble.

Instead, enjoying the calmness of his slumber; the smoothness of his skin; the tumble of his black curls.

Maggie knew it was Holly's day at Lucy's, so Matt would be at the Kingfisher. She walked down in her black miniskirt and her leather, high-heeled boots. She wore a tight, black low-cut blouse and a red padded corset underneath, the lacy edges of which she made sure were peeking out. She knew her breasts, as always, looked phenomenal and not simply great. In the cafe she hung her leather jacket on a hook by the door and spotted Matt alone reading yesterday's local newspaper, *The Daily Storm*, a mug of coffee by his wrist. After ordering a double latté, she walked over. "Do you mind?" Matt, startled, looked directly into her breasts before raising his eyes to her face.

She slid into her seat and balanced her forearms on the table. "I've seen you around." She cupped her latté between her hands and took quiet sips, her breasts rising with each sip. "It's too bad we've only met now." She extended her hand, then, and Matt eagerly accepted it.

"I know. Strange. I've seen you around too." Matt proceeded cautiously, as if he had a brand-new species in his hands. Before him, one of those Hope characters he had been content to let remain somewhere in his periphery. He had never had a chance to see her closely, had never even desired it. But now that she was this close, he couldn't think why their coming together hadn't happened before. She was really, well. Magnificent. Her cheekbones were like a model's, her skin smooth and flawless. Her large dark eyes seemed to spark. He thought that she couldn't be more than fifty-five. But wasn't she ancient? Hadn't he heard something about her being one of the originals? Yet here she was, inches from him, and one of the most beautiful women he had ever met. "You've been in Hope a while?" He feigned complete ignorance.

"Long enough!" Maggie sensed his delicacy, which made her laugh loudly. *I must relieve him of this ridiculous softness,* she thought.

"Not that you're old," he added.

"You're very handsome." Maggie addressed her coffee, then looked up and leaned forward, felt her breasts heavy on the tabletop and gently nudged them together with her wrists.

Matt turned red all the way to his hairline. He couldn't remember having ever been talked to so forthrightly, so wide-openly. Maggie was so surprised by Matt's adorable blush that she threw back her head, releasing a laugh that seemed to come from her very core. Her laugh was so contagious that Matt started laughing too, which relieved him of his worry about his ridiculous blush. What was he, thirteen?! When she stopped, she had tears in the corner of her eyes. She sighed and slid her hand under the table. Matt's hand was resting on the top of his thigh against his groin. She found it and cupped it, her fingertips barely dusting the side of his hiding penis.

"Can I take you out?" she asked.

"Why not?" Matt replied.

Maggie spent the morning, as every other, lathering a thick brown salve across her face, sitting in a straight-back wooden chair in front of her large oval mirror. The beveled edges of the mirror seemed to suck in and catch the loose ends of her hair wild around and trap them there, bending, doubling, tripling them in stasis. Next to the vanity, her king-sized bed. All the furniture had come with the house that she had been fortunate enough to buy cheap from an old boyfriend 40 years ago. He had been given the house from his grandmother who had deep Russian and Hope roots. When Maggie touched the smooth wooden canopy of the bed or laid her palms flat against the carved dining table downstairs in the formal dining room, she seemed to feel a throbbing life there; knew that the furniture at least was still humming with youth even if she wasn't exactly anymore. Now every realtor in town was waiting for her to die so they could get their grimy hands on her house upon the hill, and every priceless item in it.

The salve stunk like dead fish and tasted salty. She spread it into the sides of her nose, to the edges of her ears, and across the seal of her lips. She closed her eyes and delicately spread it across her lids. She hummed a made-up tune to herself while sitting there, waiting the requisite three minutes, and rocked back and forth in her chair, listening to it creak with every rightward lean. The tune was one she had invented one night, decades ago, after enduring a client's rough treatment. When he had awoken, he couldn't move his body, the pain in his back and ribs excruciating. He saw her smiling and naked above him, standing in a straddle, her ankles squeezing the sides of his chest like vises, her long hair hanging down over her breasts. *I'll just take this money*, she'd said, showing his wallet in her hand. *You've been a doll.* She left him there, paralyzed in pain. It was then that she realized she had abilities. Magic, the locals would come to say. But she knew they were wrong; that people were such silly stupid beings, always needing mystical or religious reasons to explain the unexplainable. But let them think what they want, she thought. The truth was simply her strength, her incredible resolve to not be overtaken or used; pushed around or told what to do and how to behave.

There were few women like her, who didn't give a damn, who hated slovenly gossip. She dressed exactly how she wanted. She wasn't afraid to show her substantial cleavage one day or button it all up another. She still wore short dresses if she wanted. Her legs were still strong and shapely if a bit loose in the thighs—who cared.

She had hated those cliquey women in Hope who owned the shops and attended the same churches; who were active in the Rotary and Chamber of Commerce; who appeared in *The Daily Storm* every time they farted. They dyed their hair according to group-declared fashion; they hated lovingly; they distrusted; they flew to Seattle on shopping trips and came back with jewelry and expensive facial cream and new supplements. When she thought of Janet, the worst of them with her fake blond hair and mansion by the ocean, with her Lexus and prejudices (of course Maggie noticed when Janet looked down at her through her black square-framed glasses, in just the way that she looked at the Tlingits or the grungy boat people or Jack the town drunk or the tattooed folk up to work the cannery all summer), she thought about Janet falling sick and simply wasting away without fanfare. And when that was exactly what happened, fifteen years ago, Janet dying from colon cancer, slowly, unexceptionally, Maggie thought for the first time that that whole process, the thinking of it, the wishing of it, the coming true of it, all did in fact signify some kind of magic. Or, more factually, some universal tendency toward justice that perhaps just maybe she had at her control.

Maggie pulled a clean, disposable facial sponge from the bag in the top drawer of her vanity and slowly wiped off the brown stuff. She had experimented for years to find just the right amounts of sea kelp, herring eggs, devil's club, sand, and lichen. She had gotten the idea from an old Tlingit acquaintance, Elga. The salve left her face fresh, clean, and smooth. Why did she still feel as if she were in her twenties? *In your heart, inside, you still are,* she told her reflection, and smiled, lips closed. High cheekbones, tight skin except perhaps a bit around the eyes and jaw, hair gone pitch black instead of white. The Chinese believe that eating black sesame seeds will keep hair black, will in fact turn it black if already gray. Nothing was beyond possibility. Life continually amused and surprised her.

The mirror reflected the world outside her wall of windows behind. In the mirror she saw the silver wash of burgeoning early morning light as it bounced between sparkling ocean and a gray sky. Just above the large dome of St. Ignatius she saw the tips of the bridge crossing the channel to the airport. She remembered when, before the bridge, locals had to take a ferry to cross the channel.

In the reflection, she admired the lines and angles of the downtown roofs; the pieces of silver ocean coming through gaps in the buildings; the spruce-thick miniature islands seemingly floating in the ocean just off shore; the white beacon heads of the bald eagles popping out here and there on the tips of spruces. There, the white fence of the sunken un-named pioneer's cabin, hiding forever in its mysterious history. It hit her, then, as it hadn't before.

None other than Hope was her elixir. There was one massive, thick root that attached to the center of her heart, tangled through her body, hot and moist and pulsing with life, and continued out of her, invisibly, into the ashen, muskeg bedrock of Hope. And there it grew and thickened and kept her like one of the island's massive, ancient spruces where it would keep her forever.

Maggie and Matt met at the Hope Lounge just as the summer sun was beginning its long, slow procession into the ocean. Maggie wore a red dress that rode her body in all the right spots—around her shoulders and breasts, at her hips. It fell loosely to just above her knees. The sweep of the neckline low enough to show off her neck and collar bones, but stopped, purposefully, just short of cleavage. Matt could see more later if he wanted, she smiled to herself. People didn't dress up in Hope; seemed to want to defy that behavior as if it suggested, at most, the despicable bourgeoisie; at least, the mainstream agenda. But Maggie had a hundred dresses in her closet and always loved the chance to wear one.

Matt wore his usual, but this time he put on the blue button-up because it highlighted his dark hair and blue eyes. Why had he gone home after work to pull a brush through his curls? Why had he checked himself once, twice, in the mirror? Why, for god's sake, had he brushed his teeth! He knew the quickening of his pulse like nothing else. It meant, as it usually always did, the beginning of something incredible.

"Aren't you . . ." Matt thumbed his sweating glass of beer as they sat perched on bar stools at one of the small round tables by the windows that overlooked downtown and the ocean. "Forgive me for being so . . . upfront." He chuckled and looked at her, took it all in at once: the red of her dress against the white of her neck, the delicate-looking bones at her collar, the firm bulge of her breasts, her long arms and fingers, delicate wrists. She had thick full lips and large eyes thinly lined in black, eyelashes long and dark. "But aren't you, well, older?"

"Oh?" Maggie smiled and sipped her margarita, licking the salt from her lips. "Don't tell me I look it."

"No! Just heard things about you." And, for the first time, he reached over and softly touched the top of her hand with his fingertips.

This is his way of apologizing, Maggie thought. The tenderness of his touch shocked her, made her want to love him instead of hating him for expressing forgiveness and, in there too, pity. Still, she had to set him straight.

"I'm seventy-nine," she watched him closely.

"What?!" He snorted and brought the hand he used to touch her to his thigh where he slapped it. "I don't believe you." He stopped laughing and took another mouthful of beer.

"Believe what you'd like," she smiled into her martini glass. It was all gone. "I'm getting another. And you?"

They ordered more, and this time food too. Hamburgers and french fries. Afterward, they split a strawberry milkshake by sipping from the same straw, just like teenagers, Maggie mused.

"I don't usually eat this much," Matt exhaled and stretched back against his chair, lifted his arms up and over his head. Maggie saw how his biceps thickened under his long sleeves. Not being able to see them completely excited her, as did the sudden urge to want to explore his body. "But it's so good."

Afterwards, when the sun had already set, he followed her up the hill to her house, watching her bottom and hips move under the silky cling and flow of her dress. When she turned and laughed at his slightly drunken amble, he noticed how her breasts and dime-sized nipples stretched the fabric of her dress there and seemed to ache against the confines of the neckline's modest V. They needed to be free! Just let them be free! He imagined one of them slipping out at the neckline. He imagined his mouth sucking on a nipple, feeling its heat and shape with his tongue. She reached back and took his hand. She led him like a schoolgirl about to lose her virginity, the two of them breathing quickly from the climb up the hill. The novelty of sleeping with someone thirty-six years older inspired Matt, as if he were a grand adventurer exploring virgin land, and he remembered again when he lost his virginity at fifteen to Melissa Adams, a senior geek who dressed terribly but was sexier than hell once she was naked and let her hair be messed with. Since then, Matt had learned that the body could do miraculous things, if you let it. If you learned to not think too deeply about it all, but just enjoyed it. Even at fifteen, he figured there were only so many decades left of his lovemaking, of any person's lovemaking.

In Maggie's bedroom, the windows bare, the walls in textured red wallpaper, the canopied bed in shadow, she stood by the side of the bed and pulled her dress over her head in one quick motion, completely naked. My god, she hadn't had any underwear on! He hurriedly undid his pants and kicked them to the side. Her body seemed to glow in the faint light of the cloudy night coming through the windows spanning the width of the wall. It was only the surprise of her eerily youngish body that stopped him, for a moment, from rushing to her across the soft wool carpet. Who gives a damn! he told himself, and went to her, pulling her down with him into the marvelous softness of her massive bed where she stayed on top, rhythmically, unceasing, until she threw her head back and hollered.

Afterward, still tingling from the effort, he looked up at the dark canopy, long, loped vines carved into it, wrapped around each other as if mating eels. With Maggie's arm across his waist, he thought about how Victorian it all felt. How he was the dashing young man who captured, scandalously, the hearts of all the ladies.

How could one ever get enough of the female? How could one ever limit oneself to just one? The eye catching, the flirting, the not-yet-knowing, the wondering, the fantasizing, and finally the knowing. The wonder of the knowing. It never got old.

Matt and Maggie had been together, most nights, for one month when Holly called.

Any more news? What had Maggie decided and when would it happen? Had she heard that there was talk that Matt had taken up with yet another woman and couldn't you just hate him for that?

Maggie took the call in the hallway on her way out to the library, her afternoon to volunteer. The antique mirror she had found at a thrift shop many years ago in Juneau hung above the hallway table, and as she talked and looked into it, she couldn't help admiring how fresh her complexion was now. How constant sex would do that to a person. How could she have forgotten? And then, deep inside, she thought what a bore Holly was. Really, why couldn't she just lighten up? Embrace the true animalistic nature of humankind. The truth of the matter was that Maggie was having more fun than she had had in years, and she knew she wouldn't live forever. But there was the matter of the contract, and Maggie had never, not once, gone against her word.

"I have my solution," she spoke calmly into the receiver while looking into the mirror and fingering some stray strands of pure black hair, tucking them gently back into her updo.

"Really?" Holly on the other end wanted to grab Maggie and give her a great big, massive hug and then plant a kiss grandly on her smooth old lips. Oh! Maggie, the earth mother goddess; the bringer of ancient magic thought long dead. Wondrous things happened in Hope!

"Listen dear," Maggie looked at her watch. "I'm late for the library. Must run. In one week Matt will be gone, love. You have my word." And it felt good for her to say those words out loud, hear them inside the dark hallway, see them grow legs and arms and run crazily around mid-air, running up against the walls and doing flips off them. Those words were positively elated.

Maggie kept having the same dream. She was young again, which meant bag-less eyes and rounder more muscular hips, a tinier waist and thick hair all the way to her bottom. She was balancing on the ridge of the crater on the top of Mt. Agnes, looking down into its center, the waves crashing 5000 feet below. The wind was blowing in from the ocean. It was warm and smelled of summer and salt and kelp. She felt the air around her neck as her hair lifted, and realized that she hadn't smelled a wind like that in decades. A chinook. She hadn't attempted the hike to the summit of Mt. Agnes in thirty years. When she turned, there was Matt, looking at her and smiling. She grabbed his hand, and they stepped off the ridge. Without falling, they flew forward across the whitecaps below. They descended just enough so she could feel the tickle of the waves against her bare toes.

One night, Maggie held Matt in her arms, naked under the silky sheets of her bed, and ran her long fingers through his curly hair. *Those fingers*, Matt thought, eyes closed.

"Let's get away," Maggie whispered into his ear and then planted her teeth into his lobe, gave it a quick, hot lick.

Matt laughed. "In the middle of summer? It's the best time to be here."

"Come on," she whispered. "You pick. Let's go. It'll be fun." And she rose up on her elbows and looked down at him, intentionally letting her nipples play across his chest.

"You're hilarious," he laughed, and lunged for a nipple, sucked it into his mouth, still couldn't get over the fact that it never felt flaccid, used, old.

She felt her body tense. He stared up at her, and noticed again the strange, loping carvings in the dark wood canopy above. Were they moving?

"You think I joke," she said it louder than she intended, saw those words brandish swords and fight each other until banging up against the carved canopy and popping.

His eyes were the most expressive part of his face. She had always known that about them, large, round, dark like bottomless tidepools. She saw in them now surprise and wonder and, most of all, pity. Pity!

"Maggie my love," he looked away to the wall of windows where a bright half-moon illuminated the bridge and the calm ocean below; cast shadows against the ocean as if the moon were a more guarded sun.

"This, whatever this is, is," he paused, "well, simply out of this world. Right?"

She was still on her elbows, watching him.

"You are . . . magical. You are other-worldly. This has been more than anything I could have imagined." He stopped and closed his eyes, though his lips still held a faint smile as if he were at that moment imagining everything they had done, had *been* together. Really, though, he was hoping the subject would drop. That Maggie would forget all about it, the fact even that she had asked it. Didn't she understand that he had José? He had Florentina and his work and his life in Hope? How is it that she of all people couldn't understand that this had been, they were, a *fling*?

Maggie, then, saw Holly's round face like a hologram before her; her deeply made-up eyes and purple-streaked hair; her astounding youthfulness. Innocence.

She sank back onto her pillow and took a deep breath. Held it impossibly long. And she had thought the girl silly, naive; was sure this would be an easy one. She had been an old fool, was losing her game or too much in her game, couldn't be sure of which. Her understanding turned quickly into despair, which was almost immediately decimated by that round, whirling ember of energy that was always there at her core; the thing that was a part of her power and control, that had always allowed her to act with disregard, conviction, expertise.

"What are you saying, Matt?" She continued to look up. He turned to her, discouraged to hear in her voice the tones of coolness he had heard in the voices of so many women over the years. He had thought, given who she was, that she'd be different.

"What we have is good the way it is, Maggie." He rubbed her thigh under the sheets. "Why would we want anything more?"

She grabbed his hand and squeezed it, turned to her side and pulled him to her with her legs. She felt his bottom ribs with her knees and his waist with the inside of her thighs. She pressed her vagina against his bellybutton. She squeezed his waist between her thighs, squeezed it just short of breaking a rib, puncturing his liver. Finally, "I can't breathe," he whispered. She softened her thighs and nuzzled his neck, kissed him with all her power, felt his erection under the pads of her fingers. They made love again, with the energy of the very young and free.

The fenced-in patch of muskeg in the center of downtown soon relayed the light of the coming day. The dim reddish light of the early morning, dissipated and enriched by the ocean at the edge of the land and the water particles somersaulting in the air above the waves, suddenly found the old cabin posts poking out of the muskeg and cast them in faint red light slowly turning orange. It spread out across the spongy, moist ground below which the cabin of the un-named man was being held in slow decay, bringing out of shade the tiny plants plastered to the ground and the bushes of ripening salmonberries. And as the light spread across the ground, it grew oranger until becoming more brightly golden, encapsulating the refractions of the lightening sky. The light found the little fence that the city had built around the plot of land twenty years ago and turned it a brilliant white. Then, there, Maggie's smooth white hand against the peeling fence. Holly inched in to find warmth there near Maggie's bird-like rib cage, the two of them bundled into wool coats and rubber boots, Holly's purple-streaked black hair covered by a purple beanie she had knitted, and Maggie's uncovered beehive updo.

"He'll be a missing person, that's all." Maggie pointed a long, painted fingernail into the center of the muskeg. "I'm sorry it had to be done." She gently placed her hand over Holly's.

"I see." Holly was aware of being so close to Maggie, finding herself strangely attracted to the old woman, some kinship there never found with anyone else, not her mother, not her aunt, not her son. Not anyone.

Maggie turned to Holly just as the sun pierced her black eyes, but she didn't shade them; she stared straight into Holly. "Are you pleased?"

Before answering, Holly thought quickly of Matt's body in there, in the muskeg at the center of Hope, the, yes, almost perfect irony of him being there in the middle of it all but, for once, going completely unnoticed, and she wondered if she could detect any regret inside herself, any sparks of sadness. There was nothing but a quickening of her heart, an almost discernible elation. She touched Maggie's elbow affectionately, respectfully.

As the sun lit the roiling sky above the ocean, clouds tumbling and moody, it continued to wash the square of muskeg there in the middle of downtown Hope (whose sidewalks and stores were unnoticeably sinking too) in large swathes of orange and yellow, the patch of land enlightening like a beacon.

The tourists were already coming in off the ships, the first ones slung heavy with cameras and fanny packs and layers of sweaters and raincoats, urgently accosting the sidewalks and streets, mission-driven in their greed.

"Oh look!" one said as she rushed ahead of her husband. "There it is! I read about it in the book. A real pioneer's cabin, honey!"

But her husband, heavy paunch leading, seemed disgruntled.

"Hmph," he rumbled to himself. "There's nothing there, Beth. Nothing there at all."

-2-

Space

One week after Hope's meth lab incident and exactly one day after Mayor Marc Randal's 30-foot boat exploded in Sealing Harbor, with one large black and white photo of the scarred thing spread across the top half of *The Daily Storm*, Alan Neuman met Blake Lindstrom coming down the trail leading from the gravel parking area to their adjacent plots of forested land atop the rocky cliffs plunging into the Pacific.

On this side of the island, the people lived in hand built cabins that merged so seamlessly with the towering spruces, draped in long beards of pale green lichen above the spongy, ashy earth, that it was hard to distinguish house from forest as one drove by on Out North Road, as if the homes were in fact eruptions of the cold mossy ground and the people inside damp creatures of the earth who had long ago refused alignment with the rest of the (intolerable) human species. The homes, well hidden from the road. No one wanted to be reminded of how close they were to civilization, and who wanted to hear the occasional passing car when they'd come this far to get away from it all? The land here so dense with forest, it was like a single living being.

There were only six zoned plots along this stretch of Out North, quickly purchased when they went up for sale 50 years ago.

Blake's 96 square foot wooden clapboard house was the only structure on an undeveloped plot a quarter mile from the road next to a tumble of rocks leading down to a sliver of rocky beach. He and his wife, Anna, were lucky enough to have bought it from the original owner, a real pioneer man, three years ago for $1,000. The furthest plot from the road, just as they wanted. There were rules to living there, though, which was part of the appeal for Blake. All owners had to sign a contract not to build driveways down to their area or cut down a single tree before first all coming to an agreement. All had some form of electricity and plumbing except for Blake and Anna and their two-year-old daughter, Sasha, who used a composting toilet outside, a wood-burning stove, and a battery-operated lantern when needed.

Their closest neighbors were the Neumans who had built a beautiful three-storied log "cabin" several years ago, with a small glass-enclosed tower from which Alan liked to watch the ocean and sky through his telescope, and a large four-person hot tub set into their wrap-around deck jutting out over the edge of a cliff. They also had installed a TV satellite that discreetly defied gravity from under their garage roofline.

When Blake met Alan that day, Blake was heading down with four two-by-four studs tied together with rope, balanced on his shoulder. He was going to frame a smokehouse so that he and Anna could smoke their own salmon instead of having to trade with friends. His right arm was slung over the load, which left his other arm free to push away spruce tree branches and huckleberry bushes in his path. His red beard barely touched the collar of his used flannel shirt tucked into a pair of brown overalls that he wore every day until Anna washed them Sunday afternoon and hung them to dry by the wood burning stove. He owned exactly two pairs of overalls, one pair of pants, and a pair of jeans he had bought used at the Hungry Hippo. He had six pairs of wool socks, one pair of tough-as-hell leather boots, and a pair of white tennis shoes that were now gray.

"Hello Blake," Alan nodded as they passed. He had a jowly, slightly too pudgy face. It suggested years when it had been a narrower, leaner face. Strands of short brown hair stuck out around his temples from under his colorful Swedish wool hat that, unfortunately, would eventually make his skin burst into a flaming itchy rash.

"Alan." Blake looked up at the older man and noticed how smoothly his face was shaved. *What an exercise in vanity*, he thought as he turned his head back down to watch his footing. *One needs mirrors for that.*

It was hard maneuvering on the trail. The studs kept flipping through the forest every time he made a turn, spraying spruce needles into his beard and across his shoulders. He also had to edge past Alan without knocking him down, though it was something he was considering. Alan and his kind were the ones who wanted it all—nature and comfort—who didn't seem to understand the true meaning behind making the conscious decision to live in the woods—the value of sacrifice and lifestyle change—who didn't want to make any real connection with the land. But there was also the thing that Alan had done, which couldn't be made less by the fact that he was simply one of thousands, millions, *billions* of idiots spreading across the planet. No, this was something Alan and Alan alone had done.

One week before, Blake and Anna were outside harvesting the kale and chard in a tiny space atop the rocky cliff they had dumped soil into two years ago and turned into a garden just below the shed. Anna stopped for a moment to take a breath and look out at the ocean, and then let out an "oh."

"What?" Blake asked, looking back to the dirt landing by the doorway to check on Sasha playing on her blanket with a wooden car he had made, sanded down expertly and polished so that Sasha would not get a single splinter.

"Look," Anna said.

And when Blake stood and looked in the direction of Anna's gaze, he saw the blinding gap in the Neuman's treeline where several tops of the second-growth spruce trees blocking their view of the ocean from their deck had been cut.

"What the *hell*," Blake felt his breath lodge as if it were a mass in his throat. He felt suddenly assaulted, violated, and yet not at all surprised. He tried to swallow.

Later that evening they wondered how Alan and his wife had managed to do it, as old and unfit as they were.

"Are we going to let them get away with it?" he asked Anna.

"What are we going to do?" she said. "Get them arrested?"

"That's a start," he had said between bites of their dinner of hot baked potato.

That was Alan, all right, Blake thought as he now kept his head down and bludgeoned his load by and along the tight trail. *Get out of my way, fool.*

"Looks like the Mayor was involved in that meth lab cover-up, huh?" Alan stopped and said as Blake was about to walk down the shallow decline in the trail deeper into the woods, eager to disappear into the one place he felt most happy. He always took this part carefully and slowly.

"What now?" Blake turned. His blue eyes shot up at the older man as he tried to remain calm, unaffected.

Blake had nothing against Mayor Randal. The mayor was against city government and was doing his best to relinquish its hold, especially on those parts of the city that seemed to be constantly demanding more money, bleeding the town dry—the library, the fire department, the police department, the health clinic, the school board, the local branch of the university, and now the ridiculous addition of an affordable housing manager who Blake was hoping the mayor could run out of town before the year ran out. Just another example of how stupid and lazy people were; always looking for a handout when they very well could secure a piece of land like he had and learn how to build something meaningful on it. It would take work, sure. He had cut himself countless times, including that time he had accidentally cut off the tip of his thumb. And when Anna had gone into labor and was prepared and ready to give birth right on the hard wood floor of their shed with the midwife right there, and when the blood started coming and the midwife was telling her she needed to be in the hospital *now, immediately*, that something wasn't right, that the baby would die if they didn't get help; well even then, they had been adamant they would birth at home, and Anna had managed to push through and Sasha came out, healthy for the most part. The midwife, who they sometimes saw around town, still wouldn't talk to them, but they hadn't thought she was that great anyway. What was the term for people like her? *Fake.*

"Don't you think it's a strange coincidence, you know, his boat blowing up after the whole meth lab discovery? And, come on, the mayor not knowing about what's happening on city property? I don't think so."

"I wouldn't know, Alan." Blake began to turn. This wasn't worth his time. The mayor's personal business was his own business.

"Well, hopefully he's out soon. Can't run again next election, even if he wanted to."

"I like him," Blake turned around from the shadow of an overhanging spruce. "He fought to keep the deep-water dock out. I'd vote for him if he ran again."

Alan looked at him from his spot higher up the trail and smiled. "Well, Blake, we're all allowed our own opinions, huh? See ya around, and good luck with that, whatever you're building."

"Thanks," *asshole*, Blake added to himself, and turned back down the trail, struggling to breathe through the anger beating in his throat, though his face was as always: expressionless, masked by red beard, eyes calm-seeming feathered by corner wrinkles that looked gentle and pure, hard-earned by steadfast work outdoors.

Last night suddenly played through his mind, and it calmed him; made him smile, even, into the tips of his boots. How he had walked over to the Neuman's house through the black woods of midnight, his ladder on one shoulder, the sky darker than usual, obliterated of stars and moon. He was careful not to get too close to the cliff edge as he listened to the crash of the waves against the rocks, though he loved that soothing sound, the crash and splash and pull of reckless water against land. Once there, he found the Neuman's satellite , opened the ladder quietly on as level ground as he could find, climbed up, balanced on the top with one hand against the garage, and clipped the wires with his large steel clippers. The job was easy, exhilarating, and satisfying. He had taken action; hadn't just sat there—never *would* just sit there as his mother-in-law did, growing soft from too many massages and manicures in her New York City life. Afterward, he carried the ladder back by the trail and, once home, put it back in the temporary canvas shelter that was bigger than their house, bringing the clippers inside where he hung them on their hook by the door. Then he climbed into bed with Anna on his side, who was nursing Sasha in the darkness.

When he reached their place, his arm was starting to lose circulation from holding the studs. He let them crash down on the ground by an open spot behind the shed that he had cleared for the smokehouse. He turned to see if smoke was coming from the pipe on the roof of the shed and saw that it was. He walked onto their deck, past the bathtub outside by the door from which they could see the ocean and bathe (oh, the pure heaven of that), and into the heat of their tight home where he saw Anna peeling potatoes into the sink and Sasha lying on her back near the wood-burning stove on a wool blanket on the plank floor, pulling her toes into her mouth and rocking side-to-side. The table was pushed against the opposite wall underneath the shack's one wide double-paned window (they'd agreed that was the one thing worth spending money on) through which was their cliff garden, the ocean, the spruce trees, the Pyramid Mountains across the bay. On the small surface of the stove were two pans of water, steam rising. He walked over to them and looked inside.

"Do you really need this much water?"

"For Sasha's bath and then the potatoes." Anna didn't turn from the sink. Her pale-blond hair, cut short against her neck, reflected the light coming through the window. "Did you get the studs?"

He told her they were out back and that he would start building after lunch. It wouldn't take long. Before they'd know it, they'd have their own salmon hanging with full skin inside, and how good would that be.

"First you've gotta catch them," Anna turned with a smile.

Blake went to Sasha and lay down on the floor next to her. The washing machine sank suspended from above, supported by a wooden catch he had built from the ceiling. In fact, it was *that* ingenious idea that had cost him the tip of his left thumb and what he suspected was a torn muscle in his upper arm. No matter. He rolled over and picked up Sasha; pushed her into the air and pulled her back down to his chest and thrust her up again, watching her smile and then laugh, guffaws lifting from deep in her chest like bubbles. He blew sounds into the hot fatty bottomless folds of her neck.

Sasha tossed and whined that night. Anna was up with her many times, leaning her bottom and thighs into Blake and then turning so that Sasha was again between them, back and forth, slinging the baby from one side to her other.

"Is she teething?" Blake whispered.

Anna rolled her to one side and popped a nipple into Sasha's whine. This calmed her and Blake hoped this meant she would sleep.

He couldn't remember falling asleep, but suddenly he was wet and jerked awake. The hip of his wool long johns was wet and warm, and Anna and Sasha were gone. His eyes burned. He got up and felt around on the mattress until feeling a large wet spot in the middle. Anna came in from outside with Sasha awake in her arms.

"I missed her pee," she said.

By the time Blake had stripped off the wet bed sheet and thrown it up in the small space in the catch by the washing machine, he was wide-awake. He listened to Anna nurse Sasha on the stripped wool mattress until both were asleep. He sat up and looked out the window at the ocean beyond and below the garden.

There was a gibbous moon nearing the height of the sky. The span of ocean directly below was a plane of pure silver that faded into the color of mercury at the farthest reaches of the moon's light until the ocean seemed to expand into dark blue and black, as if into the infinity of space. He imagined the humpbacks in there, twisting, rolling, feeding and filling up for their voyage down south to warmer waters, to procreate and return. He felt consumed by their silent presence. He wished that people would stop their damn noise every once in a while; would listen to something that wasn't them, them, them. Didn't they know they weren't at the heart of everything? The humpbacks, then, seemed to Blake like a part of the very heart of the planet, along with the barnacles closed up tight now in the low tide and the eagles tucked in for the night and the colorful foliose lichen invisibly moving across the ancient rocks at the top of Bear Bread mountain and the Pyramid Mountains silhouetted across the bay in the light of the moon. During these times, it was easy to feel both unimportant and connected to something much bigger—the soul of the planet—and he felt in possession of a deep truth that he wanted everyone to understand.

He looked at the books on the shelves he had built onto the opposite wall. He saw his namesake, William Blake, whose words he knew by heart. There was *The Complete Manual of Woodworking*, which had been very useful during his early days with wood. There was Rachel Carson's *Silent Spring* and Paul Ehrlich's *The Population Bomb*. The book on how to build your own outdoor clay oven. The collection of Shakespeare's sonnets. He debated pulling one of them down to read, but reconsidered. He got dressed and walked out the door.

He followed the same path by the cliff until he saw the Neuman's tall tower and sloping roofline, darker shadows against the dark sky. The opulence of their place disgusted him every single time. He had forgotten his gloves and his hands were already burning with cold. It will snow tonight, he thought, and could smell it in the air, one of his favorite smells, besides the smell of Anna's homemade bread baking. When he reached down for the rock, at first he couldn't make his fingers bend. He seemed to be turning into ice, his fingernails expanding and pressurizing, until he raised them to his mouth and breathed hot hair onto them, *haaaaaaaaaaaaah*. There was just enough feeling there now to reach down again for the rock and carry it to the Neuman's garage where he lodged it against the fiberglass door, leaving behind a scowling dent that made the door look soft like butter. He found another rock, a smaller one, gritted his teeth and threw it into the garage's one high window along the wall facing the ocean, blasting sound into the quiet frigid air. He wondered if Alan would wake up and catch him in the act. The thought didn't bother him, invigorated him even. And yet.

Those silent humpbacks doing their thing quietly in the depths of the cold, cold ocean. He needed to be there and yet not-there too, if he could. He had to remain connected somehow to the truth he had realized again that night; that he had maybe realized only a handful of times in his whole life. That humans aren't number one, not even close; that they are simply one part of the connective tissue that makes up the world. The truth that people like Alan would never understand ever in their whole goddamn lives. He knew he would forget the truth again, but also knew that forgetting it didn't mean it wasn't there and wouldn't be there, always, for him to realize again; pick up again like an agate collected and palmed.

By this time his toes were icy, and his cheeks were solid. He had to pee. He turned walking through the woods.

Blake worked the next day and finished the frame of the smokehouse by lunchtime just as the snow began to fall slowly, quietly over the cliff garden, over their composters, over their skiff tied up by a big orange buoy down the cliff by the rocky beach they owned. He watched two ravens tease each other through the woods, twisting masterfully through the trees, and as the snow grew thicker on the branches, the ravens' black bodies grew deeper in contrast. He stopped to watch the icy-looking white caps of waves slide across the surface of the ocean and splash across the rocks of the beach and cliff, throwing the skiff back and forth, up and down. He watched for whales, orcas; he saw instead a bald eagle, a renegade group of gulls left over from the salmon run one month ago. They would winter in town at Salmon River. That name was a disgrace, he grimaced, for it was the Tlingit's river and should have a Tlingit name.

He turned to the Neuman's house whose tree-free view stunned him like the sight of a gaping wound. He felt momentarily queasy, but that feeling quickly passed into a strong heat unfurling in his stomach, spreading masterfully into the tips of his fingers and toes, into his elbow creases and shoulder joints. He flexed his biceps and clenched his groin. He clenched his jaw.

Anna had salmon chowder for lunch prepared from the coho their friends had given them a couple days ago. After, Blake took Sasha outside to pee in the spot by the tree. Back inside, he rolled around with her on the wool blanket on the floor while Anna washed the dishes with the water from breakfast, re-heated. Sasha laughed and pulled at Blake's beard, which made him bulge his blue eyes, which made her laugh harder. He found the wooden car he had made her rolled under the bed frame and made it sound like a car as he rolled it over his stomach and onto hers. She reached for it and whined.

When Anna and Sasha were in bed for their nap, he pulled on his boots, coat, hat, and gloves. "I've got a job for John," he told Anna who was nursing Sasha with the wool covers pulled up to Sasha's ears, revealing only a little white cap of pale blond hair. The fire would burn out during their nap. He put another log on and closed the vent to a crack.

Once at the gravel lot, he swept a fine layer of snow from the windshield with his mittened hand, opened the door of their fifteen-year-old Subaru and started the engine. The car coughed and then warmed into a low growl. The six-mile drive into downtown Hope was pleasant. The road hugged the rocky beaches and harbors of the ever-present ocean, just right there, like the presence of something huge and indifferent yet incredibly meaningful. Blake liked how the ocean often looked different, whether it reflected blue clouds or gray-green ones; whether the sun was an observer, shining down and baring all, even frothy white bubbles of rogue waves, or a participant, marking the passing of silver clouds and doling out bits of crystal or pink light as if the light weren't for the clouds and air alone.

There were times when Blake liked the ocean most, and during those times he would head out in the skiff if he could. Today was one of those days, and as he turned his head to the ocean, he breathed in one long frosty breath from the car's heatless interior that even as it entered his nostrils cold, turned into a nearly malleable ball of heat at the base of his throat. There it was: the matted silver expanse of ocean, rocking, calm under the heavy gray, gray clouds of the snowy sky. There they were: the distant string of the Baranov Mountain range, named after a Russian explorer who came to these lands hundreds of years ago. *But they aren't the Baranov Mountains*, he thought. *They are simply the mountains. Some day, when we people are no longer here, they will reclaim what is theirs.* But in so thinking, he became uncomfortably aware of his own body, moving as if by magic in that old car, hovering above the road as if not connected to the land. And sadly it was so, he knew. Asphalt and rubber there between him and anything real.

For a moment he could imagine himself alone. He turned his head in time to see the houses along the road evaporate into reclaimed forest, the spruces tall and wide; the boats tied into the ocean fading into its steely silver surface. He was walking in the snow, his body and feet covered with animal skin and fringed with otter fur, and when he turned to look to his side he saw a full throng of people, brown, mostly hairless faces set firmly into the wind and snow, their bodies also covered in fur and beaded ornaments. They were not talking but he could hear voices and knew they were communicating without words; that somehow all things, the trees, the ground, the hidden bear and otter, the sun-giving raven, the human, himself—all were in conversation.

He was already past the boat shop at the bend in the road. Ahead was that side of the island's one gas station, the Lucky Laundromat, the La Iguana Mexican restaurant, the trailer park. He passed those and entered the 25 MPH zone by the elementary school and the old neighborhood near downtown, and, as if passing layer-by-layer into the heart of humanity, approached the island's only stoplight, turned left and drove along the main street until he found a parking spot by Lucy's Café.

His friend, John, had a job for him that week patching a roof in town. John was a fisherman but did odd jobs around town in between fishing runs. He paid Blake in fish when he had it; in cash if he didn't. Blake saw John's Toyota pick-up parked further up the street and knew he would be in the cafe for lunch, the only place in town where they could get a strong cup of coffee and homemade soup for a decent price.

Lucy's café was crowded with locals (no annoying tourists this time of year). It was a tiny place and pulsed with heat and conversation and the smells of food, wood smoke, bodies. Blake took off his jacket, hat, and mittens, stuffed hat and mittens into the arms of his jacket and hung it on a hook by the entrance. He nodded to several people he knew and then stopped to look around, searching for John's long dark beard and black cowboy hat that he never took off, though it was a distinctly un-Hope hat to wear, most men favoring ear-covering skullcaps. He wasn't there, but in the corner, reading a newspaper and eating a bowl of soup with a slice of bread, sat Alan. Before Blake could move his eyes, Alan looked up, smiled, and waved him over. Blake thought about simply ignoring the man, but after a few seconds he walked over, sliding past everyone he knew, and by Lucy bringing food from the open kitchen behind the cash register, her expression a combo of concentration and annoyance. Ah, Lucy!

"Hi Blake." Alan had set down his *New York Times* and looked up from over bifocals, smiling.

"Alan." Blake wasn't sure what he thought of newspapers, especially the *Times*; couldn't be sure they were helpful at all.

"Crowded as usual. Want to join me?"

"I'm here to meet John," and Blake looked around again.

"Well, sit down 'til he's here." Alan used his glasses, now in hand, to point at the chair opposite. Blake didn't appreciate people who did this, who pointed to chairs with their glasses leaving you really no choice but to accept. Nevertheless, he pulled the chair back and sat down, not pulling back in, leaving plenty of space between them.

Alan smiled and they sat in silence for several seconds. *What the hell do you want, flabby, old man?* Blake at first thought he had actually said it, but then realized he hadn't. He didn't have time for this, this superficial chit-chat.

Alan looked down, smiled at the table, looked up.

"Have you ever had a chance to look through a really good telescope? See Mercury at the horizon? Mars like a red eye? Ever caught a comet in mid-flight, frozen in time? The only other time that really happens is in a photograph. Time-capture. Snap." And Alan chuckled, as if trying to make light of his philosophizing.

"I don't know about all that, Alan." Blake's blue eyes seemed to pierce into the very core of Alan, who shifted his bottom back into the chair and started fingering the corner of his newspaper, flipping it up and down. "I guess I'm more concerned about what we have here on our planet."

"Really?" Alan stopped fingering the corner, which had become bent and wrinkled.

Blake looked at the door, checking for John. The air in the café was starting to get uncomfortably warm. The skin beneath his beard suddenly felt itchy and hot. He ran his fingers through his hair and then used both hands to gently comb his beard forward, towards his chin. He leaned in closer, elbows on the table, and nudged the paper away from him so he wouldn't have to touch it. "I'd say so, Alan." And with that last utterance, he felt himself holding back, could feel saliva sticking to the corners of his mouth.

He could hear his breath in his head, the spaces behind his ears and nose, like a wave breaking and receding. For a moment he felt himself being drawn back as if by God's or Gaia's string, pulling him with ferocious speed up, up into the universe. From above, as he wavered weightless in space, one of the celestial bodies among the moon and nearby Mars, not too incredibly distant, really in the great scheme of things, from the Milky Way and all the infinity beyond that, he looked down and saw the world overcome. Black, vibrating specks, like the single-celled organisms he remembered studying in high school biology, appeared suddenly in one spot, just two or three of them, but as they moved outward across the planet they multiplied, instantly, freakishly fast. They vibrated across the land and into other continents; poured into the oceans and disappeared only to reappear tripled, quadrupled, rising up out of the oceans, covering the oceans. As he looked down, he saw the whole thing change into a solid sphere of vibration, shaded by those living things so that the colors of the oceans and lands dissolved into the color of the sameness of those beings. *Which is me,* he thought, *which is me and you, Alan.* And at that he felt himself return just as quickly; God, relentless, fucking impotent, having thrown him back. He was awash with a horror that left him light-headed; a feeling of helplessness that angered him, at the center of which was shame, throbbing like the energy, the hot crazy power, at a star's core. What to do with all that—all that feeling—all that abysmal growth?

"Would you, Anna, and Sasha like to come over and look through my telescope some evening?" Alan was saying, though his voice seemed to be getting hitched in his throat, his words coming out gravely and disjointed. "That's all."

Blake was already up but stopped, wasn't sure he had heard right, then decided to ignore it. "See you around, Alan." Thank god John was just that moment strolling in.

After their meeting, Blake left John to buy some boards and nails at the hardware store across the street. It was snowing heavily. He pulled his wool hat over his ears and forehead and then put on his mittens. As he crossed Raven's Way, he looked up the side street and saw Alan's brand new Forester parked up the hill. Just the site of Alan's shiny new wheels gleaming piercingly black against the accumulating white made him clench his jaw.

Before he could feel himself doing it, he was trudging up the hill. By the time he was by Alan's car, he already had his pocketknife out, concealed in the palm of his mitten. As he kneeled down, feigning to pick up something from the gutter, he clenched the muscles of his hand and forearm and jammed the blade deep into the thick rubber of one of the back tires. Once there, he yanked the knife down, sawing against the toughness, leaving an uneven, silent gash in the treads. By the time he was on the second back tire, he was sweating under his hat and in his armpits. As he walked away, he turned to look at the tires that were imperceptibly deflating into the cold pre-winter air.

The snowflakes had changed. They were now as large as his pinky nail; those large, distinct ones that fall in that fine band between too-warm and too-cold. Perfect, wet, enormous crystals that freeze, truly, only moments before hitting the ground.

On his way home, Blake saw Anna walking by the side of the road with Sasha in the hiking pack. They were just about to head up the steep hill below the Catholic church. People don't need a gym, Blake and Anna had often agreed, if they're truly living as humans were meant to. He and Anna had strong, lean bodies from simple daily living.

He pulled over just ahead of her, the ocean still a smooth silver sheet below the falling snow, kept the engine running and put the brake on. Her body was covered in a fine layer of snow. Sasha's cream-colored wool Nelson's cap peeked out from the high sides of the pack. Still, he knew Anna would be warm and sweating from the walk. She waved and came to him.

"Sasha took a short nap. Then we went to the pool and showered," she said after getting Sasha into her car seat. The heater was broken in the car, but neither minded. "It was nice to take a hot shower." She smiled and pulled off her hat, shaking it on the car mat under her boots. Blake knew she liked the walk to and from the public pool; liked how it made her feel unhurried and real; that sometimes Sasha would take a nap in the pack and all would be simple and right.

Anna and Sasha were everything he could have asked for.

"I need to get over there too. How did Sasha swim?"

"She loves it. Splashes all around. Things good with John?"

"Yeah. A roof job. Probably take me a week."

"Still going to do it in this snow?"

"Sure, why not."

They reached their spot and parked. The snow was still coming quickly, as if they were in one massive toy snowball, the world shaken all around. "Sometimes it makes me dizzy," Anna said as they headed down the trail. "Swirling all around us. Can't look anywhere that's not moving."

Sasha's eyes were beginning to close in the pack, her head lolling forward. Anna sighed and said she hoped she'd stay asleep out of the pack at home, just for a bit. "For once I'd like some time to myself."

As they passed above Alan's house, Blake tried to stay focused on the path ahead, but instead noticed pieces of something in between the trees. It was white and unmoving. He stopped and turned, squinted his eyes, and put his hands to his brow to keep the snow from getting into his eyes.

"What's that?" he asked.

"Huh?" Anna kept walking.

"That." And he pointed towards Alan's house.

"What?" Anna stopped and turned.

"I'm going down." They were past Alan's trail, but Blake could easily push through the forest.

"Blake. Now?" Anna turned her head over her shoulder and saw Sasha's face sunk into the folds of the carrier, sound asleep.

"Go on, I'm just going to check it out. I'll be right there."

"Don't be long."

Blake stayed in the trees. He wouldn't be seen. He was ten feet from the house, and then there. That was it. A political sign, for god's sake, stuck leaning out of the shallow ground! Where no one could see it except Alan's stars and planets and aliens. And Blake.

Blake looked closely through the snow and saw that it was in support of Jerry Meyer, one of Hope's mayoral candidates. Jerry Meyer! Blake snorted into the cold air. Couldn't believe his eyes, and yet, yes, he could, seeing where it was. Jerry Meyer who had supported the deep-water dock even though he was also president of the Hope Environmental Society. One of Hope's worst hypocrites. Against further logging, but owner of the paper and office supply store where that shit he sold wasn't all recycled, Blake could be sure of it. Alan had put it there just for Blake, to mock him, laugh in his face! Alan knew that it would be Blake who would see it every day on his walk down. And that nothing would make him happier than knowing that Blake would hate it; that even if Blake could yank the thing right out, he still couldn't change Alan's mind; Alan's mind his own, untouchable, free, above-it-all yard sign.

Blake couldn't remember feeling so cold before, ever, in his life. Or so volcanically angry. He turned his face up into the snowy onslaught, each flake melting on his skin in a thousand places.

One of Anna and Blake's favorite things to do was to get out onto the water when the snow was falling. So when the roof job was done, they did just that.

Saturday morning, it wasn't snowing, but the gray-white sky was sunk almost to the surface of the ocean. They knew snow would soon be coming. It took an hour to get ready. They packed smoked salmon and cream cheese sandwiches, apples, bags of walnuts to snack on; pulled on wool socks and rubber boots; layered with long underwear and extra shirts, sweaters under their waterproof jackets; bundled up Sasha in wool layers and her Nelson hat; packed an extra waterproof bag with clothes and diapers for Sasha, extra socks and mittens for them. They brought a jug of water, a radio, a battery-operated lantern, their life jackets.

They needed to be back before dark to see their way around some of the dangerous boulders sunk in the water just off their beach, so as soon as Anna and Sasha were seated in the boat, Sasha on Anna's lap with Anna's arms wrapped around her cocooned body, Blake started the engine and steered the skiff into the water. 8 a.m. and not a moment too soon.

The waves were barely there. The ocean exhumed a calmness that was reflected in the sky and forest, as if all things were holding their breath for the morning's first snowflake. Blake loved the water when the snow fell, but he loved it even more just moments before, when the air smelled like ice and the water's color was both a muted gray and swirling with flashes of almost undetectable color. As the motor cut the water into rotundity, in it he could see whole swaths of green and dark yellow and purple.

It was only two miles to the other side of the channel where the Pyramid Mountains and a maze of hidden channels and pools were. They most often went there because it was directly across from their house, and the sooner Blake could cut the engine, the happier they were. For it was then that they could hear, among the silence, the musical gurgling of the ravens or the woosh, sigh of the water being sucked into and out of the creeks and crevices of the rocky shore or, if they were lucky, the powerful release of air and water from a humpback's blowhole. Once, on kayaks, they had found themselves amid three, four of them, bubble feeding. They had hurriedly paddled out of their way, but watched from the side the hundreds of herring, the masses of bubbles the whales were making to force the herring up, the lunging of the whales with mouths impressively open. What a wonder, a gift, that had been.

They were in the center of the channel when the snow began falling. At this Anna smiled and squealed *weeeeeee!* into the icy air. Blake watched her turn her face to the sky and open her chapped lips; saw how red her cheeks and the tip of her nose were turning. Her eyes were as blue as glacial ice. Keeping one hand on the rudder, he put the other on her knee and kept it there, feeling his stomach and lungs grow warmer as he felt her. And there was Sasha, whose round red face was barely popping out of her Nelson hat, mouth opened wide in a soundless laugh, blue eyes tearing from the cold, nose running. Her body seemed to be humming, as it did when Blake threw her up in the air or hugged her close and rolled with her side-to-side on the floor. She was a happy baby, and why would it be any other way?

And then there, beyond his family, beyond the rest of the ocean, was the opposite shore of an unknown wilderness. Beyond the barnacle-encrusted rocks of the shore, where the tidal pools were painfully cold and clear, where purple sea anemone and pink starfish clung, was a static wave of kelp on the beach in an undulating line. And beyond the undulating line of kelp was the forest that went on and on and blessedly on, without reserve, hiding the bear and the eagle's nest and the salmon river and the popping fungi and the subterranean creek whose watery tinkling was louder than most anything else there.

When they returned it was dark and the ground was white. The snow was still coming, alighting upon the water and instantly vanishing. Sasha was already asleep when Anna put her on the bed. Blake started a fire in the stove. They could see their breath. The cabin was frigid. Anna started unpacking the bags and quietly putting things away, hoping Sasha would give them a bit of peaceful alone time. When the wood in the stove was popping, they sat down in the dark at the table and snacked on smoked salmon, sausage, and bread. They drank beer. Through the dark between them, Blake saw a tiny smile at Anna's mouth. That's all they ever needed, the two of them. Not guffaws or loud merriment; never an excess of words or thoughts or noise.

He touched her hand and she sighed. Their hands were still cold, but he could already feel the powerful heat coming from the stove. He thought about how much nicer it was to do things the way in which they were intended; not eating by fake light, for example. Just enjoying the light barely coming through the dirty window of the stove door; or the muted light reflecting off the snow from the clouded sky outside their window. He loved how Anna's face looked in the light of the night.

When they climbed into bed, their bodies smelled like fire from the stove. Anna gently pushed Sasha over so that she and Blake could keep each other warm, snuggling into each other as they used to. Blake wrapped his arms all the way around her. Soon they were warmed up and falling asleep in the beautiful quiet.

Blake told himself that he would wake up, and he did. He could do things like that. It was still dark outside and the fire had died in the stove. Anna and Sasha were still sleeping. He didn't want to leave the warmth of the bed, their bodies, but had to.

He got up slowly so that the bed barely moved and kneeled down to the pile of clothes he'd left there before going to bed: his long underwear, his overalls, his shirt. He dressed silently, quickly, in the freezing air. He carried his jacket and boots outside so that the noise of putting them on wouldn't wake Anna or Sasha. He pulled on his wool hat and mittens and listened to the icy snow crunch as he walked to the shed and found his saw. Outside the shed he stopped and looked up into the cloudy sky. He closed his eyes and sucked in cold, clean air, so cold it burned his nose and lungs. He could feel the familiar, ridged shape of the saw's handle in his right hand through the thickness of his mittens. Finally, he turned toward Alan's house and started walking the deer trail on the cliff side.

Soon, he could make out the supporting pillars of Alan's deck against the dim light of the reflected snow. It was steep along the way to the deck, and he held the saw carefully behind him as he shuffled along the top of the cliff, keeping his left hand slightly lifted from his side in case he needed to catch his fall. It didn't take him long before he was directly under Alan's wide deck. As he turned around to orient himself among the six pillars, for a moment he felt as if he were trapped there as if in a cage. Finally, he turned around and there was the ocean; beyond it the Pyramid

Mountains, their peaks distinctly blue-white against the darkness. He stopped moving and heard the waves washing up against the rocks ten feet below.

Silence.

Snow falling in a *hush* from an overburdened branch. He felt a touch of cold air on his cheeks. In it he could smell salt and soil. The smells of strong burrowing roots and seaweed. The smells of spruce needles and decaying heart crabs. Here he was. He felt his soul growing into the ocean and forest, as if he were losing himself to them; as if he would either take root or fly away.

As he brought the saw to the first wooden pillar of the deck, he felt the muscles in his arms grow tight and hard, the muscles in his hands constrict, beginning to pulse with the blood of his body. The parts of beard around his mouth were growing unnoticeably icy as his breath came quickly in and out. He gripped the saw's handle and dug into the woody body of the pillar, carving a groove deep enough so that soon he was moving his arm back and forth with few hitches, finding a pattern of movement that excited and inspired him. Several minutes later the pillar was severed and he looked up to find another and went to it, setting his saw upon it and moving his arm back and forth. His body pulsed, his icy beard vibrated, he shifted his weight off of his knees and jumped to his feet without a break in movement, crouched this time with his legs apart so that even though the ground was icy and the night sky was light with snow clouds, his body felt remarkably hot. He could feel his undershirt wet with sweat and it was the same satisfying feeling he had while deer hunting, the sweat and pain and pride of carrying a 75-pound deer, still hot, across his shoulders from out of the mountains. The happiness of knowing Anna, Sasha, and he would have local meat to eat for the year.

"What the hell?" he heard behind him. And suddenly felt someone pull his working shoulder hard. "What the hell!" he heard again.

He knew it was Alan. He didn't turn but yanked his shoulder back and kept on sawing. Alan pulled his shoulder again, this time harder, and Blake fell down onto the ground backwards, the saw still gripped in his hands.

"What are you doing?" Alan stood over Blake as Blake looked up from the cold ground. But all Blake needed was a moment of recovery. He rolled over and jumped up and, head down, saw in hand, ran his shoulders into Alan's chest, pushing him down backward, hard against the rocks. Alan tried to get up but lost his balance and tripped on the edge of a boulder, falling on his bottom and sliding further down the cliff side. He caught himself and pulled himself up as Blake edged toward him, coming carefully on the icy ground. Blake's cheeks were flaming, his beard disheveled.

Alan watched Blake's eyes that even in the darkness looked bright. *It's come to this,* he thought, and pushed himself up and swung an arm so flaccid and unused that he felt his whole body hum after slamming his fist into Blake's jaw. Blake twisted and fell. Alan immediately brought his hand, broken feeling, up to his face where he cradled it and blew warmth into it. He exhaled a low, warming *ohhhhhhhhh* onto the tip of his chin. When he let his hand fall, Blake was on top of him.

"I thought you were a decent young man," Alan breathed. "Oh, I was wrong, so wrong."

"I am, Alan. You cut down trees. I'm here to tell you, you can't do that. You can't do that! You disgust me. Don't you know I hate your kind? *I hate you!*"

It was uncomfortably true. Blake was somewhat aware that somewhere inside him was a deep pulsing unlove. There had been nowhere to let it out, but now, finally, the urgency of it came out through muscle and breath and heat. Through the intensity of none other than his very life. It was time. It had been time a long time ago.

And as Blake blew his hot breath into Alan's gaping mouth, Alan grew slack under Blake's grip. His body sank into the icy rocks of the earth, the earth that seemed to want to reclaim him, to hide him until the time was safe. Alan could feel the cold rocks like chunks of ice against his back and bottom, which illuminated suddenly the pain throbbing still in his fingers and knuckles and a colder more distant pain resonating in his chest bone. He looked up past Blake's shining eyes, black planets hovering in the space just above, and beyond them were the tops of the trees all around, dark blue against the snow clouds of the night sky of the wilderness.

-3-

The Swan

What a surprise when the swans started coming to Hope two years ago. They would settle on Loon Lake for the winter, elegantly easing through the water like vacationers until the week or two when the whole lake would freeze. Then they would walk across it awkwardly; stay tucked-in in pairs asleep in the cluster of trees and plants by the water's edge where it was a wonder the bears didn't get them. Locals began to come with bags of old bread, let their children excitedly throw out pieces to inspire the grand birds to come closer, closer still, just so they could see their long, white necks; their massive white bodies; the folds of their wings and the beautiful, deep blackness around their eyes. And when the swans came, they seemed to come forward as if knowingly crossing into a baser world.

When the snow came, it covered the world in white. It heightened Hope's stunning natural beauty and erased all of Hope's ugliness—the cracked roads and gravel driveways; the piles of used car and boat parts crowding patchy, muddy yards; piles of wood, rocks, shells, fishing net, bones, tin cans and glass jars, defunct ovens, odds and ends that people saved, the stuff they held on to like tenders to life. Also all the things already long buried. The snow comforted it all, as if those collections in fact reflected the people's great anxieties and compulsions and in themselves needed reprieve, just for the few weeks every year they could go covered, unnoticed and free.

The swans, utterly white themselves, could escape notice when the snow came, unless a person purposefully sought them out; walked down to the Lake to stand or sit on the cold bench to watch them in a sort of meditation. Then a person, perhaps, would see them soundlessly cutting the ice-free center of the lake, their necks looped like S's, their bodies made even whiter by the blackness of the water. And when the snow actually fell–those big fat flakes that forgave the world and eased everyone's troubles and soothed all noise–the swans floated through the snowfall slowly, contentedly, disappearing and appearing like ghosts in the clean, cold whiteness of it all.

Last winter, alas, only one swan came. It remained through the summer and into the current winter. Unpaired and alone, it popped up in conversations at the library, Seaside Hardware, Lucy's Cafe.

"A young one, you think?"

"Alone. Hopefully not lonely."

"Why not leave? Why stay in Hope?"

"He's fed, that's what it is. We feed him."

"He's beautiful, isn't he? Just there like that in all this."

People came to expect its solid white body. Its silent, peaceful presence. When they drove past on their way to middling, mind-numbing jobs, they searched for it and found it standing on the grassless land near the water's edge, head down to the ground searching for food, or in the middle of the lake, floating with its head up as if testing the weather. "More will come later," people took comfort in the thought. But even if it continued to be just the one, that would be all the people would need. Just to know it was still there seemed to give life in Hope a tinge of something no one could exactly put their finger on.

*

Dusty's Grandmother hasn't been able to throw out the expired milk for years, so she stacks it outside on the tiny backyard deck that is already piled with forty gallons of milk in various stages of curdling and in a spectrum of colors. And there too she leaves the moldy bread she promises herself to take down to the swan on Loon Lake, though she rarely does because it's never top of mind. She also leaves out there the frozen turkeys she buys in bulk when they're reduced at Hope Grocers, and the old whole chickens no one in the family ever eats fast enough. There's a sliding glass door to the deck off of the dining room, but the wooden planks started growing soft several years ago (no sun can get through the forest of spruce in the backyard), and no one except Grandmother has been out there for years. When it is winter, as it is now, she trudges out back and places the milk and meat directly on the deck to save her having to put them into the fridge. A Hope winter, however, means few days of snow and ice; many weeks of wavering between freezing and glorious, cold downpours.

Dusty pauses Halo on the PlayStation, pushes out of the plush brown couch that is sinking in because of the time his big brother Johnson pulled out a knife and slashed the cushions, drunk and angry from his high.

He emerges out of the darkness of the living room. Keeping it entirely dark, blankets tacked up and over the one large living room window, keeps the experience of his gaming alive and pulsing. Plus, he's grown up in the cave-like environment of Grandmother's house and not only feels cozy, as if in his mother's womb again (something he can't even begin to imagine, though the

57

subconscious desire for it is there nonetheless), but invisible, as if he could do anything and no one would ever know. There is some comfort in that, but there is also the constant, rumbling desire to be noticed.

On his way to the fridge to grab a Coke, he sees in his periphery how the plastic gallons of milk are now tumbling off the decaying deck onto the muskegy backyard. The moldy bread is still recovering from last week's freeze. The turkeys and chicken, all fifteen of them, will keep until the first winter rain when they will begin to reek so strongly that the bears, though Dusty suspects it's the same ol' one, will come for an unseasonal visit.

Last week he saw a bear devour two enormous partially frozen turkeys. He watched it, heard its long mouth and saliva work away at them, while sipping an ice-cold Coke. It was like watching a movie, the best kind.

The next morning, the mesh bags wrapped around each turkey were in pieces across the ground, like confetti, and bits of turkey fat and bone were laid out everywhere as if they had exploded. Dusty went out there around through the front door just to see the crazy glory of it. He hadn't ventured out there ever before. No reason to. He bent over to touch the white, slightly yellow skin stuck like gelatin against some meat. It felt like human flesh, but soggier. The stink was all-consuming. The Thompsons next door must have complained about it, like they always did, because the police came to their door not long after. Told them to clear it all out. That this had to stop. So Grandmother, unable to throw it away, buried the stuff herself as she always did. She dug into the spongy, cold, patchy ground in among the roots and moss, and buried every last turkey and chicken so deeply that she thought the bears wouldn't easily find them. The milk she shoved into the dark space beneath the deck, which left the deck free for more.

It had felt familiar to her, as she sank on her hands and knees into the dried spruce needles across the lichen and mosses of the moist ground and shoved in the sharp point of her trowel. When she got to a spot full of roots and rocks, she tossed the trowel aside and used her hands to pull everything out, making a pile of roots and plants and rocks next to the hole. By the end of the burying, her fingernails were cracked and bloody, but it felt marvelous.

She will never forget burying her baby back there, fifty years ago. She had been fifteen. Uncle Josiah had lived with her family since coming upon bad times. Those bad times, she assumed, entitled him to the visits he made to her bedroom every week in the middle of the night. Now she can barely remember them; has no details at all. So when she simply came out of her bedroom that one morning long ago, proclaimed to her parents who were eating cereal at the table that the baby had gotten sick and died in the middle of the night, everyone left it at that. Might have been relieved, even. She still remembers the feel of the wet, cold ground, though, as she dug. She remembers the weight of her two-day baby, a girl she had yet to name, wrapped in a garbage bag. She had suffocated her. It hadn't been hard.

When Grandmother buried the turkeys, she thought maybe she'd find the baby's tiny bones somewhere, like the almost violent pleasure of discovering an unusual amount of sugar-covered raisins in her bowl of Raisin Bran or discovering the swan sleeping by the lake and raising its elegant head when it sees her. Instead, the ravens hung their black heads from their perches in the spruce trees. Their eyes on her. She felt them even as she kept her head down toward the digging. The ravens knew everything, of course. One day, she knew, they would eat her alive; return her to the mercy of the earth.

It's almost the end of winter break, but Dusty hasn't been going to school for weeks; threw away the notice when it came one afternoon. Suspension. "Ha!" he'd laughed into the hot stale air of the house, shut in tight against the outside as Grandmother liked it: plastic stretched across every single window so that they could never be opened; the heat cranked up to 85; the front door locked three times over.

Grandmother never asks to see a report card. He hasn't washed his hair in weeks and she hasn't said a word. When the gym teacher, Mr. Till, caught him once strangling that weirdo Barry during lunch time out against the tree line at the farthest reaches of the field behind the high school, Mr. Till threw him down and he fell against a root. He was never going to hurt Barry; just do enough to scare the shit out of him for being so weird and into chess and good at math. It didn't take much convincing to get Johnson to go with him to Mr. Till's house one night, the both of them jacked up on too much Coke and gummy worms and that sweet, sweet natural high from pure adrenaline, and throw the biggest rocks they could find right into the windows of Mr. Till's precious orange Honda Element.

Grandmother tells him that when the white people, the Russians, first came to Hope, they destroyed their culture, which is why his parents overdosed when he was a baby. The white people are also why his Grandfather shot himself drunk one night ten years ago in the bathroom off the bedroom. There are faint brown spots still in places across the moldy tiles; those places where the blood just can't come clean. This also explains why his Uncle Baxter is stupid, a dumbie, and likes to fiddle with himself in the bathroom whenever Dusty needs to go. The white people led Johnson to meth. They're also why Grandmother keeps all her money in a boot box she bought her Sorels in thirty years ago on a rare trip to Anchorage, which she keeps hidden behind her piles of second-hand shoes on the top shelf in her bedroom closet.

All those bills squeezed in there to make $100,000 and growing. Money she gets from the tribe, money from the government for Baxter's stupidness, money from grandfather's death, it's all there in the cluttered, dark, moldy privacy of her jam-packed bedroom closet. "Don't use the banks," Grandmother told Dusty. "Can't trust 'em white folks places."

Dusty couldn't care less about any of that shit.

It's 11 o'clock and the house is quiet. Grandmother is in bed. Uncle Baxter closed his bedroom door 15 minutes ago. There's only so much Halo a person can play, and Dusty has been at it for five hours. One of the downsides of living in Hope is that there's nothing to do and hardly anyone to do it with. It will be Christmas in four days and his one good friend, Will, is in Seattle visiting his aunt and uncle and cousins. Will doesn't know it, but that aunt is actually his mom who he's been told died in a house fire months after he was born, which is why there are no photos. He's been raised by his grandparents. Dusty's Grandmother spilled the truth once to Dusty after she'd had one too many whiskeys like she often does after the sun goes down. Will's mom and dad were hooked on heroin just like Dusty's. Will's parents, however, were sponsored by St. Ignatius Russian Orthodox Church and put into a fancy rich-persons rehab in Seattle. Will's dad didn't make it; committed suicide in some one-bedroom there. Will's mom never came home, instead stayed to marry a white guy, get her degree in communications, have two light-skinned kids with dark eyes. Dusty will never tell Will because why would he?

If Will were there Dusty would call him up and they could do something. Dusty has always had a hard time sleeping. Most nights when Baxter starts snoring like a fat cow, Dusty barrels into his room and smacks him across the side of his head. He laughs when Baxter shoots up into the air like a man paralyzed from the waist down who's just been shot in the face.

So, he does what he often does. He sneaks into Grandmother's room while she sleeps and quietly opens the top drawer of her cheap peeling dresser. It's buried under her cotton underwear, nylons, socks, and a loose stack of B&W photos that have gotten wrinkled and bent from neglect. He thinks he recognizes Grandfather in one of them, dressed in his regalia. Maybe that's his mom. Maybe that's him, as a baby. It's hard to tell, and he doesn't really care. Dusty pushes through it all, wrinkling his nose in disgust from having to touch Grandmother's underwear and feathery nylons, her old-woman smell emanating outward like the decaying food does in the backyard. There, against the grain of the drawer bottom, is the Kel-Tec pistol Grandmother bought in Juneau three years ago. Why, who knows. It feels refreshingly cool against his hands.

It's not like he hasn't fantasized about it a hundred, a thousand times. Lain in bed, wide awake, waiting for sleep to come when it just won't. Instead, getting up to grab another Coke, hoping the sweet coldness of it will spur on the sleep he's come to view in the same way he views good grades, a handsome face, anything beyond tomorrow: elicit, impossible, laughable.

At night, he can conjure it all, like a wizard sitting in front of his book of spells, thinking of the people he will make pay. Teachers and neighbors; smarty-pants and dumbies; policemen; Larry, the dumb rich fuck who sells Johnson his drug of choice; the stupid shitty mutt two houses down who barks at him every time he passes. He's held that Kel-Tec in his hand, in bed under the sheets and blanket; held it until it became hot like a living thing; until he could feel its heartbeat under the metal. He was giving it life; he could make it do what he wanted. He had power buried deep beneath his skinny chest, the kind of power that didn't lead to good grades or lots of friends or fabulous families. It was the kind of power that went beyond all that superficiality; the kind of power that could see right through society's bullshit and call everything what it was.

Which was, largely, injustice and unhappiness. Though he couldn't be sure exactly what unhappiness was. He knew, though, that unhappiness wasn't what happened at night when he held the gun in his hand. Unhappiness wasn't him standing in front of his bedroom mirror nailed to the wood-paneled wall, dusty and greasy from years of unclean and recycled air. It wasn't him standing in the center of the mirror where he could barely make out his face from a spot he'd wiped nearly clean with the sleeve of his shirt, and raising the gun to between his eyes. It wasn't him seeing himself press the trigger and watching the bullet explode the head of the dog two houses down. Mr. Till's head needs two shots just to make him stop. Barry's head he fills with bullet after bullet so that afterward he is nothing but a headless, neckless, body. Uncle Baxter gets a bullet. And when it comes right down to it, just to see what it's like, Grandmother gets one in her right eye; Johnson gets one; his mother and father get one. He lines them up, temple-to-temple, shoots, and watches the bullet go through and out his father's far temple. He can control the speed of each bullet, which means that he can see the bullet go in and out slowly, in all bloody detail, or he can see it go in swiftly, the bullet like Superman, able to move faster than anything except, maybe, light. The last bullet he always saves for himself. *Boom*, he whispers. The beauty of the whole thing is that he always comes back from the dead, and so does everyone else. He is that masterful.

Now, the gun in his hands, the bodies of Mr. Till and Barry, the dog, Grandmother, Johnson, Uncle Baxter, mother, father, headless and bloody and reeking around him like the thawing headless turkeys in the backyard, he says *boom* into the mirror and catches himself squarely between the eyes, directly above the small bridge of his wide-ish nose. *You're dead.*

"Get up, shithead!" Dusty had fallen asleep on the couch and the pistol had dropped from his hand onto the brown shag carpet. It is still dark, though silvering outside. Johnson is punching him in his upper arm. He will see a fist-sized bruise there later. "Someone's been into my box. Someone's been into it!"

Johnson has been working at the movie theater since getting out of jail, but someone, Grandmother or Baxter because Dusty would never, had been stealing bits of his pay. $20 here; $10 there. It added up. He tried hiding his stash in his room, but someone always found it. "I'll be outta here as soon as I can," Johnson had told Dusty not long after returning from jail. "Gotta get outta this fucking place." But he needed the first month's rent to be able to go anywhere, and in order to do that, he actually needed a chunk of money. So, two weeks ago he started burying the money in an old shoebox out front in a wall of salmonberry bushes by the road, just deep enough to stay hidden; not too deep to retrieve, at night, for a deposit. It was hard, though, saving for that first month's rent. Drugs were expensive, and so was life. Rich, white kids had it easy, Johnson often thought. They could afford to have it all: the fun and the necessities.

Dusty comes to with the stick of Coke in his dry mouth. "Stop hitting me, asshole," he narrows his eyes at Johnson. "What do I care about your shitty box?"

"Huh? What'd you say? Huh?" Johnson grabs him around the head and jerks him to sitting. He starts slapping Dusty, first on one cheek, then the other.

"Ok, ok," Dusty, even in his sluggishness, quickly has his arms up over his head. "Stop it! Just stop it."

Johnson sits next to Dusty and stares at him. His body seems like one mass of vibration, and even though he sits, his right leg keeps bouncing up and down; he keeps crossing and uncrossing his fingers as he brings his hands together and apart, together again.

"Where is it? Tell me!" Dusty notices the sweat on Johnson's face, how he keeps opening and closing his eyes.

"How should I know where it is?" Dusty looks down at his feet and shakes his head, hoping to clear his way into wakefulness. Time for another Coke. Time to cut his toenails.

Johnson heaves a tremendous, wobbly sigh. "Man, I need that money. Fuck! It's my money. It's *my* money! I can't *believe* this!"

They sit in silence. Johnson, though, can't stop bouncing his leg. Every once in a while he gives a full-body shake, like a wet dog drying off. Dusty knows he won't get any sleep until Johnson has it.

It's obvious, suddenly.

Dusty gets up without a word. Johnson follows him down the dark hallway to Grandmother's room. They pass Uncle Baxter's closed door. He is remarkably silent in there. Dusty opens Grandmother's door exceptionally slowly until it makes it past the angle of the hinge's stubborn *crack*. He's had plenty of practice, though he's never gone into her closet before.

Grandmother is on her back, the blankets and comforter pulled up to her chin. The one window is heavily blanketed so that the room is black with the darkness it has grown accustomed to. Grandmother keeps the blanket on her window at all times and the window always closed so that her room has become a creature all its own—dark, smelly like old woman and mold and something else, damp and dead. The room seems to find solace in its isolation and darkness and stink, its communion with Grandmother. The fact that it exists and thrives seems to thrill it. It is some grungy, hapless creature, its brown shag carpet the individual parts of which rise like hair that covers all kinds of minuscule creatures. The whole room seems to hum with forbidden life.

A hazy glow spreads from behind the dresser against the wall opposite Grandmother. It's her nightlight, casting barely any light at all. Dusty, with his eyes on Grandmother, quietly walks past and to her closet. The challenge will be to get the box without making any noise, which will mean clearing past empty boxes, piles of clothes, shoes, and hundreds of trinkets she scavenges for at garage sales every Saturday morning. He knows Johnson's box will be there, right next to her own jammed box of money.

Dusty turns around and points his finger to show Johnson to stay put. Johnson peers into the dark closet with squinted eyes, can't make out anything but shadows of piles of things and clothes hanging from hangers packed against each other like nightmarish slivers of people jammed together in some alternate universe. Dusty enters the closet as if he were crossing a land plastered with mines. Once he gets to the shelf above Grandmother's hanging dresses and skirts, he slowly pushes aside the piles of old shoes and cracked faux leather boots. There it is, Johnson's box, directly on top of Grandmother's, caked with dirt. He reaches for it and, without thinking, takes both, balancing them one atop the other. The concentration he needs soothes him, makes him feel bodiless and mindless. He is a spirit floating above the shag ground, doing what he has to do.

Back in the living room, he exhales and suddenly feels immensely proud. He feels as he did, once, running through the woods behind Grandmother's house, dodging trees and jumping over soft, moist cassocks and protruding roots. His heart, running wild inside him. The sweat, sliding down his back and from his armpits. He had felt effervescent, dreamy, ghost-like. He was convinced he had actually lifted from the ground!

The early morning light is struggling to pierce between the edges of the blanket and the sill of the window in the living room. Dusty knows he'll not be able to fall asleep now, but it hardly matters anymore. He isn't even mad at Johnson, feeling as good as he is.

"That crazy bitch," Johnson grabs his box and flips off the top. Inside, a few twenties and tens; bunches of fives and ones; some change and clumps of dirt; a fine dusting of soil over everything. He dumps out the money and begins counting. The coins fall into the carpet and get lost; the dirt, too, settles to the unseen bottom. "$235. It's basically all here." He snatches it all and stuffs it into the pocket of the jacket he hasn't taken off. "What's this," he sees the other box. When he tears off the top and the money erupts, his body freezes for the first time. His mouth opens. He stays like that for seconds. "What the fuck is this," he whispers.

"It's Grandmother's," says Dusty. "She says there's a hundred thou in there." Why he took it, he doesn't exactly know, if only to have something, for once, laid fully bare; out in the open and known.

"A hundred thousand fucking dollars!" Johnson throws his head back and hoots. He slides the box into his arms as if it were a baby, stamps the lid back on though the money all wants to come out, and takes it and his own box, which he palms like an afterthought. As he walks out the door, he looks back at Dusty who is still standing in the middle of the room, feeling like a spirit, but that feeling beginning to wear away. Johnson looks pointedly at him so that Dusty knows not to talk, ever. That Grandmother's box will remain one of those terrible mysteries.

When Johnson is gone, the house seems to have never had him, and Dusty awakens completely, remembers the gun he had dropped in sleep by the couch. He can't imagine going back to Grandmother's room after all that, so instead he hides the gun under the pants in his bottom drawer and thinks about what to eat for breakfast.

*

When Dusty skips out on fifth period algebra after winter break to meet Will at Will's house for gaming, he first drops by his house to grab something to eat and to just chill out a bit. Things often got wild at Will's place, and he has to be physically and mentally prepared. Will tended to have bags of mushrooms and marijuana, which they could partake of with abandon depending on their mood. Once, in the night, Will had convinced Dusty to go out with him in his grandfather's Jeep Cherokee. Will took the keys hanging by the front door, started the beast up, and off they went, cruising the streets of Hope at full speed. Neither exactly knew how to drive, but they couldn't wait to get their licenses. In the meantime, there were always alternatives. The max speed limit out to the ferry at the northern end of the island was 45, but they had that Cherokee going 90. With the windows down, it felt like flying.

Dusty opens the front door, throws his pack on the ground, and walks to the fridge where he grabs a Coke. He also pulls a Snickers bar from the top drawer below the microwave where Grandmother keeps the candy hoarded from years of Halloween sales. The first thing he sees is that the gallons of milk and the loaves of bread have cascaded from off the deck and the sliding glass door is open, letting in the smells of the outdoors and something sour-smelling and sharp that makes the inside of his nose burn.

There is Grandmother in the backyard, slamming a shovel into the thawed ground. There are three frozen chickens up against the side of the house. She has already brought up several of the buried turkeys, lying in pale, putrid piles about her. He sees that many of them are already fully in the process of decay, their pale brown bones beneath soppy flesh and muscle, in some instances, no flesh or muscle at all anymore. She has already dug up great

68

swaths of the backyard that have thawed since last week's first big freeze. Among the turkeys are piles of ground, skinny roots, and clumps of lichen and moss. Occasionally, something starkly white catches his eye—the shocking complete whiteness of bones long buried and preserved, unearthed.

Grandmother is going into the ground with one foot on the shovel. She leans her body up and over and into it over and over again. Every time she heaves down and forward, the covered mass of her breasts convulses. Her sweater is on the ground, her arms and shoulders bare from under a turquoise tank top. The skin on her upper arms sags and wobbles, swings and shudders. The site of her flesh so fully revealed brings up into Dusty's throat the dankness of lunch.

The ends of her baggy brown pants fall over her rubber boots and skim the ground. She doesn't notice Dusty until he is on the deck, and he hasn't once been on the deck in his life. When he steps on it, he puts first one foot then another, testing it, then very cautiously walks through the open doorway and all the way onto it. The stink hits him like a heat wave; he seems to feel it against his cheeks and nose and forehead, a cellular, rippling barrier that he must just punch through. But it keeps flowing into his mouth and nostrils, clogging every opening, gumming the back of his throat. He breathes through his mouth, but his throat keeps narrowing. On the deck, it at first feels like he is balancing in a boat on the ocean, but when he fully understands in his body that he is in fact *there*, and it is not falling or wavering beneath him, he nearly feels on solid ground again. From there he sees the sweat on Grandmother's face. He hears her humphs and grunts, the pound and crunch of the shovel as she digs into and brings up the ground, tossing each shovel-full frantically to the side. She throws the ground back not caring at all where it goes. Sometimes she throws so forcefully that bits of dirt fly through the air and splatter across the closest, blanketed window of her bedroom.

"It's gotta be back here somewhere," she mutters.

"Huh?" Dusty says. He is feeling something strange inside, something that makes his heart sound in his ears.

"I know he took it," she's digging her way through the whole yard, but still has a way to go before the edge of the forest. "I know that asshole brother of yours took my money."

She stops, then, frozen with her back hunched over the widening hole in the ground, and stares at Dusty who has not moved from his spot on the deck. He has to turn away, so he does. Grandmother's eyes are flaming. Looking at them any longer would have incinerated him. He looks down at the ground and, peripherally, notices the milk and bread; sees how one of the gallons has ruptured and is leaking milk, which strikes him then as one of the sources of the horrific stink.

"I'll kill him, you know that," she says quietly, as if she were talking exclusively to the trees near her, the piles of turkeys and upturned ground, the slender root clumps and innocent-looking lichen and moss, the pale white bones here and there. "I see him, I'll *kill* him." She straightens, unwavering. "You go find him for me, Dusty. You find that asshole brother of yours."

It takes some time for Dusty to find his voice, which is still in that process of maturation. He hopes that someday soon it will be low, low, low, like a true man. Someone who can command attention and not be pushed around by people's bullshit. When he's a man, he will know exactly what to do. He will wield his power as easily as pulling floss through his teeth. But now, with the backyard in piles and the sloshy turkeys around like big fat piles of bear shit, and those strange, tiny white bones catching the light amidst the darkness of the ground and nearby forest, and Grandmother piercing the ground again and again with the swoosh, clomp of the shovel, now he can only breathe. Breathe.

Blink. Eventually begin to feel the tips of his fingers and move them just to make sure they are still attached to his body.

"What do you mean?" his voice catches, for a moment, in his throat. He can't take the smell anymore and is pinching his nose with the fingers he has just found.

"Don't you play games with me," Grandmother freezes and looks at him. He has to look away again. "In fact, you, you were the only one who knew about it." She stops and looks down at the hole below. Her whole body shakes then. She throws the shovel and it lands on the ground with a crunchy thud. She turns and starts walking to Dusty, her head low but her eyes on him. When she accidentally walks over a turkey, it splashes below her boot, making the sounds of a shallow puddle.

She steps onto the deck and grabs Dusty's upper arm, which makes him lower his hand from his nose. She is the source of the smell, it seems. He opens his mouth to keep from having to smell her, though the hotness of her wafts into him and hits the back of his throat. With both of them on the porch, it cracks and creaks. It seems to want to sail off above the ground and into the forest before them.

"Are you the one behind this? It's you, isn't it." She smiles, and for the first time he sees the black between her teeth, as if she had been eating the ground.

"No!" Dusty jerks his arm back. "I don't know what the fuck you're talking about."

"Language." She looks at him and jams a finger once, twice into the center of his chest. Grandmother has never before touched him. He lowers his head. She turns and slumps back to the shovel; lifts it and starts digging again.

She then collapses onto her bottom, her knees up by her chin, and starts howling. The sobs coming through her body remind Dusty of the way he and Will made Will's grandfather's Cherokee zoom across the road; her body, like the road, merely the passageway.

That's it, Dusty says to himself. His fool Grandmother must be left to herself and her stupid, shitty ways. She is old and losing it. What did he care? Before he can make it away, though, she speaks. It is her normal voice, completely free of sobs and tears and craziness. A switch flicked.

"At least help me collect these bones." She is pushing herself up, dusting off the bottom of her pants. "Help me collect these little bones, Dusty." And she begins going to them, the bones scattered around the piles of upturned ground and cradling them in her tank top that she has pulled out to make a hammock.

No, he isn't going to help her collect those bones from whatever had been buried back there. Isn't going out onto that rotten ground. Isn't going to defile himself with his Grandmother and her sweat and tears, her sounds and smells. He has shit to do.

The Snickers bar has partially melted in his gripped hand. When he rips open the wrapper, the chocolate is sticking to it so he has to lick it off before biting into the rest of it. He hates when that happens, prefers to eat it wholly. He eats it in three bites and washes it all down with the rest of the Coke he had left open on the counter. Immediately, though, he has to vomit it all up and runs to the bathroom. Uncle Baxter is on his bed reading a comic book. After Dusty flushes it down, Uncle Baxter calls out with a snicker, "Dude, you sick?"

It would be the swan, of course. Dusty always knew it would.

He hated those things, how they seemed to claim Loon Lake all for themselves every summer, and then decided to stay year-round, all-of-a-sudden, as if Hope was theirs. And you couldn't help but have to see them, passing Loon Lake on the way to downtown to catch a movie or to Hope Grocers or to, basically, anywhere one wanted to go in their tiny town with its twenty miles of road. The way people would come to admire them, as if they were the most fabulous creatures known to mankind, and feed them their old shitty bread, tossing out those precious morsels as if to gods in sacrifice. And the way the swans' necks arced, puny and weak, toward the surface of the lake. The way they floated across the lake effortlessly, smoothly, cutting through the snowfall white-on-white like from something out of a stupid fairy tale. But now there was only that one swan left, a young dude, he liked to think, who couldn't get married and who had been kicked out by his folks. *Time to grow up. Out you go.* And the sickening thing about it was that the swan seemed okay with it. That arc of his white neck, that gentle gliding through the as-yet unfrozen lake, that agreeable approach toward locals with stale food in their outstretched hands, all said how okay he was with his life, with his peaceful, beautiful life. All seemed to show how life was one big lake of shitty happiness.

"Wake up, people!" Dusty had wanted to scream so many times.

Dusty has the pistol, but Will wants nothing to do with it, chickened out at the last minute in a spasm of nervous, frightened sighs. He stays in the driver's seat of the Cherokee.

It is midnight. The swan is sleeping in the plants by the edge of the lake, his head tucked into his wings. Dusty's eyes have already gotten used to the dark so that the fine wash of gray clouds across the sky seems to be generating silver light. He slowly walks to the swan, carefully one foot in front of the other so that he makes as little sound as possible. *My ancestors walked like this,* he thinks, *when hunting the deer.* He chuckles inwardly. He impresses himself with his patience and agility. *I could be so fuckin kickass at gym if I wanted,* he realizes. When he is a few feet away, the swan lifts his head and stares. The deep blackness and slant of his eyes against the whiteness of the rest of him, make him look regal and pure. But now that Dusty is close, he sees that the swan isn't purely white; that he is actually covered in a fine layer of dirt. The swan continues to look at him, doesn't make a noise in fear or anger; doesn't ruffle his feathers or back away. He looks at Dusty like, perhaps, a best friend would, anticipating a joke or a plan or hot food to share.

The Kel-Tec feels heavy in Dusty's hand, even though he has held it dozens of times. He realizes that is because he is so relaxed; that his arm is hanging loosely, and the gun is pulling his arm to the ground. If he is any more relaxed, he will drop the thing, let it fall onto the ground with a silent thud.

It is not as cold as it will be during one of Hope's winter freezes, coming again, soon. The swan, however, would stay, even then; would continue to maneuver the frozen lake like a cartoon character or a creature incapable of knowing shame. The people would come to feed it more food, but it would eat just the normal amount despite the cold and snow and ice, because it would be happy there like that. It would be completely at home and at peace. It would not be hurting in any way. Its layers of feathers would keep it toasty warm. It would seem to love the quiet fall of the snow; would tolerate the week or two of ice skaters before the thaw.

Dusty, even though he has on only his light jacket and hat and no mittens, does not feel any cold; can feel the gun perfectly in the palm of his hand. He clenches his hand and pulls the gun into the center of his palm, feels the trigger against his finger. The nearest streetlight is far away and all the house lights are out. Yet still he sees the swan before him clearly, how he seems to glow against the darkness of the tree trunks and lake like an enormous hole.

The first bullet misses entirely, which causes Dusty to clench his back teeth and see great swathes of pulsing darkness before him. *Idiot!* he thinks as the swan rises and starts hissing, neck outstretched. Dusty backs up, trips, and lands hard on his butt.

Once, twice, those times he doesn't miss. Their sounds ricochet through the dark night like unseasonable thunder. The swan simply drops to the ground, hissing still. He puts his forehead down, his long neck arced balanced against the ground as if in some weight-defying, graceful move. The bullets had gone right in, and as he balances there, forehead against the ground and neck bent above, held there in stasis, the blood begins to spread and drip. He falls to the side, then, but keeps his black eyes wide open. He looks at Dusty, but Dusty's body is reflected running away in the dome of the swan's black eye, and Dusty is suddenly aware of the sounds of the wind and his boots against the rocky ground. He had done it!

Will, eyes wide and darting, has already started the engine when Dusty throws open the passenger door, plops onto the seat, sticks the gun in his jacket pocket, and tells Will to "get the fuck outta here."

"You did it, man!" Will hoots.

Dusty is jittery. "I have to piss," he says.

Up the street, Will pulls over and Dusty pees in someone's junky front yard, making a steaming puddle between a rock and a rusted-out boat engine.

In the morning, Dusty is religious in getting up at the first sound of his alarm, eating a reasonable breakfast of cold cereal with milk, and making it to first period well before the first bell. He can't account for the energy he feels. It makes him feel like a true someone, for once. Like a man.

Last night comes to him as a dreamscape, the possible source of what he senses inside, which is part energy and part an uncomfortable sharpness, as if something is beginning to just barely pierce him deep in his gut like from the blunt tip of an ancient knife. The problem, as he trudges up the hill to the high school, taking wide heavy steps, head down, his backpack nearly empty but still on his back, is that there is nowhere to go to get away from that piercing. It inhabits him like the beginning of a fever.

Last night, alone, he had returned to the swan. It took him twenty minutes to walk to the lake, the patches of snow illuminating the darkness. He had to make sure he had actually done it. He wanted to find the swan still alive, though he hated it. But when he saw it there, having grown stiff in death so quickly, he found a resolve in himself. Which was the resolve to carry on that, on his walk back, turned into a resolve to muster some strength in his secret action.

When the police were called to the swan the next day, it made the front page of *The Daily Storm*. The black & white photo of the swan's body covered the front page. *If anyone has any information at all,* the article ended, *please contact the Hope police immediately.*

"It is horrifying and a disgrace," mayor Marc Randal said later that week at the beginning of the Assembly. "Let me just say that this will not go unaccounted for. We will find whoever did this, this evil thing."

People talked. In Lucy's cafe, at the meeting of the Chamber of Commerce, the Rotary; at work and church and the Hope Grocers. Some thought it was the town drunk, Frank, who roamed the streets and taunted walkers in a perpetual state of drunkenness. Wouldn't he just die already? Others kept their thoughts to themselves, barely willing to admit that it could have been their uncle or son or father or daughter, people they knew hovering near, at, already over the edge.

Two mothers and their twentysomething daughters sat cupping their mugs of lattes in Lucy's Cafe one morning. They all attended the local Assembly of God and met once a week at Lucy's before work. Their hair was impeccably blond and their eyes the bluest shade of blue. Once a month the mothers would go together to get their nails done at Sherry's Salon next to the Hope Hotel. "Can you imagine?" said one. "Who would do something like that? Who?" said another. "I don't like it," said the other, urgently sipping her coffee and taking a hasty bite of her cranberry scone. The crumbs stayed on the corners of her mouth until her tongue flicked out quickly to each corner and wiped them clean. Again and again, the tongue flicked. Her head shook once violently. "Let's just not talk about it. I don't want to even think about it!"

Grandmother, meanwhile, had put everything back into the yard. There were great sections of it smooth and patted down and buried deep and perfect.

-4-

Home Range

Bear tended to be shy and docile, and on top of that, had a particularly heightened startle reflex. He didn't like heavy rainfalls (last year it had rained without stopping for the entire month of September) or aggressive ravens or falling trees (there was a natural wind tunnel in the forest near Salmon River where trees fell regularly and snapped surprisingly). This is why he preferred his aloneness, hugging the margins between town and forest, and dreaded coming across any of the strange bears that tended to come down from the mountains at the end of winter. They would pick fights over the bright yellow shoots of the baby skunk cabbage, but he knew better than to hold his ground. Standing, he was only eight feet tall. He had been born the smaller, weaker one, yet it was his caution that kept him from being shot as his brother had last year. The humans were scary and unpredictable; stinky and noisy. They carried around guns that killed immediately, or if they didn't, as in the case of big, old Silver Face Bear who had lived on Bear Bread Mountain and roamed it like a sentry, they would kill gradually after days of leaked blood and anguish. Silver Face had returned to his spot by the creek to die. Bear had avoided that spot for months, eventually cautiously coming to it again when the smell had disappeared, finding there several massive rib bones picked and washed completely clean by the rain.

Where Silver Face went after death, Bear didn't know. But there were entire populations of human ghosts in the woods. They were children and parents – families roaming incomplete; Tlingit warriors and Russian soldiers; contemporary folks looking, by their dress, more like the living than the dead; most in clothes, some not. Bear saw them all the time and knew without specifically knowing that they had always been there. He watched them walk in circles in Totem Park at night. They bumped into the totem poles and climbed to the very tops of the spruce trees. They fell into rivers and creeks and walked aimlessly into the ocean waves over and over again, out until they toppled and the waves brought them back in or carried them farther down the rocky shore and bashed them into massive half-submerged boulders covered in knife-edged barnacles.

Everything could see the ghosts except the humans; the trees, the ravens, the eagles, the heart crabs, the deer, the river otters, the salmon could even sense them – Bear had once watched whole schools of them shudder away from the strange, living shadow a ghost in jeans and a long-sleeved shirt had cast across the river. When Bear felt antsy and aggressive, sometimes when he felt hopelessly powerless, he would attack them because he knew he could. He had knocked one over, once, just to do it, but also out of irritation, and the ghost, a young girl with long black braids and in a beaded dress, had simply gotten back up. He had knocked her down again, hard, and she had again risen. So he hit her over and over until growing bored.

All winter Bear roamed, alone with the ghosts and the owls and the ravens and deer. When the snow came, he buried himself into the forest floor and found warmth from the body of the earth. When the snow melted, he arose and found his favorite tree to file his claws on and to scratch his back. The rough bark dug into his skin, and it felt good.

The winter, so-far, had been mild. There was still skunk cabbage to dig up, their roots still delicious though tough and old. There was a cranberry here and there, tiny and sour. There were voles, but hard to catch beneath the cover of the forest. Bear, however, had learned how to access the human world to get exactly what he wanted, which is why he was rarely ever hungry. Perhaps he had grown a bit out of shape eating human food, and sometimes it made him sick and tired. But mostly, it was easy. Like finding whole salmon carcasses in garbage cans, just sitting out there in front of the houses at night. Once, one can had been too hard to open, so he simply lifted it and threw it. It landed with a bang on the ground and spilled out all kinds of strange delicacies and, glorious! chunks of hacked-up salmon and rockfish including their most delicious heads and eyes.

Occasionally, the ravens chatted with him. Mostly, though, they mocked him. "Hey, shrimpy!" they called, tilting their heads and eyeing him with precisely their one eye. "You smell like human food," one said to him from a branch way above. "But also just your nasty bear smell. Isn't it too bad you can't fly?" And she threw back her head and laughed into the quiet, cold forest air. "Must be tough having to stay down there all the time, finding places to hide." Bear lunged up into the tree's lowest branches. He tried reaching for the pesky thing but fell several feet short.

One night, in a growing snowfall, he found himself down along the one downtown street. The town, once he had grown brave enough, had surprised him in many ways. It was loud. Even at night there was a constant humming and buzzing that underrode the crashing of the nearby ocean waves. The sidewalk didn't give under his paws. There were few lights here; a streetlight every so often. As he walked he sniffed, preparing himself for having to meet a human, but not thinking beyond that because behind every window were things the town was showing him that baffled and amazed him: headless humans with clothes on, frozen; flower arrangements in colors he had no concept of; miniature houses and cars; a train stopped in its tracks; there, in a doorway, a big stuffed bear standing on its back legs, a strange nose and goofy eyes that shocked him; a place, across the street, still humming with dim lights and sounds, the piercing, sour smells of humans inside.

One stumbled out then, head down, and vomited on the sidewalk, slowly spreading darkness against the snow. The smell was overwhelming. The human finished and then looked up, saw Bear, and froze. Bear stopped too and stared. His shyness and fear, for the moment, had abated. This human was seeing him and doing nothing. It reminded Bear of the ghosts that roamed the island, and Bear worked his nose more quickly to make sure. It, however, smelled terrible. Suddenly, it held out its hand and started making a low, quiet rumble; it stepped directly into its vomit and began to cross the street.

The snow had started falling heavier. Bear noticed a change in the smell of the air. The street between him and the human was smooth with fresh snow. Bear felt the cold wet of the snowflakes on his nose. The human marked the street with its procession, its hand out, its eyes on Bear. Eye-to-eye made Bear uncomfortable, even though the human smelled like crazy and weakness. Eye-to-eye is what happened during fights.

The human was coming after Bear in the spirit of the living. It seemed to be having problems seeing, though, and beneath Bear's burgeoning feelings of fear and anxiety, Bear wondered if he could use this strange fact to his advantage. Could simply walk up the side street and disappear under the old Russian tower on the hill until the human left him alone. Instead, Bear stayed. When the human tripped coming off the sidewalk and fell onto its knees and elbows, Bear jumped back, startled, and ready for fighting or running, whatever came. But the human simply dropped down altogether on its stomach, making terrible noises, and licked the snow, its little pink tongue jutting out once and bringing into its mouth a small ball of snow. It then rolled onto its back, still laughing, and looked up at the sky that had cleared moments before and was awash in stars barely visible above the muted glow of the streetlight nearby.

It seemed to Bear, then, that this human, though not a ghost, was similar to one, straddling a line between both worlds; occupying some new, strange home range that included the living and the dead and the island and Bear too.

The human rolled back to its stomach and pushed itself to its knees, its head still hanging. It took some time for it to rise all the way. When it did, it began leaning one way and took a quick step before falling down again into the snow and then pushing itself up again. In the street it walked slowly; it kept its head down and its eyes on Bear.

"Hey bear!" it shouted.

The noise, like a gunshot, punctured the quiet. Bear's skin trembled and instinctively he let out a low growl. He'd never get used to the humans' noise. They were, ultimately, nuisances, and this one he could take.

"Yo bear, yo sorry bear," it talked softer now as if its own sound had also startled it. It held out its hand and came slowly across the street, closer. It left long swaths of cement behind in the snow. It kept its head low but its eyes on Bear. Still, Bear knew the human couldn't quite see him, and so he relaxed again, only somewhat unsure. The humans had brought such crazy lights, after all, and so many things in the shop windows. The humans left out meat and threw out perfectly good fish. They had concocted breads and cheeses and thin, salty meats. They owned live animals that so easily spilled hot blood. They had boats that bobbed in the harbors and made tinging noises in the wind. They decorated their buildings with colors and lights; they erected totems and built sidewalks on which to lumber down that were easy though cold and hard and ungiving. They were givers and takers; he just had to be sure of which one he was dealing with.

"So, bear," it was ten feet away. Its smell came so strongly now that Bear blinked his eyes, once, twice. Shook his head.

It was time to run.

He knew he was a weak, foolish bear. He knew he shouldn't have lasted this long; that all he really knew how to do was run and hide. He would die before growing old, whether from sickness or gunshot or the aggression of another bear. That had always been clear to him. But now, he wondered if there might be something not bad coming, whether it was food or something else. How many times had a full living human, though quite possibly half in the ghost world, come directly to him, talking, weak, unafraid? Never. Surely this was something to stay for.

"So, bear, my man," it stumbled forward. "I been comin' to this place for as long assss shiiiiit, assslong as I can 'member. Which ain't too long, lemme tell ya." And it laughed. "I can 'member yestuhday. Yeah, I can 'member comin' yestuhday." It turned momentarily and gestured to the bar behind with its shoulder. "This place's my home 'way from home. My peeps." It stopped, then, and stood for a second, two, and then stepped up onto Bear's sidewalk. It concentrated for this. Bear watched it carefully lift first one foot then another up and over the curb. When it made it, it stopped again, six feet from Bear. It was close enough now to see Bear's large hump of muscle on his back. Bear's halo of coarse hair around his wide face and cheeks. His long black nose and tiny close-set eyes. Somewhere, deep inside, the human sensed this was foolish. Yet the sky was star-full and the night was pure silence, and its head was buzzing with the quiet, soothing static of a certain, gorgeous, normally unattainable peace.

"A fuckin' bear," it mumbled. "I'm standin' in front of a fuckin' bear. You ain't gonna kill me, man, are ya?" It stopped for a moment. "Hey!" it shouted too loudly. Bear shivered, backed up. His growl was too low to hear. "My ancest'rs run way back with you, ya know? They prob'ly been here just as long as yours been." It began walking to Bear again, its hand outstretched as if it were about to pet a giant puppy.

He could kill it, Bear decided then. It was stupid and small; skinny. Long straggly black hair; hardly anything on. It smelled like something long spoiled, about to be fully obliterated like the mushrooms in the forest after a month of nonstop rain.

When the human touched Bear's nose, barely, just grazing the nose with a fingertip hot and tiny, Bear huffed and tensed; his paws, his claws, tried to grasp the cold, hard cement ground. The humans had killed so many of their own. The ghosts roamed and roamed and went nowhere, endlessly.

"You," it wasn't looking directly into Bear's eyes; instead, at Bear's large black nose, right there. "You always been here," it was saying so quietly and its hot breath made Bear's skin instantly contract.

Bear didn't know what to think of the touch of the human's fingers, the hot, strange sensation of which was still there across the top of his nose. He couldn't take much more of its smell and was suddenly intensely uneasy and boiling angry.

"Me, I'm a half-Indian fuckin' *drunk*." And the human raised its eyes and looked into Bear's close-set black ones, speckled with brown and gold [like the eyes, *how could they be?*, of his girlfriend who had recently told him, in one of their fits of mutual anger, that she had been unfaithful; she had been unfaithful for years, and how was it that he, dumbass, had never known. He had gone after her, then, not trembling, but in control, clear-headed like he had never felt before. His hands fit all the way around her throat, a female's most vulnerable spot, though there were so, so many. Her throat seemed to welcome what was coming, easy, like smashing in a salmon's head once it has been reeled in, lost its fight, into the boat. A given. What was meant to be. His hands were superhumanly strong, a metal vise, and they squeezed, squeezed the air right out of her body. There was no air at all for her. She made no sounds, just looked at him with her eyes wide, pleading, afraid. That there could be a combination of pleading and afraid, delighted and surprised him when he saw it. For she had deserved it. But it was also something to see what came after that, those base reactions, which were pure and simple biology; her body shaking to continue to stay alive, to subconsciously revive itself; her eyes glazing over as if in some kind of post-haze high; her body falling limp, which meant the full weight of her was suddenly then on his hands. Throwing lighthouse closer to the indifferent ocean by the skirts of Mt. Agnes had been hard but required. She had been so heavy, overweight, too many Doritos and beers. He had always wanted her thinner. When he rolled her over the side of his boat, she almost tipped him, but when she was gone into the darkness of the waves that were reflecting the darkness of the night all around, pure, pure darkness like only the complete wilderness can give, she left him light-feeling and so awash in relief that he felt like he had to go, right then and there, and so he peed into the gently thrashing waves. Now, staring into Bear's eyes that looked exactly like hers, he began to feel afraid, which bled into a growing sense of regret, and whether that regret was the alcohol talking or his own puny conscience (for he had never really given much thought to the idea of a conscience just like he had never given any thought to the God they all prayed to at St. Ignatius when he was a kid and was made to attend mass with his grandparents on Christmas Eve), he couldn't know for sure. Up to that moment, he had believed he loved Bear with every living, sinewy strand of his body. But now, there was no time for that, for love–a fantasy. Now, he would have done anything to have his gun. He felt his body, then, really felt it as if his physicality had suddenly been given a presence like a bubble reverse-popping into the freezing air; felt his bare arms and jacket-less torso; felt the snow from his fall slowly melting into his jeans]

For Bear, it had been too much minutes ago. He huffed into the air, leaving clouds of heat behind. He started rocking from paw to paw, moving his head side-to-side, but never taking his eyes off the human, who reeked. Who was challenging him with its touch and closeness. With the fact that it was even there. When could a human ever be trusted? When had he ever seen a human relinquish the upper hand? He had never seen that.

When Bear pushed himself off the ground and stood, he looked down the two-and-a-half feet at the human's glossy upturned face. The human couldn't stop looking into Bear's eyes even though it was shaking with cold and terror and was suddenly making sounds too loudly.

When Bear came down with all his weight, almost as wide as he was tall, the human simply lowered its head.

[In that moment, he had only one memory, which was of him as a boy collecting herring eggs with his grandmother from the hemlock branches she laid out every year several feet off Jackson's beach. They would skiff over and he was the one who got to bring the branches in, dripping, the water cold, the eggs plastered like bulbous gelatin across the branches and needles. The eggs he liked to eat straight from the branches. One-by-one he picked them, even as tiny as they were, and he popped them between his front teeth, releasing pure cold salt.]

Last second, Bear changed his mind. There was something about the human, ineffectual, weak, bowing to the ground, half-alive half-dead.

When Bear came down, he left enormous marks in the snow inches from the human's stained, booted feet. He turned and ran around the corner and up the hill. As he ran, his whole muscled body vibrated like the way light reflected from the sky moves on ocean water. His breath left behind explosions of steam.

At the hill he slowed, he walked, knowing the human wouldn't be following. It would be spread on the sidewalk; soiled, stinking. Half-alive. Moaning.

It wasn't yet close to dawn, so Bear headed back to the house with the frozen turkeys in the yard. His stomach was aching with hunger. He'd had too much excitement and confusion for one night. The thing was, though, is that he knew he could have killed; that even though he was a small bear and timid, and now most assuredly a "towny," as the ravens called him, he was still a bear. And it was suddenly clear that all this home range, *all* of it, was his.

Now, at this house, by way of the delicious fishy smells of the canneries and past the town's stoplight by the hospital, and then up through the houses like decaying mushrooms up the gentle slopes of Bear Bread mountain where a nervous dog or two left out in the cold whined as he passed, he smelled out a buried turkey and dug quickly, easily, until finding one as if it were waiting just for him. Easier than squirrel or vole or mouse. Not hot, not satisfying exactly like the wild food was, but easy and filling in its cold, salty, shallow way. With the ravens sleeping and the snow falling again and the spruce trees and muskeg before him ready to hide him when he was finished, the world was quiet and dark, almost like total, unblemished wilderness. As it had been long, long, such a long time ago.

Within the pulsing faint blue light of the shaded house, though, stood a boy.

The boy had been awake playing video games for hours; had always had trouble sleeping but then could never get up for first and second periods in the morning and was going to fail yet another year. His parents, one Tlingit the other white, were long dead. His grandmother, who was not right in her head, didn't care.

The boy watched Bear and brought the can of Coke to his lips again and again; sucked down the sweet, cold, stimulating liquid. The boy watched Bear and, unlike hardly anything else in his life, wanted to love him.

$$-5-$$

The Dead Girlfriend

If someone had said, this will be your life, and then *this* will be your after life, I would have laughed in his face. Full-on *in his face*. Because, guess what, there's no leaving the place you die in, but you don't find that out til after, there being no clues about it in life, ever, anywhere. Hawaii would have been nice. Maybe Mexico. The Caribbean. Hell, Nepal? I never been to Nepal. You know, some place like that. But Hope? *God!*

Recently, though, I've come into some money, which ain't half bad even for someone in my condition. Johnson came running into Totem Park last night, into the very center of the forest where it's dark as hell (which I know *for sure* it ain't, which is the joke, right?). He fell a couple times, banged himself up a bit, which I wasn't sorry to see because he's an asshole. Always was, even when I was with him. Too many asses in Hope, actually. Took me way too long to figure that one out. Crazy guy was probably hyped up on something, and when he gets to the very middle of the black forest, these skinny spruces all around him, half of them dead it seems like, he drops to his knees and starts digging. Crazy, frantic-like, no shovel or nothing which is why it takes him foreeeever. He buries something, and then he turns and runs away. *Stupid.*

We ghosts are all over the place. But I was the only one who saw him. I'm beginning to think after so many years of this, no wonder these ghosts lose their senses; just keep roamin around like dummies. But not me, no way in hell is that gonna be me. So I go to that spot and I unbury whatever Johnson wanted so damn much to hide, and I'm laughing to myself because he's so fucking stupid he don't even know there's, like, a whole other world around him of stuff he can't even see! And sure enough, what do I find? A box full of fucking *cash*. It's as real as flesh, and there I am holding it because somehow I can. Never seen so much money in my life. Guess I'm gonna now that I'm dead!

Morning comes, though for us ghosts it don't really matter because we don't never sleep, and the thought pops in my head, what's a ghost gonna do with so much real-life cash? Specially if Hope is the only place she's got to be in. Then another thought pops in my head, is that I gotta hold on to this box with *my life* because there's no telling what these others might do. Some of these new ghosts, like me, we're a little more hyper. Nothing like those Indians walking around in full regalia, all serious like, or some of the others, damn Russians looking like they just walked out of one of those books I had to read junior year high school, all Victorian like. They just roam. They don't even talk or look at you. I've seen relatives, like people I've only seen in my grandma's photos. Honest. They don't even know me. Whatever. There was that girl, Tanya, who got stabbed last year. All over the news because they couldn't find who did it and no, I don't know neither. Sorry, no superpowers. She's around and I kind of knew her, and wouldn't you know she's still just as much a bitch dead as she was alive. Soon as I knew I was dead and that all these people around were dead too, and that this wasn't, like, heaven or hell or what the fuck this is cause it's obviously way too full to be purgatory, I saw her and immediately went up to her because I, like, knew her not too long ago.

"How we get outta here?" I asked her. And she just looked at me like I was disgusting, like she had always kind of looked at me, she being prettier and thinner like she thinks she's Tlingit royalty.

"We *don't*," she said like I was stupid.

"Well, you even try?" I said back, a little tougher for her having talked that way to me.

"I been told."

She wasn't even looking at me; seemed to be about to turn away as if she were so busy and just had to get to somewhere *so* important.

"Don't you know there's a force field around us?" She was looking at me now and talking way down to me, like I was a little kid. So I just smacked her, right in the nose with my fist, and she fell back like a cheap punching bag, that easy, but then just got right back up and laughed at me. Then she started pointing out over the ocean and around to the mountains and up at the sky, like she was some crazy spinning toy.

"It's everywhere, Jill. You can't leave." And then she looked right at me, all wise-like though I know she ain't; she's just looks is all she is. "You better get used to it."

Well, I had to smack her again for that. She was one of those tramps, hanging out too young in the bars looking for men without knowing she gotta be *tough*. Me? I'd fight all of these ghosts for this money box; they're as easy as sliced pie. Which by-the-way, I could go for a piece of pie right about now. But we don't eat. Don't need to. The food goes in but just falls right out, and that's some nasty shit.

So I got this cash. Haven't counted it yet, but it's *a lot*. I'm thinking it might be what I need to get out of here once and for all. Because I've always wanted outta here. Just been tied too tight, and, yeah, I guess I was a someone here, and my parents were someones, kind of drunk all the time but with their peeps at least and grandma stopped the drink once she turned Jehovah's Witness. Actually, my roots in Hope go *all the way* back to the very beginning; my ancestors were the *first*, bitch. Okay, so maybe that might have been hard to give up. Whatever. But now that I know that *this* could be eternity? Roaming around all the usual places without having any e-ffect? It's boring, is what it is.

It doesn't take long. One day last week I can't even remember. Woosh. It's gone. I've seen it. Ghosts are only fresh for a few months, maybe at most a year, and then they start to go really dead, as if dead weren't dead enough. Brain dead. Or soul dead or whatever you wanna call it. This morning I looked down and couldn't remember what my hands were called. "Hands!" I had to tell myself over again when it came to me. Wiggling my fingers is what did it. But look, my pointer finger won't wiggle.

Yeah, it happens like that.

I always got myself mixed up with the wrong men, for the excitement, I guess. Those were the only kind of men I knew. Thank god I ain't no psychologist, but maybe those were the only kind of men I really wanted. I was a big woman. A true Tlingit woman. Not a pansy-ass whitey with their skinny asses and delicate, prissy laughs. "Oh, ha ha ha!" I loved bar fights and I loved roughing up my men a bit; needed them somewhat weaker than me cause it was so much fun to push them around and get a kick from that like a boost of energy and, yeah, probably self-esteem. Whatever. And the sex had to be rough, and oh, now that was fine. And the men didn't mind that at all! Rob should've known there were others; that that was the kind of woman I was. Fat, extra large, big pussy, loud and in charge, the kind of stuff men love. Or the men I knew; the only kind of man that really mattered.

But getting the life choked out of me, now that was something I wasn't expecting. *Fuck!* And the fact that Rob, puny and drunk most of the time and never knowing his right hand from his left and barely able to scrounge out a living like any reasonable human can do, was so damn *strong*. Yeah, that took me by surprise. He lifted me up so high that my toes could barely touch the ground. And my body knew it was over before I did, and the next thing I knew I was in the water by crazy Vic's lighthouse, swimming to shore, not cold at all. Actually, not feeling a single thing.

Revenge is a glorious bitch, let me tell ya. I've busted one or two noses in my life; women who were getting all up in my face over some man or another, and there was that time I had to beat up that girl in high school for calling my older sister a cunt. Sure, I saw plenty of people beating up on each other growing up, like families do. But most of the time they were just drunk or high, and I guess I just never liked that stuff. The few times I got drunk it made me weaker. I didn't like that shit. Why give an ass-kicking if you're not really going to *give* one? I've been in so many fights I can't remember now. But there's no revenge as ghost. I've crept into Rob's apartment at night and sat on him and strangled him myself, but my hands are useless and he never feels me, which is the first time in my life I haven't been felt. Fucking weird. Other-worldly. I even tried to get a knife into him once. It went into him and came right back out clean. Nada. I do it anyway, when I feel like it. Just to feel a little better.

Whaddya gonna do with your one true life, some poet said somewhere. Well, that's a good question. And I'm thinking about that now. I really am.

If I were alive, I'd take this box full of cash and buy myself a one-way ticket to, shit. Paris? Florida? I've been to Juneau and Anchorage. Never been out of Hope for long; never left the great big state of Alaska. The Final fuckin' *Frontier*. Spent my time working the counter at the Fisherie, serving out fried fish and ice cream to stupid tourists. Spent some time at the car rental place 'til I quit, just walked out one morning because the job was as boring as shit. Spent some time in the jail after putting Wanda in hospital. Just minor injuries, really. She forgave me, but we're distant cousins. She'd have to. A live person wouldn't fool around with this much cash. She'd get out while she could. She'd maybe start over somewhere. Learn a new language. Pretend she was an Asian instead of Tlingit. I could pass. I've passed before with some of those whites up for fishing; their big, expensive, outdoorsy vacation where they get to pretend to be real "outdoorsy men" for a week or two. Get their kicks out of laying a real live Indian or an Asian or a Latina. Whatever they want. And I never minded taking their cash, though no one ever came right out and said "hooker" because I ain't no hooker. That's one thing I'd never do.

For the first time in my life, I've made a plan. I keep thinking of what that poet said. Makin' something out of your one true life or whatever. It's a pretty quick walk to the airport over the bridge. I didn't walk much when I was alive because why walk when you can drive?, but now I'm sort of able to hover-walk, which makes getting places easier. I really could've used that when I was alive. But oh well. *Tough*. You know? Like there's gotta be at least one good thing about all this.

I got myself to the airport this afternoon. It's always fun hangin around the airport, being around all those people when they come off the flights three times a day. Their heat and noise. Kinda jovial. The runway is full of us, mostly dummies who're probably lost or something because the runway begins and ends in the ocean; there ain't anywhere else to go around there unless you can figure your way across the bridge and back to the main island, which most of them probably can't. I've watched the airplane just cut right through them, like fog, and me, I can walk right through people without them even knowing a thing. Sometimes, that can feel a little lonely. Ya know?

At the airport I saw my uncle Jesse, once, but he's been dead for fifteen years and didn't know me from nothing. Hanged himself in his room at the men's recovery center. But now he looks just fine; neck ok and all.

I got myself to the airport this afternoon *with* the money box because I ain't takin any chances at all, even with an island full of stupids. Now that it's not tourist season anymore (ha, ha, like we're hunting them or something, which most of us locals wouldn't mind doing) there are only two flights going south to Seattle. 7 AM and 6 PM. I'm planning on the 7 AM one tomorrow. If there is a force field, I'm gonna find out. It's gonna have one angry bitch to deal with.

So here I am. Sittin on this chair. And now that I'm gonna do this, I'm kinda excited in a nervous way. Like, being unseen like this makes the whole world feel really open, like I could walk into any club or country and no one would say a thing, stop me at the fuckin door. No passport. No bags. Just this money box because, who knows, I might need it. It's conceivable. "It's conceivable." Ha! Did I just say that? Like some smart-ass! "It's conceivable" my big fat Indian ass.

I keep looking around for this "force field," and guess what, I don't see it, which makes me think that Tanya don't know nothin, which ain't a surprise at all.

People start showing up early, 6 a.m. People get nervous about flights. Especially the white folks with their matching bags and made-up faces and little pinched mouths. When security opens, I walk right through and nothing. Actually walk right *through* the people standing in line, going through security. Whaddya know, machines can't detect us! Not at all. When I enter the waiting room that's when I see it.

It's like a wall of water, see-through but rippling, right at the entrance to the walkway to the plane. This is some serious sci-fi shit, and, yeah, wow, I'm scared. Scared like that time my dad came after me or like the one and only time I tried cocaine and passed out and hit my head on the counter. Yeah, scared like the moment I realized Rob was going to kill me and there was nothing, nothing, I could do about it. But also scared in a more real way because this force field looks like God, maybe, or gods or whatever you want to call the spiritual stuff that's not anywhere, actually, until I see *this*. Like I'm in some movie or dream and none of it's real; it's like pure imagination. But the water wall is moving, rippling, and it's right there between me and the plane.

The stewardess opens the door to the walkway and people start lining up so fuckin nervous. The wheelchairs first and then the rich people pulling their fancy, leather carry-ons behind them. They look so stupid and mighty with their little wheeled suitcases. The stewardess smiles fake-like at everyone. They just pass through. The wall bounces and moves around them like jello but no one notices a thing. And then there's me.

I gotta get through that thing.

I'm ready for it. People are all crowded up around me, bumping into each other, faces looking stretched-like, all anxious to get onto that plane as if it was gonna leave without them.

"Relax, people!" I say out loud even though I know they can't hear me.

"'Cause I'm relaxed. And I'm about fuckin ready to enter this Star Trek-looking force field, which as far as I know is gonna explode me or send me to hell or whatever happens to dead people when they die again."

I step up to it but before I get any closer it sends out these lines that zap me all over, and it fuckin *hurts*. Which is, like, a surprise, to hurt like that. So after a few minutes I turn around and head in backwards, but same thing. These lines come out and knife me all over, is what it feels like, but I'm not bleeding. I'm not nothing except hurting so bad and frozen. People are all over me, itchin to get onto that ramp and into their seats. They're passin right through me. And I'm *hurtin*. Bad. Like couldn't they just *stop* for a minute, let me just recover a sec. Because this force field ain't playin around. It's fuckin *supernatural,* and all I can think is that it's not fuckin *fair*. I should at least have a chance. So I get mad, which is what I usually do. Anger ain't such a bad thing. These people are gettin on my nerves. I shove through them 'cause I need the space. I need the whole waiting room.

I'm fat, yeah, I'll admit it. But being fat never meant I couldn't move fast if I wanted to. I can move fast. So I run. My breasts and tummy hurt as they bounce. I haven't full-on run since middle school. My knees feel like they're gonna pop any second and I won't make it. I'll lose my lower legs right at the knees. I'll be a fuckin crippled ghost forever. But I think of something as that wall gets closer, rippling and wiggling before me. Before the lines get me I take the money box like I'm about to punch someone in the face and I throw it as hard as I can right into that wall, and the strangest thing happens.

This big hole opens right up around that box and the cash goes flying and wherever the dollars touch, holes appear and close like mouths yawning, but these mouths have these big wavering lips that suck themselves close almost as soon as they open. But the hole in the middle from the box grows bigger before getting smaller, and I just go for it. My shoulder first and then my head and I'm jumping through that thing like an Olympian. A fuckin fat Indian Olympian!

It slices me all over, going through. I feel like I'm in pieces, like some serial murderer just cut me up into all my body parts. But guess what? When I open my eyes, the people are walking right on top of me. So I get up and behind me that wall has closed back up, and before me is that long, beautiful covered walkway into the plane.

I can smell it, that airplane smell. I can smell the places I'm gonna go!

I run! I run to the airplane because guess what? Jill did it! Jill did it again.

I gotta sit. I ain't standing and I'm gonna be civilized about it, no sprawling in the aisles; so sittin' on anyone's lap, though there's a cute guy in first class. And for a sec I really, really regret that I'm not still alive getting first class service in first fuckin class. "I'll take an orange juice," I'd say. "The steak, please. Coffee with cream, no sugar, please." I'd have one of those designer carry-ons. I'd be on my way to some big-shot conference in Switzerland. Sure, I'd be twenty, thirty pounds lighter. I'd treat myself real well, and I'd have a steady boyfriend who's a lawyer with a penthouse in Seattle that we'd meet up in on weekends in between trips to France and Italy. "What do you want?" he'd ask me when we'd go shopping. Bloomingdales, Nordstrom. Some rich person's store like that. "I'll take the diamond earrings," I'd say. Whoot! Can you even imagine? Now that's some funny ass shit.

So I find a seat with the stewardesses. There's an empty one. A little cramped, but not bad. A little window to look out of. And as the plane takes off I see Hope fading away below so that soon it's just ocean and ocean and mountain after mountain, and Hope is this teeny tiny nothing. Like, I've never seen it like that before. And for once I'm not thinking about how wrong Tanya was, there being no way out, skinny dumbass. And how stupid everyone is down there. I honestly just don't know myself at all because I suddenly know all the answers. I see no separation. Like, bam! Just like that. Everything everywhere anytime is just all there laid out like the galaxies. I know it all, and it stays with me and settles into me so that I'm like the air itself, not weighty. Like I've been let loose into the universe and it's all me everywhere. In the ocean and in the air; in the trees down there and the clouds covering the view. In the whales hiding under the waves. Memories, poof! Desire, nadda.

That's me. Everywhere.

$$-6-$$

Larry and Marc

Oh, the feeling of the gavel in his hand during city assembly meetings. Now that was something Mayor Marc Randal never got tired of. And if he happened to be just the slightest bit high, well that helped him cut off the chief of police when he just kept going on and on about the need for more police. That helped him address the man as "dude" instead of "Chief Kularsky." And it certainly helped him tell the Tlingit elder, Lawrence Peters, to "get with the program" upon hearing that the clan wanted city money to help build a new clanhouse in the gravel parking lot by the seafood processing center.

People were a fucking nuisance, he often thought during assembly meetings where he squinted his eyes in what he thought was a commanding, menacing way. He couldn't always hide, however, the way he nervously tapped his index finger on his knee or the habit he had of jerking his head to fling his brown hair, stringy and long despite the U-shaped baldness on top. He knew that the masses were too dumb to govern themselves. They needed a leader, that's all, not an assembly of local jackasses with their "ayes" and "nays." He could, he would, be that leader. His older brother had made the Senate ten years ago. Robert, the college graduate, the lawyer. Marc wondered when he'd stop hearing his father, *why can't you be more like Robert?* Yeah, well okay then, *father.* Marc had his eyes set on the Alaska State Senate next year and wouldn't let anything get in his way.

So why was it that his oldest friend, Larry, had gone and ruined everything? And why was it that here he was, now, digging a crater the size of his mom's two-door Honda in the open space behind his and Larry's outlaw cabin up Bear Bread Mountain, big enough for all those bottles of pseudoephedrine, acetone, ammonia, and phosphorus, because there was no way in hell he was gonna waste even a little of his hard-earned stash? *He always thinks he's so fuckin' smart,* Marc attacked the ground with the rusted out shovel. *Now look who's smart!* He stopped to shout it at the treetops into the crisp, quiet mountain air. The thought made him realize just how muscular he actually was under all his skinniness, and he brought the shovel up and back and down with all his strength, as if it were a sledgehammer, just so that he could feel his arm and back muscles pop. Pistons! Firing! God, he was good. The challenge was making any damn mark in the compact, ashy soil under the wet moss. There was also a whole bunch of god-awful roots all twisted up and co-mingling and conspiring down there to keep the whole ground down like the mafia.

It's not as if Larry had wanted to spend the 125th night of his 30th year in Hope's one-room prison before Marc started hacking out his hole. He kind of liked the sound of it, though, "drug lord." That's what officer Schmidt said as he pushed Larry into the cell. Officer Schmidt was a total dumbass and had been since high school. But still, it had a ring to it; a certain CEO-ish feel to it. Besides the Grady boys, who didn't really count because it was their father who owned the bars and one of the gas stations, Larry was Hope's only thirty-something millionaire, having the previous year transformed the empty lot at the corner of Main and Fireweed into a three-storied megalith of cement and steel and moved everything over from his smaller shop down the street. It was a lot his parents had bought for him for his 25th birthday, and to finally see it bear the load of his dreams was just about as perfect as it got. The other shop owners complained at city assembly meetings that Larry's Radio Emporium blocked the view of the ocean and didn't fit in with the cute and rustic, old-fashioned look of downtown, which is what drew the tourists, after all.

"A little modernization never hurt anyone, right?" Larry had told Marc afterwards, who took pride in consistently being the sole vote either for or against the majority unless it was for something he was truly passionate about, like building the road across the island ("good for business, folks") or stopping the building of the deep water dock ("an eyesore and bad for the fishermen") or capping the already ridiculously high city hospital admin salaries.

Larry hadn't forgotten to build the penthouse suite atop Larry's Radio Emporium he had always promised himself and his parents, with stunning views of the Pyramid Mountains, the Baranov Range, and the wide-open ocean past the gentle bend in the bay. One of the first things he did, even before installing the surround-sound music system and the hot tub on the deck, had been to move his parents out of their old three-bedroom ranch— the tired, wallpapered place he had grown up in—and into their very own wing of the penthouse. His dad, large, slow, and quiet, now spent most of his days lifting flat screen TVs and 5.1 stereo systems out of boxes and into the store, taking close stock of where things were placed and if anything needed ordering. His mom, short, round, and spunky, helped Larry with the sales because the only thing she enjoyed more than seeing her son's store full of customers, was listening to him explain to one the difference between Panasonic and Sony. Many times she had said to his dad, "Giving Larry that fifty grand to open his little store ten years ago was the best move we made, Jack. You know? And then the lot.

Remarkable boy, huh?" And Jack had simply nodded because his wife always had such a good way of saying things that there was no reason to add any more. Their son was quite conceivably Hope's most successful resident ever, they conceded to each other.

By senior year of high school, Larry had subscriptions to *Forbes, Businessworld,* and *Money.* He began buying and selling stocks on the little Mac his parents had bought him for his sixteenth birthday. On Thursday, March 21, 1994, he had sold $2000 worth of stock BXGT, making it a record-earning day that he had noted in the little journal he had labeled "Stocks" in black sharpie on the cover, and which he kept religiously. Before money, he had been into chess and birding, which he still enjoyed, though he hadn't done the annual December Hope Bird Count since he was twenty when he had had Hope's highest count. He also played a mean trombone that he still got out occasionally to play in the bathroom because he liked the acoustics there and the big mirror. But his destiny had always been money. Before he turned twenty, he had taken out loans and purchased a few cheap properties, bought a fixer-upper near the ferry terminal that he later sold for 125% of what he bought it for, and had decided that what Hope needed, and what most of the Filipino cruise ship workers seemed to want when they roamed downtown, was a damn good electronics stores. Now, if one wanted to buy Sennheiser wireless headphones, one went to Larry. And it was at that point, when one wanted to buy Sennheiser wireless headphones and one went to Larry, that he stopped looking at himself in the mirror and seeing a short, fat, pale boy with no chin, and started seeing someone who actually *knew* things and was now quite rich.

Drugs hadn't been a part of the plan. He had just sort of fallen into them during a trip to Hawaii the winter of '01 where he met some nice, local guys who convinced him that drugs were an amazing investment, and they had a whole string of investors and buyers from Alaska all along the Pacific islands to the Philippines.

Imagine! It had turned into a nice side thing, and though he could have enjoyed his own drugs at discount, he mostly stayed away from the stuff, preferring instead to remain clear-headed. He did enjoy sex with coke, though, and liked to throw parties in his new place. And who didn't smoke marijuana? It wasn't long after Larry's third month in his new store that private detective Linda Booth, acting on behalf of the Hope Police Department who had been watching closely for about a year, discovered that Larry's Radio Emporium was also Hope's and the outlying villages' number one source of cocaine, mushrooms, marijuana, and heroin.

Linda couldn't have done it without twenty-year-old Kyle Anderson who offered to do whatever he could to bring Larry down after discovering that his girlfriend of two years, Stella, had been sleeping with "fat ol' dickwad" for months. It was an easy job because Kyle was one of Larry's regulars, every payday eagerly retrieving from Larry at the counter of Larry's Radio Emporium a sealed white envelope with his name written in black across the front. In plain daylight. In front of everyone.

"No one even notices," Larry had smiled. And he firmly rubbed Kyle's neck like he tended to do with people because he had read in some magazine, hadn't he?, that it made people feel trusting and at ease.

And no one had until Kyle had. Started caring about who was fucking his girl, and how it wasn't fair that she got for free what he had to work hard for. It was both those things. And so it was nothing for Kyle to walk into Larry's penthouse one Saturday night with a wire across his chest and party like he never had before, even if it cost him one week's pay. The Hope PD had reimbursed him for that, but he hated the pigs as much as everyone else, and even though he wanted to rip up that check into a hundred little pieces, he didn't. He went to the ATM immediately. He deposited that thing before he had it five minutes.

The cabin would be the thing that would keep Larry from talking. His prints were all over the pots, his purple coffee mug, the toilet seat, the matches. Sometimes Larry helped Marc separate the crystals into baggies, though usually Marc liked control over the whole thing. And as tempting as it was to tell their friends, to bring the girls up for a night or two, they had shaken on it: it was their space. Their secret. Yet there was the fact of Larry's flabby mouth and the way he could just go on and on about whatever. When Marc had been paired with Larry sophomore year at Hope High so that Larry could tutor him in algebra, Larry wouldn't shut up about chess or birds. Had to be one or the other. Marc knew he'd shoot either himself or Larry before the semester was out. But by the time Marc had passed algebra with a C-, he had gotten used to, maybe even kind of liked, Larry's fact-full, innocent babblings. There was something so unpretentious and real about Larry that had sort of made Marc feel as if he didn't have to work so hard to be the cool guy, though, admittedly, that mostly came naturally.

Last night played through his mind like an endless repeating of a horror movie he knew would end bad. As soon as he found out that Larry had been arrested and was definitely going to get out on the $25,000 bail (because any fool knew this was chump change to Larry), he immediately left his father's transportation business where he worked as ground manager, raced home in his dark blue GT, and spent the following hour deleting every single e-mail he and Larry had shared. The normal ones about fishing and hanging out, but also the recent ones inviting him to the penthouse parties, and especially the ones asking about the latest business, which was the meth that Marc conveniently made in high-quality small batches on his 25-foot boat, The Little Lady, and also knew was being poorly made by a couple of dummies on city property at the old sawmill at the end of the road who gave him a cut to keep it hush-hush.

That night he drove down to Sealing Harbor and efficiently dumped five gallons of lighter fuel over the beautiful wooden planks of The Little Lady, which had been his father's old boat (he figured he would conveniently collect insurance on the thing and upgrade, finally). When he lit the match, he noticed for a moment how little impact the light of the flame had on the darkness of the harbor; how there were probably animals out there in the jet-black water doing their thing without anyone seeing them at all. The flame roared into a fire immediately and then the boat unexpectedly exploded, singeing Marc's eyebrows and nose hairs. Dammit, he had forgotten about the couple bottles on board. "Must have accidentally left the hot pad on in the kitchen," he told the firefighters when the explosion awoke all the boat dwellers and suddenly he was the attention of every loser in Hope.

With each shovelful and swing of soil, he felt the muscles in his arms and back tighten and move. Pistons! Firing! Though on the water fishing is where he really liked to be, it was peaceful there in the woods too, just the sound of the thrushes and the *tick, swoosh* of the shovel penetrating impossible ground. The impressive sound of his own breath, firm and steady. He was surprised to see to what degree his abilities could turn, and he knew he was *past* 360 degrees; that he was operating on some super-human level of speed and efficiency and strength. Skinny, weak, my ass! he told himself, remembering suddenly all those times he'd lost to his brother wrestling, monkeying around. Then finally, to see all those precious bottles half-buried like silent little children and then to cover them, putting the earth back in its place. That was him, changing the very earth itself, planting strange new hybrid seeds among the roots, and only he would know!

When the job was done, he jogged across the spot and scuffed it up with his boots; threw some spruce needles and plant detritus on top and jogged across again, then stood back and looked at it out of the side of his eyes to make sure it looked natural. Not quite, but then maybe it was just the way the late afternoon light streamed through the spruce trees, making things appear and disappear in bars of orange and blue.

It doesn't matter, he told himself. It's as good as done. There was no way in hell anyone would think to dig. When he walked back into the cabin, he seemed to notice it for the first time and fell relieved and sweaty into the couch with his jacket and boots still on. He could smell the smoke from the thousand fires he and Larry had made in the stove, now a part of the wood grain in the beams, the cotton fibers in the couch and drapes. The thrushes trilled outside. He thought that perhaps there was a bear trudging around somewhere out there. The way the sun piercing through the lone large window opposite the couch seemed to shift suddenly, at which point he felt the ball in his stomach from all those Power Bars he had lived on over the past 24 hours. He could really use a steak. Hot, salty, juicy. Some mashed potatoes. Creamed spinach on the side. Tall glass of cold Alaskan Amber. There was a spot waiting for him at Raven's Bar and Grill. Food he could count on; the family discount besides the one for being Hope's youngest mayor to-date, which was fucking predictable for him, like wasn't he always going to be that! And the guys around the pool table and Jasmine the Indian waitress who looked just like a Japanese princess to him, but who was taken so it didn't matter anyway, but to see her walk, sway her hips, carry a tray of drinks above her shoulder. Damn.

The erection he always got thinking of Jasmine inspired him. He jumped up, set the volume on high on his iPhone on the table and clicked the Sting Greats album he had meticulously created several years ago. He centered himself in the middle of the floor by the couch and began to jerk his hips, first to the right and then to the left, in perfect timing to "Stolen Car." He shrugged his narrow shoulders up, back, down. "Oh the smell of the leather always excited my imagination," he sang though he had never been able to carry a tune, eyes closed, flushed face turned to the wooden beams. Every time his shoulders pulsed forward in the consistent groovy circle they made, his head and neck followed as if they were being unwillingly yanked forward, and then his entire body in a shuffle-step that was meant to look so stupidly cool. His arms wiggle-jerked by his side until he got to "Please take me dancing tonight!" and then he leaned back, creasing at his low back where his vertebrae clicked and cracked (and which hit him only in retrospect as a painful maneuver), lifted his arms, and shook them to the sides and above like just-beached salmon. With his eyes closed he jerked, shuffle-stepped around the room, his arms flailing about him, his head circling around and around so that his long hair hit him across his face giving him the sense every single time of being a young rocker in some ass-kicking metal band. He jerk-danced to his jacket hanging on the back of one of the dining chairs and plunged his right hand into one of the pockets, retrieving a joint he had expertly rolled that morning. He put the joint just barely between his lips, danced over to the kitchen where he found some matches in one of the drawers, and lit the beauty up, sucking the sweet, sharp smoke deep into his lungs where it hung and blossomed before he opened his mouth and let it waft out like visible laughter.

After, sweat sliding down his back and ribs, utterly exhausted, he sank onto the couch, threw his arms across the back, took a big sigh, and closed his eyes. He thought of Larry. Fat, dependable, dorky Larry who had always been game; always ready to muck around. When they were sixteen, it had been Marc's idea to break into Dirk's Party World on Muskeg Way. They had been just drunk enough to enjoy hoisting a huge rock through the side window and crawl through. No alarms. No nothing. They took a dozen stink bombs and spray confetti and a hundred balloons. They filled up on helium and sang "Smells Like Teen Spirit" and "Happy Birthday" and "Even Flow" until the drink began to wear off and the ocean water outside the shop began to lighten in the dawn.

Marc listened to the mechanical trilling of the thrushes and then silence, and *trill* and silence and *trill* and silence. The thing about the woods was that it was so quiet you could hear yourself think, even. The uncanny notion that what you were thinking was being projected into the universe; heard, seen, by you and whatever else was floating around, if one believed in spirits and ghosts or such stuff. Being on top, the boss, telling people what to do and how to do it, it was all one ever wanted in life. And only some got it.

It couldn't end. Couldn't end with him this way.

He stretched his arms above his head before using his stomach muscles to pull himself up. Pistons! Firing! He looked around. The place was clean but not too clean; like-it-was-barely-used clean. Like maybe he came up here every once in a while to hunt or get away. The coffee mugs in the sink. A clean one in the drainer along with a plate, a knife and fork. The coffee tin on the counter. The little wooden table bare; two chairs pushed in. Four beer bottles in the paper sack under the sink along with the Power Bar wrappers. He unzipped his duffle bag and threw what he needed inside.

Larry couldn't talk. Marc ground his back teeth; felt the muscles in his jaw. Pistons! The dough-boy couldn't talk.

How the hell did we get so close? Larry wondered that one night he was in Hope's pitiful little one-room jail listening to Officer Schmidt sipping his coffee, over and over again at his desk. He felt like punching Schmidt right between the eyes. Yeah, he remembered. It had started when Mrs. Richardson paired him with Marc sophomore year who didn't know jack about math or anything else, for that matter. "If you could just *do* this for me,"

Marc had smiled grimly, like it took him some effort, "then we could be done with it."

Larry had been so naïve then, just a kid. He had been shocked to think that Marc wanted him to cheat; had stared at Marc with wide eyes, like a Northern Saw-whet Owl, which he had had the great fortune of seeing up Waterfall Trail the previous month. "Come on, Larry!" But Larry had simply looked down at his algebra book and shook his head. Marc had pleaded, "pleeeease," and then when Larry continued to shake his head, Marc socked him hard on his upper arm where Larry felt shock waves rippling through his flesh. "Ouch!" Larry had practically screamed. "Stop it!" And Marc told him to "shut the fuck up" because they were in the school library and the last thing Marc wanted was more shitty teacher attention. In the end, it had worked out. Marc had passed, and Larry had discovered that Marc wasn't such a bad guy; that he could actually be a friend, and Larry had had very few of those.

They began to play Dungeons and Dragons in the woods behind the school. Once, Marc agreed to go on the Christmas bird count. Who cares that he had made fun of Larry and the other birders the whole time; had scared away with an enormous fart an uncommon Red-throated Loon as they sat hiding behind a salmonberry bush by the estuary. Larry had even taught Marc how to play chess, and twice Marc had beaten him, though Larry had always thought it was a fluke; that probably he had been smoking the weed Marc occasionally brought over and so he hadn't been in his sharpest mind.

The next morning, Larry's mom was waiting for him. She rose on her toes and squeezed him to her, though she couldn't quite get her arms all the way around him. "We'll get you out of this mess," she said.

In her Lexus, Larry sunk appreciatively into the brown leather seat. The jail cell had been more uncomfortable than he'd imagined, and he'd also had to share it with Stan the junkie who was scratching himself bloody in the corner. "Ha-ha!" Stan had kept laugh-choking, revealing a mouth full of holes. "They finally gottcha! Gottcha, gottcha!" And with each "gottcha" he had thrust out his arm and grabbed the air between them with bulb-knuckled fingers.

It was only a five-minute walk from the station to Larry's Radio Emporium, but he figured his mom wanted him to have some privacy, and so the Lexus. He loved her so much. "We'll get you out of this," she spoke to the windshield. After a minute she added, "I imagine the police are exaggerating, huh?" She looked at him. "Why would you do something so stupid, Larry?"

Larry turned from the window and looked at his mom, noticing how her small nose and mouth and eyes all congregated within the center of her fat face. His white forehead rippled into half a dozen fleshy mounds, his eyebrows raised, eyes watering. "How could you believe them, Mom?" He liked the thought of being known as "drug lord" only in certain circles, but most certainly not by his mom. Everyone knew he wasn't a bad guy; had never, ever been a bad guy!

She wiped away a tear and looked ahead as she pulled into the in-ground garage below the store (the only one of its kind in Hope), which Larry had paid a fortune for and had been an engineering nightmare. She parked next to Larry's black Porsche and turned off the engine.

"You're smart, Larry. You sure you've been hanging around with the right people? You wouldn't lie to me?"

But Larry couldn't find the breath to answer such meanness from his own mom. He opened the door, shut it, and hurried to the elevator. He just needed to get back into the store; back into his world.

Upstairs in his penthouse, Larry crashed on one of the leather couches in front of the huge glass fireplace. Oh, the smells and comfort of home again! The smells and sounds of his store below! He needed a hot shower and a massage. Needed a shave. It took a moment before he realized he wasn't alone.

"You must be exhausted, Larry."

Across from him on the other couch sat the lawyer his parents had flown up that morning from Seattle. The man, tall, dark-haired, abnormally skinny like he was one of those hard-core cyclists who was actually probably on some illegal substance at that very moment, casually reached over with his long arm and big, impressive hand.

"I'm John McDonald." His handshake was the perfect combo of firm and tender, and though Larry didn't much like his fancy suit and slick purple shirt and shiny black shoes, didn't care for his rich-looking haircut, he admired the guy's efforts. "Larry, your mom has filled me in." He sank back into the couch, his long legs crossing, assuming a posture of ease and instant adaptability. "Seems like they've got you for one night and one night only. And who knows how reliable this 'informant' is, right?" He turned his slick head and gazed out the floor-to-ceiling windows that wrapped around the curve of the ocean-facing side of the penthouse. There, the Pyramid Mountains in all their glory, boom, like some insane 3D movie; the rippling slate of steel-blue ocean; the tree-covered islands studding the harbor and channel; the wide expanse of the Pacific just past Mt. Agnes.

"This is some place." He turned back and smiled, and Larry noticed just how stupidly white his teeth were. Only fools spent money on shit like that.

The lawyer stared directly into Larry's eyes. "You do any business with anyone who might wanna talk? How many friends you have? You made a mistake, right? One mistake. There's nothing about a drug ring; buying and selling. Nothing like that at all."

Larry hated this guy, but he knew he needed him. Sometimes he wished his parents were just a tad more reckless.

He was pretty sure he could guess who talked. If he was wrong, then, oh well, at least he'd get his message out. Hope was such a small town.

After the lawyer left for the Hope Hotel, he called his friend Vince who wasn't squeamish about getting physical; who hung up the phone and immediately drove to Kyle's apartment. Knocked on Kyle's peeling door and when Kyle opened the door bleary-eyed from sleep, *bam!* Vince punched him right on the nose, cracking it into the cavity behind so that Kyle passed out, hit his head on the soft arm of the sofa, and came to minutes later, remembering with a shudder Vince's face: unexpressive, calm. It was clear. He would take a vacation; hop the ferry to the mainland; wait it out at his sister's until he got a good sense.

The next morning, refreshed and clean and with a full stomach, Larry went down into his store. His bliss. All of it, his. The TV screens, some black, some reflecting the silver-blue light of morning from the floor-to-ceiling windows that spanned the ocean side of the store, each one a massive eye, some kind of primordial sentry standing guard. The crisp racks of CDs, the walls of DVDs. The extension cables and cable-less microphones; the Panasonic stereo systems; the Bose speakers; the noise-canceling earphones. The sweet, sweet smell of new.

When the customers started coming, some looked at him as they shuffled through the CDs, as if they hadn't really noticed him before: chubby, skin too white, eyes too small, nose too pig-like. He who had simply been the guy who knew everything there was to know about everything they wanted to buy. But now, kind of famous with *The Daily Storm*'s front-page article. Friends, family of friends, came up and told him to "be strong, you'll get through." Or people from his parents' church who said, "we'll pray for you," which he had to take with a smile even though he knew he didn't need any prayers; the deal was as good as done, didn't they know who he was? He was sure there were probably some who wouldn't come to his store for a while; who would "boycott," the word made him chuckle. But they'd end up coming back. They always did.

Business had been slow that day, Larry admitted to himself, but that's exactly what he had expected. He also knew that it would pick up; that people would need their latest whatevers. Also, that in another month the tourists off the cruise ships would start coming. Those Filipino cruise workers came like clockwork, buying whatever they couldn't find back home or was cheaper here. The dumbest question he had ever gotten from a tourist? Easy: "Was this stereo made here in Alaska?" He wondered even now, if he had said "yes," would it have sold? But he was more ethical than that, and what did people think he was, some fat-ass dumbie?

As he locked the front doors and went down the aisle turning off the TVs and left his mother to run the cash register tape, hearing its comforting whirring in the emptiness of the store, he kept thinking of what the lawyer had said. *You do any business with anyone who might want to talk? How many friends do you have?* Well, he had friends. Plenty of them. And probably most of them by now had gotten his message. And yet. Marc. He hadn't seen that guy for almost two days.

Why couldn't he spell his name with a "k?" Like did he think he was foreign or something? A small town boy like him? He was nothing. But how well did he really know Marc? He was a Randal, after all, and Randals could do things in Hope. Had done things in Hope. When Marc had been arrested for stealing when he was sixteen, all his dad had to do was show up at the police department, throw his weight around a little bit, and walk out with his arm around Marc's shoulder. Larry knew because he had been there, waiting, like a friend, for Marc in front of the station.

Would Marc say anything?

Mayor Marc Randal. Hope's protector and leader. Getting rid of the "bad guys." What a load of bullshit! And was he, Larry, was he a "bad guy"? Didn't he like watching the gulls fly in ever tightening circles as they followed the seiners and trollers into the harbor, full of fish? Didn't he love the sky full of stars? Didn't he love the quiet of Dead Man's strait, anchoring his yacht there and then turning off the engine, listening for whales or eagles or looking for rafts of sea otters or rare seabirds? Wasn't that just the best place to be right before the throes of a storm, right when the black clouds were escalating from over the ocean, all moody and dramatic?

Larry conceded to himself that hardly anyone knew how much he loved the wilderness, the watery world around him. No one knew how much he truly loved Hope and its regular, every-day people. Bad guys didn't like stuff like that. Bad guys didn't sell stereos and speakers and flat screen TVs. Bad guys didn't stock Disney DVDs for all of Hope's children.

After closing, his mom asked if he wanted to join her and his dad for dinner. He smiled and declined, said that he was going out with a few of the guys to Raven's. "Be careful," she said. "They're looking for any excuse." "I know, mom," he said and took the elevator up. It would get cold later. He went to the hall closet and grabbed his puffy North Face jacket and mittens and then stopped. Listened to the static of silence. Decided. Went into his bedroom and pulled out the hand gun from the dresser, cold, exciting, silver-shot, and when he felt it in the palm of his hand it registered more in his groin, which gave him a momentary flash of Kyle's sexy girl, her face and breasts and vagina like bulbs exploding in his brain.

So this is how it will be, he thought, tucking the gun in the pocket of his jacket. Up to the cabin, then.

When he fell into the brown leather seat of his Porsche, it suddenly occurred to him that it could go another way. That after all, he and Marc had always been buddies; could shoot the shit like nobody else in all those fine moments in the cabin or watching a game over satellite or, in the good ol' days, playing chess and looking for birds. He pulled down the sunshade and slid open the mirror. He looked at himself and laughed. Why was he making such a big deal out of this? They would talk it out or fight it out like they always did. No biggie.

The thought made Larry smile as he turned the key in the ignition and felt the beautiful vibration of the Porsche's engine deep in his chest where the soul was, he speculated. The thought of his soul made him feel suddenly magnanimous and he told himself he'd do something, donate something, something big to starving kids in Africa or somewhere, when the whole thing was over.

Marc sat sunk luxuriously on the couch until the weed wore off, and even then he remained with arms outstretched and head leaning back with eyes closed to the beamed ceiling. He had spent the past day-and-a-half working his ass off and didn't he deserve a little R&R? All he needed was a bit of quiet time; some time to collect himself, take a few deep breaths, reestablish himself. He was a Randal, after all. *Mayor*, for god's sake, though he was terming out soon. *Elected* by the majority of Hope! Now more than anything he wanted that steak and beer. He wanted to feel himself grow hard watching Jasmine cross the sticky floor of the bar.

He collected his arms and raised his head. He realized he was cold, but oh so relaxed. Life was grand.

The meth had been his idea, even before those low IQ-ers started their thing at the abandoned sawmill. Larry at first wasn't sure, said that the market was already saturated. "Yeah, but this is something new and better!" Marc had said. Larry had needed to "think about it" before putting in his "investment." Marc hated when Larry needed to do that. Sometimes a person simply had to act on instinct; not be such a fucking dweeb.

It had taken more than a year, and boy had he worked at it. He could still see the glorious stuff across the table in the cabin that afternoon two years ago, proving Larry's initial caution wrong and himself absolutely right. He had always thought he had more of a natural business sense than Larry; he just didn't take himself so damn seriously. He knew how to chill. He had more immediate access to "the zone."

"This is good." Larry had run his fat white fingers across the little zip lock baggies Marc had ordered in bulk on-line. "Nice and organized." Marc was proud of how he had arranged them into columns and rows across the table, tastefully overlapping each other like designer ties in a boutique. Larry randomly picked one up and placed it on the scale. "I'm organized, Larry." Marc stood with his arms crossed, squinting. There were times Larry's attitude got on his fucking nerves.

After Larry weighed the bag, Marc grabbed it and carefully put it back. "Why you hafta weigh my fucking bag, Larry? I got it." Larry laughed. "Ok, ok, chill. It's just business, right?" Marc squinted and tossed his hair. "Well, we're business partners. S'posed to trust each other." Larry smiled and drew Marc into a fleshy side-hug, aggressively rubbing Marc's neck. "Ok, let go now," and Marc pulled away and went to the fridge where he took out a couple beers, tossing one to Larry who barely caught it in the catch his arms made against his chest. "Now for the best part."

Marc slid a sheet from the counter and carefully walked it over to Larry. Marc had spent hours on the design. It was perfect.

At first Larry wasn't sure what he was seeing, kind of cute little stickers of a red dragon and a blue dragonfly, intertwined. The dragon had narrow eyes and long human hair hanging in a ring around its pointed ears and scaly domed head. The dragonfly seemed to have Larry's very own eyes, shrunk, but bulging like balls from its spindly head.

"These for a kids party?" Larry asked. Marc reared back and looked at Larry as if he were crazy, for once opening his eyes wide. "Whaddya mean, 'a party'?" He smacked Larry on his hefty upper arm, feeling no muscle there at all. "It's our signature, dude! Our business motto! Put these on every bag!" Larry snorted. "These are for a kids' party, Marc." He threw back his beefy head and laughed, and when he finished and was wiping the tears from his eyes, he turned to Marc with the expression Marc called "le professeur," which Marc hated more than anything.

"We want our customers to take us seriously," Larry said. "You know, as much as you tried, ok, I give you credit for that. But," and he started laughing again, spitting out his words in between attempts at breathing, "design's not really your thing, Marc. And do we really want to be identified, you know? Like is this really a legit biz?"

Marc simply lifted his right arm, made a fist, and punched Larry square on his temple. Larry fell into the table and instantly Marc was on top of him, Larry's back and head across all the tight little baggies. Larry started moving his fat arms up and down as if he were making a snow angel in the bags, which went flying off. He grabbed some and threw them in Marc's face where the sharp plastic edge of one nicked Marc in the eye. Marc shot back howling, which gave Larry enough time to latch onto Marc's chest with his fleshy arms and throw him back onto the couch. On his way down, Marc grabbed the ceramic lamp on the end table and it came down with him and shattered on the floor. Pinning Marc on the couch between his huge thighs, Larry started slapping Marc across one cheek and then the other so that soon Marc's cheeks were hot pink and he couldn't feel them at all. Marc brought his knee right up into Larry's dick. With a muffled "uh" Larry fell back onto the ground on top of the broken lamp.

For several seconds they just breathed. "That was a fucking cheap shot," Larry finally said from his curled-up position on the floor. "Yeah, well, real fuckin men don't slap, Larry."

Marc leaned forward on his knees, his cheeks flaming. He could feel pockets of soreness beginning in strange places across his back, chest, and neck. He couldn't imagine Larry being strong enough to have got him in all those places. Everyone knew Larry was really just all flab. The thought made Marc giddy. He tried to suppress his laughter, which only made it come out in explosions of saliva and hot air. It was kind of like being high without having taken anything at all. Wouldn't you know it, all one needed was a good fight every once in a while!

Larry didn't even bother to get up when he turned to Marc and shot him what he hoped was his most disgusted-slash-menacing look ever, lips slightly flared, nose wrinkled, eyes slits. This had been his first fight and now he knew why. Why would anyone in hell fight their own fights when they could get someone else to do it? Now he was hurting and would probably be bruised and sore tomorrow. He'd need a dozen ice packs tonight after a good long soak in the hot tub. Fighting was for thugs and idiots. And yet he had a sense, as he slowly pushed himself up to standing, accidentally jamming his palm into a sharp chunk of broken lamp and crying out "shit!," that he had somehow arrived; that getting rough and dirty had been the final element. The realization made him feel suddenly magnanimous and he leaned over, reached out a chubby pale hand, and pulled Marc from the couch. "I resent that I'm the dragonfly," he drew Marc into a hug and immediately released him when they both grimaced from the pain. Marc nodded toward the side of Larry's head. "Hope that didn't hurt too much." And they set about gathering the bags that were now scattered across the floor beneath the table.

Now, Marc gurgled with laughter to remember how hard he had kneed Larry in the balls, and how it had stopped Larry cold. Larry had just toppled over like a fucking statue! He'd probably never been kneed before in his life! Probably never had a genuine fight before either.

Marc left the cabin with nothing more than his duffle bag. Inside: the ledger with the names of everyone he'd established business with, the $5,000 cash he had recently collected, and a small shotgun that he occasionally used for deer hunting but mainly for scaring away bear. The sun was setting on the other side of the island, leaving the cabin in darkening shadow. The forest was as dark as night though the clouds above were still pink and purple. Instead of looking up, though, he stood still; looked ahead until his eyes had marginally adjusted, then started walking down the deer path to his car parked on the abandoned logging road below.

Marc's eyes had adjusted to the dark woods, but he still couldn't see well. *I'm getting old.* He tripped on something, his foot getting caught so well on whatever it was that he fell down and caught himself with one hand, feeling the pain of a hundred spruce needles and twigs and tiny rocks imprinting into his palm. It hurt so much that he moaned and startled himself hearing it in the quiet of the forest.

When he got back up, once again securing the duffle over his shoulder, he saw something dark move sideways across his path into the woods. He stopped, listened, and heard the shuffling of branches. Bear, he thought, and threw the duffle down, unzipped it, pulled out the shotgun, put his finger on the trigger and aimed.

"What are you doing, dumbass?" Larry seemed to have been hiding behind a tree but at the moment of Marc's taking aim, stepped from behind it. He could have been a bear. He was one large, puffy North Face jacket.

"Larry, fuck you. I thought you were a bear." But still Marc held the shotgun up, finger on the trigger, as if he weren't yet convinced.

"I'm not a fucking bear." Larry was walking now towards Marc and the cabin. "Put it down, dude."

Then it occurred to Marc, as it never had before, as if seeing Larry again had suddenly gifted him with insight. It occurred to him that Larry would talk; Larry would tell the police, the stupid detective, everything for immunity.

"I just came to hang out," said Larry. He kept walking, as if he were about to assist a customer. "You know about, well, I'm sure you do." And he stopped for a second to scratch the white flab of flesh below his chin that bulged from over the top of his jacket and flashed in the dark like the breaking of a wave in the moonlight.

That Larry had struck a deal with the police, with "Chief Kularsky." Larry wouldn't go to prison if he spoke. Marc could hear Kularsky's Kermit-the-frog voice, "Who else is involved?" Larry wouldn't be able to leave the island. Hope would be his prison for thirteen months, but, fuckin hell, Marc knew Larry didn't want to leave anyway. And the dough boy couldn't pass it up.

Larry had given it all up.

Menacing, Marc thought. Damn fuckin annoying. And as Larry walked forward, a fat puffy stupid bear, head down to see his footing across the dark forest floor, Marc stood there.

Aiming.

Waiting.

-7-

Lauren's Child

Lauren had spent her adolescence in a drugged haze, her twenties addicted to the beautiful numbingness of Jack Daniels while running with a band that did weekend gigs and never quite made it, her thirties in healing, crystals, and recovery, and now, in her late forties, married, mom to the world's most beautiful six-year-old daughter, Lucy, and a counselor in one of the local psychologist's practices.

She wasn't very nice. She knew that. For her, niceness had always been a sign of weakness and stupidity. She had, however, miraculously found a very nice man named Jim who lumbered at 6 foot 3 and wore oversized glasses. He ran his own nonprofit helping troubled adolescents—there were so many of them in Hope—and wouldn't even swat a mosquito, though with this she always took issue because, really, mosquitos were a fucking nuisance. He didn't even drink the occasional glass of beer like people tended to do, which was perfect because when they met she had been five years sober and intended to stay that way until she was six feet under.

With him she could eventually be honest, though this was something that came slowly over many months and was largely due to Jim's innate gentleness. For a big man, he seemed to have no desire at all to use his size to his advantage. He sensed almost from the beginning that she needed to be handled carefully. She was overly cautious and prickly, though she had given him a slight smile the first time they'd locked eyes in the downtown Juneau bookstore. And he had fallen immediately for her red hair and big green eyes and her pale face awash with freckles. With him she talked about her past addictions. How she still had them but was living a good life, now, and wanted to keep it that way.

Because she had never valued niceness (though made sure she had married, at least, a nice man), she wasn't one of those women who laughed and shared intimacies. In fact, she didn't like those women at all. There was something about them, the way they so easily smiled and shared stupid little confidences, that made her want to smack them. She didn't go to spas or get her hair done, though she did visit the chiropractor every Friday afternoon for an injured neck. She had never told anyone, and never would. Twenty years ago, she had been driving high and drunk and had hit a kid. It hadn't been hard; more like a 'tap,' really. She'd simply found herself veering, for a moment, along the quiet road and then meeting the kid's bike tire with her bumper. She had felt something and then over-breaked and her head snapped forward and met the steering wheel. She had blood on her face when she came to and noticed the kid on the ground. As she frantically drove away, she was convinced he was getting up. Even now, it felt more like a dream than reality, and at times she could convince herself that it never actually happened, though the pain in her neck reminded her like a clock tolling the hour.

Occasionally, she'd see blurry images of the whole thing over and over again in her sleep; the child's face, the road, the trees, none of it, clear. So many, many things from her past, unclear. Intimations only. She had recently taken up knitting so she could distract herself through knitting's moving meditation. She also did yoga and on occasion meditated. She had learned that it was important to think positively and in the moment. Coming to Hope, after all, had been the opportunity to lock the door on her old self and create a whole new present.

She was confident, cautious, and discerning, and she had never felt so on top of her game.

So the matter of Lucy's teacher irritated her to no end. At the last parent-teacher conference, there was Ms. Bateman on her high horse as if she could know more than *the mother,* saying with creased brows in her high, soft, confessional way that Lucy showed no restraint on the playground; that she pinched others when she didn't get her way and had more than once picked up a stick to smack a child over the head and across the ear, drawing blood that one time. Thankfully, there had been no "permanent damage." "There hadn't been any damage at all," she had told Ms. Bateman in her even, cold voice. But there was more. Lucy wouldn't sit down for story time. In fact, when Ms. Bateman or the assistant reminded her to stay seated, Lucy seemed to take this as a cue to get up and wander even more; to finger all the other students' projects; to, once, stick her tongue out at Ms. Bateman and go over to the math station *deliberately* where she scattered the math tiles across the table. "Though it's typical at this age for kids to *adore* the teacher," Ms. Bateman had smiled warmly at Lauren, as if they could possibly in any discernible universe become friends.

Imagine that, Lauren had thought. *Friendship!* The thought at once amused and irritated her. Friends with someone who didn't understand her very unique, brilliant, and high-energy girl? Well, Ms. Bateman was dumber than Lauren thought. It had been obvious to Lauren from the beginning that Ms. Bateman didn't understand Lucy; wasn't allowing Lucy to express and be her own dynamic, original, spirited self.

"Is it possible Ms. Bateman could be right?" Jim asked that night as they laid in bed. Lauren had been talking for a good half hour about the situation, watching the ceiling, stretched out in bed as if she were on a therapist's couch, the thought occurred to her.

Lauren pushed herself up and stared at him incredulously. "How could you even suggest that?" she said. "I just. I can't *believe* you'd even say that! I can't believe you're taking a side *against* your own daughter."

She suddenly had a hazy image of the child she had hit those many years ago. Had it been a boy? A girl? She fell back on her pillow and the whole bed shook as she plummeted. "You can be such an idiot sometimes," she added to the ceiling.

He turned and gently spread his chest and arms over her and nuzzled her neck. "I'm not taking sides, hon." He raised his head to look into her eyes, though she was gazing toward a corner of the ceiling, feeling hurt and betrayed by the only person she loved in the world beside Lucy. She felt a piercing ache in her stomach, and began counting her breaths like she had read. "You're right," he whispered. "Let's just pull her out. We'll find something else."

Oh, sweet relief! She turned to him, then, and hugged him, clung to him like her raft. She needed him so much, so much did he even know? Her eyes suddenly filled with tears that she held back because she hated tears almost more than she hated people like Ms. Bateman.

Night after night she lay in bed, contemplating the educational alternatives in Hope, which had taken no time at all because there were only two: the Evangelical Christian school, and the alternative school for troubled kids. But perhaps there were positives to the Evangelical school? Could it work? She knew of several of the families who went there, though, and none of them were impressive. They were the kinds of families who bought processed foods at the grocery store and let their children watch way too much Disney. They most certainly spanked. The kinds of families who had voted for Bush and all hung out together every Sunday after their brainwashing sessions at the Assembly of God. So very mundane and mainstream and stupid.

Jim had suggested homeschooling, but she knew there was no way in hell she could do that, be around Lucy, as much as she loved her, 24/7. Besides, she had her clients. Why couldn't *he* do it? she had asked. He had the temperament for it. But he also had his nonprofit. When she really thought about it, she knew that he was far too social to be home all day with a kid. It wasn't normal for parents to be around their kids *all* day. On the other hand, she knew that Lucy was unquestionably bright, independent, and better than any other child her age Lauren had ever met. Lauren wasn't about to see Lucy's intelligence, spirit, and uniqueness be stomped upon by some run-of-the-mill teacher. Life was all about fighting against that awful tendency for the majority to shove their normalcy and stupidity down everyone's throat.

So, at last, one sleepless night as she tossed in bed next to snoring Jim and felt the sweat begin to coat her back and armpits, she had the miraculous notion that it would be the Tuttles.

Jennifer and Dylan Tuttle and their eleven children were obviously a part of some religious sect (invented or real, who-really-cared; this was Hope, after all). They all dressed as if straight from *Little House on the Prairie:* the girls with long hair covered by bonnets, long-sleeved dresses that scraped their ankles, lace-up boots; the boys in slacks, button-up shirts, and suspenders. Mr. Tuttle wore wide-brimmed hats and a beard. Mrs. Tuttle wore just what her daughters wore, though she kept her hair uncovered and pulled up in a loose, puffy bun that revealed her possible amorousness and, really, drop-dead gorgeousness. All their children were taught at home and, besides the religious bit that Lauren supposed she could put up with in moderation, were most definitely receiving an education better than what was going on in the public schools or the brainwashing sessions at the Evangelical school.

She had seen and been impressed by how spunky Jennifer was at operating the family's salmon jerky and salmonberry jam business out of a tiny shop downtown. Not a docile woman at all. And all the children helped; operating the cash register, assisting customers, carrying the products in a wheelbarrow they walked down from their house a quarter mile away, even the girls though their walking was somewhat hindered by their long, heavy dresses and low-heeled boots. Lauren had never seen such polite, happy, busy kids in her life. Lately, she had driven by the Tuttles' sprawling house in the Old Hope neighborhood several times just to take in their enormous garden, the forearm-sized kale and cabbages, the large greenhouse, the immaculate house and large wrap-around porch, the goats and chickens that wandered their property happily, as if they'd found the best place on earth.

Lauren's eyes super-focused on the dark ceiling and seemed to see it for the first time. It was settled, then! She would contact Mrs. Tuttle as soon as she could.

Jennifer Tuttle was reluctant and Lauren loved that.

"We don't follow the ways of the world by any stretch of the imagination," she eyed Lauren over the counter of jams at her store.

"Well, yes, I know," Lauren replied with an eagerness she was trying to hide. "And that's why I'd love for you to at least *consider* this. Jim, Lucy and I aren't much into the ways of the world either." She gave a boisterous half-laugh, as if her spirit were hitched on something buried deep.

"Let me talk with Dylan. I'll get back to you." And she returned to stocking the shelves with pretty jars of jam.

Jennifer Tuttle was one of those kinds of people whose eyes never wavered and who didn't readily smile, which gave her a spirit of dominion. Lauren respected, envied, that kind of forth-rightness because it showed justified power instead of silly compassion. However, though she desired this for herself and knew she was like this with her patients, having it directed at her also made her vaguely uncomfortable. With relief, her half-laugh allowed her to avert her eyes for a moment and take her leave.

One week later, Jennifer called Lauren to say that she and Dylan and their kids had agreed to "take on" Lucy. They'd prayed about it and decided that this was something God was asking them to do. That Lucy could start the coming Monday, if Lauren wanted. She wouldn't need to dress like the others, but would need to keep her head covered during morning prayer. "A simple scarf or handkerchief will do." She said that Lauren and Jim would have to be okay with Bible study every morning, no questions asked. That, yes, instruction would include gardening and tending the animals, helping with the business, "doing some hard labor, probably, and, of course, school subjects, reading, writing, math." Lauren loved the sound of it all! It would keep her active little Lucy busy and happy, working her muscles, not sitting still all the time needing to conform. They agreed on a price that would be paid at the first of every month.

Lauren could hardly believe this was actually happening! She felt immensely proud of herself for having figured this one out. She knew there was no way she was going to jeopardize her own daughter's well-being and personality just to satisfy some public school teacher's goddamn opinion.

Jim was at first skeptical; said he wasn't sure it was such a good idea to stick Lucy in "with a bunch of fundamentalists." But Lauren assured him that she'd seen the Tuttle children in action at their store and around town; they weren't depressed- or solemn-looking. They were happy and energetic and were given the freedom to *do* things. "And Jennifer knows we're not religious. She said herself that Lucy doesn't need to dress like the others. She can be herself, Jim! What more could we ask for?"

Later that night, Lauren awoke from one of her nightmares, tears down her face. She had been sobbing loudly moments before awakening and quickly checked to make sure Jim was still asleep.

In her dream, she was driving on a golden-sand beach that seemed to go on for miles. An aqua-blue ocean sparkled on one side. She felt free and utterly elated, as if she had no body at all. She felt the dull pixelated sensation of the simultaneous buoyant and gritty traction of the tires on sand. It was harder to bring the car to a stop on the sand, and yet that's not what she wanted. She was driving fast. It must have been a convertible because her hair was flying everywhere. She threw back her face to the hot sun and hooted. When she turned back to the windshield, the child appeared out of nowhere. In between strands of her hair, she could see slices of the child, chubby, no more than three, with a little shovel in its hand and its legs splayed out, fat knees bent around a bucket. She felt the child's body all the way under the car, yet she kept going. There was a sense that she could simply drive fast enough away from the child, though it seemed to be stuck underneath.

Awake, she stared at the ceiling and let the tears dry. Oh, she was a weak fool to be harboring this grief, this ancient mistake, for so long. Enough, enough, already! And yet what relief to realize that it had all been just a horrible dream, and that she hadn't stupidly cried out loud, waking Jim and inciting his concern. *Dear universal spirit,* she began in her head in a way that she assumed was prayerful. She knew there wasn't a God, but she felt that there had to be a certain "something" out there that had brought her this far and had uplifted her this high. *Let Lucy know just how wonderful she is. Let her never, ever be hurt. May she learn to fully be herself at the Tuttles. To not bend or be made weak.* She stopped and listened to the vague hum of the silent room. Was it a spiritual presence? She felt her heart and mind settle back into the peacefulness of fatigue, of calm, which confirmed that true happiness wasn't a conformity, a disciplined action, but rather a simple coming into the perfect shape of oneself and nothing more. Sleepily she added, *Just let Lucy be. Protect her powerful soul.*

Lucy had been pulled from school not long after the conversation with Ms. Bateman, and Jim had agreed to stay home with her until they could find something. When Lauren came home that evening to break the news to Lucy about the Tuttles, Lucy screamed long and hard. "*No!* I won't like it!"

She had been baking with Jim for the afternoon, which was his way of distracting her from drawing on the walls. Lauren had insisted they not use the word "no" with Lucy; that excellent parenting, especially for someone as high-energy and brilliant as Lucy, was simply a matter of distraction and redirection. Lucy had flour in her hair and around her eyes. The corners of her mouth were dimples of melted chocolate. The small two-bedroom condo smelled sweet and buttery.

"Oh sweetie, it'll be wonderful!" Lauren tossed her leather bag on the couch near the door and sauntered to the kitchen, taking in the flour on the floor and the counter piled with bowls, measuring cups, and ingredients. She smiled widely and kneeled to gather Lucy into her arms. "You've seen the Tuttle children. They get to do *lots* of cool stuff, and they have *goats!*" Lucy was accepting Lauren's embrace though her arms were by her side and she was scowling into Lauren's neck and releasing little whimpers that sounded entirely fake.

"You've been having fun with daddy!" Lauren changed the subject. She felt Lucy's hot little body against her chest and smelled Lucy's beautiful Lucy smell, as she called it; a smell she had known as soon as Lucy was born.

"Daddy's no fun," Lucy whined into Lauren's neck.

"Oh?" Lauren pulled back.

"He was on the computer all day," Lucy looked teary-eyed into Lauren's eyes.

"Oh really?" Lauren looked at Jim who was sweeping the flour on the counter into his hand and dumping it into the sink. He turned immediately and tried to act nonchalant, as if the matter of his being on the computer wasn't something Lauren had made an issue of before. She had told him plenty of times that it was imperative that when Lucy was around they should give her their undivided attention *at all times*. Weekends meant 100% time with Lucy. Days-off too.

"That's not true, little love," he smiled at Lucy.

"Lucy's a liar?" Lauren stood and stared at Jim. He sighed. They'd had this conversation too many times to count, and he was tired. He'd known from the beginning that being with Lauren wouldn't necessarily be easy, but he also loved her spirit and strength. The intensity of his love for her at times shocked, surprised, him.

"Lauren, of *course* I'm not saying Lucy's a liar. I was on the computer, checking work stuff, for maybe ten minutes."

"Longer than that," Lucy looked at Lauren with her big teary eyes.

Lauren released a tight burst of air. "I'm tired of the same old thing, Jim. I'm tired of always hearing the truth from Lucy and not *you!*"

Jim silently turned back to the counter and began cleaning again. He knew it was no use talking to Lauren now because she was mad and convinced that he was the bad guy. How tired he was of always being the bad guy! But there he was, cleaning up the kitchen after having spent the entire day with Lucy and not saying "no," and now it was time for him to prepare dinner because what would they eat otherwise? Lauren forbade eating out on weekdays, said it wasn't necessary and was lazy, unhealthy, and expensive.

They argued later when Lucy was in bed, and their frustrations came out in quiet spurts for Lucy's sleeping sake, both of them jammed into the tiny kitchen, the place farthest from Lucy's room.

Early on in their marriage, Lauren had insisted that they never go to bed angry, and they never had. And so tonight, though Jim hugged Lauren afterwards and they both said "sorry" as they went to bed, there was still the sense between them that the other was *wrong*. Jim believed, though would never say, that Lauren coddled Lucy, and he hadn't seen Lauren coddle anyone ever. Now, for the first time, he couldn't coordinate in his mind this contradiction. Why so loose with Lucy and so cold with everyone else? And Lauren felt again as if it were she and Lucy against Jim. Why couldn't the three of them just be a team? Didn't Jim know she was just doing the very best she could?

Jennifer Tuttle was extremely organized. Lucy came home after her first day with a very neatly written (because the Tuttles didn't own a computer) schedule for the month, detailing each day's activities down to the minute. Lauren loved everything about the schedule except the hour-long Bible study daily 9-10 a.m., which seemed just a tad long, but she thought she could talk Jennifer into reducing it to 45 minutes at least for Lucy. The Bible was certainly a part of a Western education, after all, the stories of which Lauren really did want Lucy to be familiar with. She also liked that Lucy was getting a bit of spirituality among people who were independent thinkers and doers, and not mindless, group-think Christians like the Assembly of God-ers. After Bible study and before lunch was something called Workshop, which Jennifer told Lauren was when the children did their projects, whether it was designing and building a new chicken coop, pulling the ready dried salmon from the smokehouse and cutting it into strips to sell in the shop, feeding and brushing the goats, writing a play version of a Bible story or their own creative one, and so on. Each daily activity braided together all the academic subjects, Jennifer explained. "My kids are learning *more* than their age levels in all the subjects."

"Do you do art?" Lauren asked Jennifer one morning at Lucy's drop-off.

"Art?" Jennifer looked baffled. "We are not to make images in the likeness of God or anything God has created. But we stay on top of painting the house and the shed. The children act out Bible stories and make their own costumes. God made us creative, after all, didn't he?" And then she smiled at Lauren and gave her a big hug. The fact that Lucy would not be receiving any art instruction at all suddenly didn't seem to matter. Naturally, there were a thousand ways to be creative that didn't entail mere drawing and painting. Besides, she and Jim could do art activities with Lucy at home if they wanted.

On Saturday morning, Lauren got up early and spread the dining room table with all the art supplies she had bought the day before. When Jim awoke, he was at first confused to find the bed empty, Lauren's spot cool. There was the smell of brewing coffee. When he walked into the living room, Lauren was squeezing dollops of paint from twenty-five different bottles onto plastic plates arranged around Lucy's place at the table. She had fanned out an incredible selection of paintbrushes. There were tiny, thin brushes with hardly any hairs, and extra fat ones. She had also bought a twenty pack of colorful molding clay and some stainless-steel shaping tools. Near the edge of the table was a stack of pure white canvases.

"A little art project?" Jim tried to kiss Lauren on her lips but she offered him her cheek.

"Sorry, hon, just a little busy. I thought it would be good to do art with Lucy on the weekends just because she's not really getting this kind of thing at the Tuttles, you know?" She stepped back and assessed the table. Lucy would like it.

Jim walked to the coffee pot and saw that most of the coffee was gone. He tossed the remnants into the sink, rinsed the pot, and pulled out the tin of ground coffee that Lauren always ground ahead of time so that the sound of the grinder wouldn't wake Lucy in the morning. "Are we going to eat standing?" He had sort of meant it as a joke.

"Well, get creative," she sighed and gave him a semi-annoyed look. "The floor is just over there."

"Pancakes on the floor, then!" And he began gathering the ingredients for the chocolate chip gluten-free pancakes he made for Lucy every Saturday morning like clockwork.

Lucy squealed with delight when she walked into the living room, her eyes still tired-looking and in her hands her most beloved and used stuffed animal, Rose the Rabbit, which she immediately threw down so she could grab a canvas and start painting. She went through all fifteen canvases in less than 30 minutes. Her paintings were expressions of vivid imaginings, Lauren thought—her strokes quick and reckless, the colors merging and tangling and looping. Lucy treated the canvases as if they were without boundaries, rushing the brushes slathered with globs of paint over the canvas edges so that the table was soon streaked with paint. When Jim said the first pancake was ready for Lucy, she said "not now," and

Lauren smiled to see how vibrantly and thoroughly Lucy was getting lost in her artwork. Her vivid, bright little girl. Lauren plopped herself playfully on the living room floor and ate the first pancake off a plate on her lap. When Lucy had exhausted almost every item of art and had paint on her cheeks and in her hair and across her forearms, she said she wanted a pancake and joined Jim and Lauren on the floor where they all giggled like children. "It's like camping, inside," Jim said.

"Do you want to wash your hands?" Lauren asked as she saw Lucy pick up her pancake and take a large bite with paint thick across her fingers and palms.

Lucy shook her head.

A rare morning sun was streaming through the large living room window. Outside, the ocean sparkled. Lauren listened to the soft sounds of her family eating. Now was the perfect time.

"You know," Lauren licked the corner of her lips where an errant chocolate chip had lodged, "there are many ways of being spiritual in the world. There's Islam and Judaism and Buddhism and Hinduism. Right, Jim?"

Jim sat leaning with his back against the couch, his second cup of coffee in his hands. He looked at Lauren and raised his eyebrows. He shifted slightly on his bottom.

"Oh yeah," he said, "many ways. Lots of religions in the world."

"Buddhists don't even really believe in a god," Lauren smiled at Lucy who was jamming a second pancake in her mouth. "They believe we can all eventually become holy. And Muslims believe in Muhammad. Hindus believe that there are gods in just about everything." She paused. "Isn't that cool? Holiness everywhere!"

"And the Tuttles believe in God and the Bible," Lucy said with her mouth full, "because we read the Bible every morning and pray. Why don't *we* pray, mom?"

Lauren felt a pang of guilt and for a moment had nothing to say, and then remembered.

"Well, I pray, and so does daddy," she smiled widely and reached over to palm Jim's knee. She had never heard Jim pray, but assumed he did what she did sometimes in her head. "But we pray to a spiritual *presence*, honey. The Tuttles are just *one* way of connecting to the spirit. Hey, let's do a prayer now!" She turned gleefully to Jim and pulled him towards her. He chuckled, amused at how playful Lauren could get with Lucy around, and cinched forward. Lauren reached for his and Lucy's hands and told them to make a circle. "Yay!" Lucy grabbed Lauren and Jim's hands as if they were about to begin a fun new game. Lauren felt Lucy's hand sticky from syrup and paint.

"You don't have to close your eyes or bow your head," Lauren said. Lucy kept her eyes wide open and her head up, looking eagerly at Lauren. "Dear spiritual presence," Lauren began. And when Jim didn't say anything, she squeezed his hand, and he repeated, "Dear spiritual presence."

"Thank you for dear, sweet Lucy, the best daughter in the world," she smiled at Lucy and gently squeezed her hand. "Thank you for daddy and our house."

"Thank you for pancakes and paint!" Lucy shouted and rocked happily on her bottom, her legs crossed. Her red curls bounced.

"Thank you for mommy," Jim smiled at Lauren.

"Help us to always be true to ourselves and to know that you always forgive us when we do something we shouldn't." Lauren was smiling, but Lucy suddenly frowned.

"Why if we do something we shouldn't?" she asked with furrowed eyebrows.

"Well, we're learning," Lauren said a little too loudly. "We make mistakes and that's how we learn. It's good for us!" She released her hands and leaned over to gather Lucy into a big hug. She didn't want to worry Lucy, who was already very, very sensitive. "That's all. No biggie. You know, let's not even call them 'mistakes'! They're *not* mistakes. Let's call them 'experiences'!"

"Ok," Jim pushed himself up and his knees popped. He smiled at his little family on the floor. "That's enough spirituality for one day! Who wants to go on a bike ride?"

And because Lauren didn't want Lucy to feel too *serious* about it all, instead wanted her to associate the spiritual presence with sweet pancakes and paint and her loving parents, she said that was a great idea and released Lucy with a tender kiss upon her warm, Lucy-smelling head.

"I'll only go if I can get ice cream, daddy," Lucy crossed her chubby arms and faked a pout that Lauren always found so mind-numbingly adorable. Her dear, dear daughter. Such a sponge, taking it all in, ready to take on the world.

Two weeks in, Jennifer Tuttle thought it would be a good idea for her and Lauren to meet for a quick check-up. Lauren admired her initiative and forthrightness, and instantly agreed. She went on her morning off, parking her car in the short gravel driveway of the Tuttle's sprawling property. There was that crisp tinge of fall in the air; the smell of mushrooms and dying leaves and humus was more poignant here at the cusp of the forest starting up the mountain behind the Tuttle's house. She flicked the latch on the gate and walked through into the wide patchy yard, more full of wilderness than domesticity, feeling herself instantly relax as she took in the large greenhouse and outdoor garden, enormous bright orange pumpkins—some soft and slimy in decay—zucchini, squashes, kale, chard. Goats, sheep, and llamas were idling in a gated section in front of a red barn on the side of the property under overhanging spruce trees. There was a thick tangle of raspberry bushes against one side of the leaning two-story house; three smokehouses not far from the outhouse. The Tuttles had no indoor bathroom. Lauren hadn't been sure Lucy would be able to use the outhouse, she was so squeamish, but she hadn't heard a single complaint. She looked around for Lucy but only heard her voice, happy, among the other children in the large shed by the barn. *Woodworking maybe*, she smiled to herself. *Another big project.*

She walked up the sloping wooden stairs and onto the large wraparound covered porch. There was a chair swing and three food dehydrators one after the other. Clothes drying from a line. She knocked on the door. Jennifer Tuttle welcomed her directly into the kitchen, brightly lit by an overhead lamp. The whole place effused heat and the smells of fresh bread and what appeared to be a big pot of soup simmering on the stove. Jennifer's hands were sticky with dough and her cheeks were flushed, giving her what Lauren ashamedly thought looked like a very vibrant, post-sex glow.

"Hi Lauren. Take a seat. Let me just wash my hands." She thrust her hands into a big bucket in the sink. She dried her hands on her apron and brought over a plate of steaming sliced bread and a small plate with butter. On the table was a jar of salmonberry jam already open with a spoon sticking out. "We always have the jam out." She smiled.

Lauren eagerly helped herself to a slice of bread and generously slathered it with butter that melted immediately. The soft bread warmed her fingertips. Oh, wasn't it the best bread she'd ever had, the creamiest butter! She held the first bite in her mouth for a moment, letting its salty rich warmth sink into every crease and crevice. She felt herself perceptively sink into the wooden chair, the security of the wood along her back and against her shoulder blades, which made her realize just how clenched up she had been. Was she always like that, so tight and anxious? She would definitely have to do something about that.

"Lucy gets the gluten-free bread, of course," Jennifer said as she took a big bite herself. "But it's not the same," she said with her mouth full and a slightly mischievous smile.

It wasn't funny, but Lauren burst into laughter anyway, she felt so good. It *wasn't* the same, was it?! It all made her feel *good*, for the first time in, well, a while. It was the beautiful, solid wood dining table and the pale blue tiled counters, everything clean but not too clean. It was the soup simmering on the stove and the hot, comforting smells of garlic and oregano and tomatoes. It was the loaves of bread in the oven and the intimations of pureness and comfort she glimpsed through the kitchen doorway into the dim wooden-beamed, wooden-floored rest-of-the-house. For as big of a family as they were, the kitchen was remarkably ordered and clean; ceramic jars neatly lined up on the counter against the wall, towels folded and hanging on bars below the sink. And then she remembered that was because the children all helped to clean it daily. That last week Lucy's job had been to wash the dishes and scrub the counters after lunch. Imagine! Lucy would never do that at home.

Jennifer put her elbows on the table, a thick slice of bread held casually between the thumb and forefinger of her hand, and smiled at Lauren's head-thrown-back laughter. "I don't think I've ever heard you laugh, Lauren." And she took another bite, letting the crumbs stay in the corners of her mouth, a smudge of jam on her upper lip.

Lauren wiped her eyes. "It must be the bread." And she gathered herself and strengthened her face. Swallowed. Cleared her throat. This wasn't like her at all. Laughing, *giggly, for god's sake.* "I'm just glad this worked out. Really, Lucy seems very happy."

"Well, I think it's clear that Lucy just needs more boundaries," Jennifer looked into Lauren's eyes. "There've been times I've had to keep her from pulling the goats' tails, which she just loves to do for some reason. And there are times when she complains and stomps around because of the chores she's expected to do. Well, no one especially likes to scoop the animals' poop or mop the kitchen floor, right?"

Lauren held her second piece of bread in front of her mouth and then lowered it a bit. "Oh?"

"Oh, don't look so distraught." Jennifer reached over and patted Lauren's other hand.

"She's a good girl." Lauren replied, brows slightly furrowed. She was completely collected now, had been under some strange spell before.

"I'm not saying she's not. We're happy to have her. Very." Jennifer patted Lauren's hand again, once, twice, and then got up and brought over a stack of papers that were on the counter. "Here's some of her work."

Lauren put the bread on the table and brushed her hands on her jeans, cleared the corners of her mouth with her tongue. Oh my. Page after page of Lucy's beautiful writing, and she could see a difference between the first pages and the most recent.

"Her daily journal," Jennifer said.

Lauren read. *Brushd Stars hare. Now I kno why she is called Star, she has a wite star shap on her forhed! Sawd for frst time! It is hard but not to hard.* Pages of math problems, harder than Lucy had ever done in Ms. Bateman's class.

"She's already doing subtraction," Jennifer said. "She's good at math."

There was a page on an experiment she'd done with solids, liquids, gases, "with the older kids," Jennifer added. Finally, there was a little booklet she had sewn together with hard, waxy string titled, The Creation of the World. On the cover, a wobbly picture she had drawn of the planet, a big moon, and enormous yellow stars. There was also a giant man standing above the planet with a long beard and wearing a cape.

"I told her that we can't possibly know what God looks like," Jennifer said, "and that He doesn't have a form at all. But she wanted to draw Him anyway this *one* time." Jennifer looked at Lauren who felt compelled then, as if she were again under some strange spell, to look up from Lucy's work and into Jennifer's eyes. "I told her not to do it again. That there are no images for God who is beyond all representations of our wildest human imaginations."

"Oh. Of course." Lauren returned to the booklet. She read Lucy's slanted, slightly irregular writing. *God creatid hte planit in six daz, and on the sevnth day he restd. We ar to rest on hte sevnth day and do no werk, even the wemen.*

"Well, we don't really believe this, you know," Lauren said as she carefully folded the booklet, inwardly stunned by Lucy's writing and accompanying pictures and by the fact that she put it all together in a carefully sewn book. "We believe there is a 'higher presence,' of course, you know. But just to be clear. I'm okay with a *little* of this as part of her education. But we already talked about that."

"Has she recited any of her Bible verses to you yet? She knows a lot. She doesn't always like to memorize them, but like I said, 'boundaries.'" Jennifer smiled at Lauren and pushed back her chair. She smoothed her apron and turned to the stove where she leaned over the soup and smelled it. She turned and said, "lunch today," and turned a dial on the stove and covered the soup.

Lauren put the papers down. Though The Creation of the World was utter nonsense, it was so remarkable, as was Lucy's other work. Yes, this would do until Lucy was a little older, until she had outgrown the Tuttles. It was cheesy, and she abhorred stupid phrases like this, but the world *would* be her oyster. And the world would know that Lucy was *her* daughter!

Jennifer came back and sat down like she really meant it this time. She eased into the back of the chair and relaxed her shoulders. She loosely crossed her arms atop her apron and took a big sigh. Before her, Lauren seemed to be witnessing the picture of contentedness. Jennifer, at that moment, was timeless, of no era despite her late 19th-century attire.

"David and I used to be heavy into drugs back in our twenties," Jennifer said. "In California we met a man, Father Jacob, who taught us how to reach enlightenment without drugs. He also taught us the Bible and how seriously we have to adhere to it. He brought us up here, in fact. He moved on with the others to Palmer. We stayed. We love it here."

Lauren couldn't believe what she was hearing, that someone as holy and put-together as Jennifer had had *a past*, and now she was here, living like this.

"Freedom has many faces," Jennifer continued, "and I'm sure there are many ways to come into God's grace. This is just ours, and it works nicely for us." She smiled, as if the latter statement was a sudden realization. "'For faith is being sure of what we hope for and certain of what we do not see,' Hebrews 11:1. A little faith is sometimes all we need."

Lauren didn't know that verse. She didn't know the Bible at all. She wondered how much of the Bible Jennifer had committed to memory, and then it occurred to her that Jennifer was probably very bright. That in another life she could have been a CEO or judge. They sat in silence. Lauren wondered when she could go. There came a low, resonant gong from an invisible clock somewhere in the house.

"Well, I should get going." She gathered her purse and began to push back her chair. She realized then that she hadn't bothered to take off her jacket, and she felt clammy and hot.

"Just one last thing." Jennifer stayed seated. She tucked back into her bun a loose strand of hair.

Lauren froze on the edge of her chair.

"Lucy is so smart. She'll continue into multiplication in the next few months and begin essay writing. We'll be starting an animal study next week." Lauren realized she'd been holding her breath. She quietly exhaled, relieved without knowing why, and genuinely smiled. She pushed back her chair and got up.

"I'd really like to start seeing her *connect* with us and the animals over the next few months," Jennifer continued. "A little I-give-you-give. But you're a therapist, right? You probably get all that."

Jennifer's words socked Lauren in the gut, just in the rare moment when she was simultaneously relaxed and happy, and wasn't that always how it worked? A person couldn't get one, happiness, without the other, despair. She knew that.

"Connect?" Lauren's mouth was suddenly very dry. "I don't understand." She didn't want to, but she could hate this amazing woman if she had to, for Lucy's sake.

Jennifer arose and walked around the table and pulled Lauren into a hug. "Oh, connection, you know, so she can really know how wonderful she is and be able to give that back to people."

Jennifer's hug was hot and deep, the kind that Lauren imagined people gave to each other who were locked in tight communities, which was maybe alright for some, but she felt would never, could never, be for her. When Jennifer pulled back, there lingered in the air between them the smells of fresh bread and yeast and vegetables and earth. Lauren wanted to cry but instead pinched the inside of her palm between the fingernails of her opposite hand. The pain was sharp and utterly relieving.

"Fine," she looked down, pushed in the chair, and turned to the door before looking back at Jennifer, making sure she locked eyes with her, casually, firmly. "I'm glad things are going so well. And I'm sure Lucy will come into the other thing, the . . . connecting. As you know, she is bright. I have no concerns. Let's meet again before Christmas, sound good?"

"Good." Jennifer followed Lauren onto the porch and began pulling down the dry clothes from the line. "I had my qualms about this, but it's working out so well, isn't it? Probably best not to interrupt Lucy in her work. I'll tell her you came."

When Lauren left the Tuttles, she decided to drive out to the end of the island where she parked her car in the parking lot of the ferry and sat and watched the waves cap over and over again upon themselves. She looked for sea lions and sprays from submerged whales, but saw nothing.

Two months later, Lucy *wanted* to dress like the Tuttle girls, so why couldn't she? Lauren took Jennifer's advice and let her handle the clothes ordering and measuring. Jennifer used a company out of Montana and could easily order everything Lucy wanted; in fact, it was about time for another bulk order, the children were growing so quickly.

Lucy had previously had such a love of dinosaurs and fairies, but now there was nothing but Bible stories and questions about God, wanting to know if Lauren felt He existed and if He had really created the world in six days, which Lauren felt like she nicely answered in open-ended ways. And did Lauren and Jim know about Moses and how he was put in a basket and floated down the river? And Jesus was from the line of David, which meant he was the rightful Messiah, which means the Son of God? Did they know all that? She came home smelling of chickens and goats and salmon and spices. Her fingers became stained from picking salmonberries and thimbleberries and wild blueberries that they'd blend and heat into sticky jams and syrups. She developed a very healthy glow that Lauren assumed was from spending so much time outside and in movement. She filled out. Still, Lauren wondered about the dinosaurs, and were there other things from before? Well, yes, there had been Lucy's wild imagination; her interest in fairy tales and trolls and gnomes. She still had a closet full of costumes: cloth butterfly wings that she had loved to make fly in the wind; princess dresses and plastic crowns; a snake with a long thick tail; an alligator, a pig, a penguin.

One afternoon after school Lucy came into the living room with her arms full of her costumes. She let them fall to the floor in a soft pile.

"These all have to go," she looked at Lauren who was reading one of her psychology journals on the couch. Lauren looked up and momentarily thought Lucy was in another one of her costumes before realizing it was simply the outfit she wore at the Tuttles – the long dress, the slip underneath, the wool tights, the apron over it all. She hadn't taken off her bonnet yet, affixed by a neat bow tied under her chin. This meticulous, proper, covered little girl at first seemed like a complete stranger, and for a second Lauren felt like ripping the outfit off and letting her sweet girl free.

"Oh?" she smiled, taking in the pile of costumes on the floor. She was sensing a spark of panic inside, that same spark that in years past had spurred on an intense desire for whiskey and crank and loud music. The best thing to do now would be to smile just a tad wider; to ignore, again, that old familiar feeling.

"But why, sweets? Won't you miss them? You *love* to dress-up!"

"The Tuttles don't have any of these things. Mrs. Tuttle says to be what God made us."

Lauren took it all in. There before her, her most amazing daughter, her little chest and stomach, her tiny shoulders, all covered by a long brown dress that looked somehow too heavy for her. She suddenly wanted to see Lucy running freely in her underwear through the condo, as she had done before; wanted to see Lucy's skinny, freckled arms, covered in soft almost invisible white hair; her soft still-round little girl belly, white like moonshine. Instead, Lucy stood there, and though her blue eyes and red eyebrows were in the shadow of the bonnet, Lauren saw how confidently Lucy stared at her, the pile of her most treasured costumes before her on the floor. Such a poignant gaze inflated Lauren's heart with pride, and she felt her panic subsiding. She sighed. "Are you sure?"

"Of course," Lucy said, and as she turned back to her bedroom she said, "Mom, the Tuttles are great."

Lauren watched her daughter, dressed like a miniature pioneer woman, her tiny shoulder blades riding beneath the stiff cotton of the heavy dress, walk down the hallway and turn into her bedroom. Her daughter was happy. As an afterthought, though, which was ignited by an intense desire to see Lucy's red hair wild behind her, she called out, "But Lucy dear, don't you think it's time to take off that bonnet?"

There was also the matter of the library, which Lucy now insisted they not step inside of because it was "full of untruths," such as books on the dinosaurs, which were *not* in the Bible, and evil things such as witches and fairies and talking trees and dragons.

"There are books in there that say the world wasn't made by God in six days," Lucy said.

Lauren supposed it would soon be time to talk to Jennifer about Lucy's science education, which she wanted to make clear would include *other* theories about the origin of earth and life.

"What the h-!" Jim had stopped short one Saturday morning after Lucy refused the library, remained sitting at the dining room table in her dress, drawing, coloring, and gluing one of her masterpieces. He looked wide-eyed and somewhat amusedly at Lauren, as if the whole thing were one big joke. In fact, he'd never heard something so crazy in his entire life, and the fact that it was coming from his own daughter made him want to burst into laughter!

Lauren, however, gave him a little shrug that was meant to assure him that, yes, this was *really* happening and, no, there was nothing he could do about it. To just let it be. The library book bag was already on his shoulder and his baseball cap on, ready for the mile walk to the library. Instead, he clenched his jaw and looked at his shoes, already on. He said quieter and calmer, "Well, I think I will go by myself, then." He smiled at Lauren. "Anything you want, hon?"

She said curtly, "No. Enjoy." Jim turned and walked out the door. He *would* enjoy it, he thought. He would enjoy some goddamn peace by himself in the world of the sane again.

It was November and the days were shortening. At 6 o'clock, it was now completely dark. Lauren, Jim and Lucy ate dinner within the circle of dim yellow light cast by the hanging overhead lamp. Lucy sat with her bonnet on, which made it difficult to see her face as she shoveled macaroni and cheese into her mouth.

It had been Lauren's day to make dinner, so she had baked a chicken with baby potatoes and rosemary and lemon. She had made a salad with sliced almonds, spinach, broccoli, and sweetened cranberries. She knew Lucy wouldn't eat the chicken, so she made macaroni and cheese from the box for her. In fact, Lucy rotated between this, hot dogs, and ground beef tacos for dinner every night, and would only touch uncooked broccoli and carrots with Ranch dressing for dip. She would also only drink milk ever so slightly warmed.

Jim and Lauren ate their chicken, potatoes, and salad while Lucy dipped her raw veggies and scooped her pasta. Last week, as a sort of experiment, Jim had served Lucy the same thing he had made for himself and Lauren – steak with mashed potatoes and creamed spinach. Lucy had stared at her plate and burst into tears. *I hate this!* she had said. So Jim had frantically boiled the water for her macaroni instead. Later that night, he had agreed with Lauren to just let Lucy eat what she wanted. It wouldn't last forever, and at least she was eating broccoli, right? And wasn't raw better than cooked anyway?

That night, as they ate, Jim said how good the chicken was, so tender, and Lauren smiled and touched his hand. Work had been good for both of them that day. Lauren loved the segue into a Hope winter; how the sun set so early over the ocean; how there was that purple-tinged silver glow over everything afterwards. There was that lovely crispness in the air and the underlying smell of mushrooms and wet earth. Jim mentioned how they should maybe take a hike on the muskeg trail over the weekend to see the change in the colors. "It's subtle, but it's there."

"How was school?" Lauren smiled at Lucy. Lucy looked up. There was yellow cheese around her mouth, a small glob of Ranch dressing on her cheek.

"I memorized all my multiplication tables!" she said. "Sarah, Ruth, Levi, and I helped Mr. Tuttle measure out the new smokehouse. It'll be bigger so we can sell more smoked salmon in the shop." She scooped another spoonful of pasta into her mouth. "We learned about Absalom who got his hair caught in branches. He was trying to run away from his dad, King David, and God, but he got caught."

Lauren had distant memories of sporadically attending Sunday School as a child. She had a sudden memory flash of one of those Sunday School scenes erected on a felt board with the felt character Absalom hanging desperately from his hair tangled in an overhanging felt tree. She remembered his mouth opened in an almost perfect "O" of pain and surprise. What had been the message of that again?

Lucy picked up a raw broccoli with her fingers and dipped it in the small bowl of dressing Lauren had set for her. She took a bite.

"We shouldn't run away from God," she looked at Lauren matter-of-factly, as if she were telling her about one of the PBS kid shows she had liked to watch before the Tuttles. "Have you ever run away from God?"

Lauren laughed and then stopped when she saw Lucy still staring at her, expecting an answer. She turned and smiled at Jim, as if she were sharing with him a sweet moment of tenderness over something adorable their daughter was doing. Still, the question made her feel something she didn't exactly want to place. She had done plenty of "running" in her day. No reason to dwell on those faraway times. If she didn't think about them, then maybe that meant they were completely gone. There was no way to resurrect the past, after all; what was done was done and long gone, and here she was raising a miraculous daughter in a miraculous place in what was her incredible Alaskan island life. Current events, that's what life was all about, especially a life as good as hers. Jim was sucking on a chicken bone without much concern.

"Have *you*, daddy?" Lucy turned to him. He still wasn't used to her bonnet and how it shaded her face. It made her blue eyes seem darker than they were, and he hadn't seen her red hair loose and free in weeks.

"What was that?" he said as he put his bone down, sucked clean, and wiped his hands on the cloth napkin on his lap.

"Have you ever run away from God?"

Jim tilted his eyes to the ceiling, as if he were seriously considering. That was one thing Lauren loved about Jim – he always treated Lucy seriously and respectfully; he never, ever talked down to her in that annoying way most grown-ups talked to children (and, really, each other). Lauren couldn't stand that. She was curious – how would he answer? Wasn't this such a *cute* wholesome conversation they were having!

"Well, if I believed in a god, I wouldn't believe we could run away from him or her," he moved his eyes from the ceiling to Lucy and smiled.

Lucy's eyes widened within the shadow of her bonnet and she threw her broccoli down onto her plate. She started crying; real, desperate-sounding tears that sounded, to Lauren, like the precursors of honest-to-goodness depression. Lauren quickly got up, shot Jim a look, pulled Lucy off her chair and took her into her arms as she balanced Lucy's body on her knees. She ran her hand tenderly across Lucy's bonnet.

"Can we just take this off?" Lauren began slowly untying the strings under Lucy's fatty little chin.

"No!" Lucy stopped crying. "I like it!"

Lucy was mad, then, and pointed a fierce finger at Jim, though she stayed encompassed by Lauren's embrace. Lauren realized that Lucy was getting heavy, must have done some growing over the past weeks. She couldn't stay for much longer kneeling and balancing on her feet while holding Lucy. She tried lifting Lucy back up with her onto her chair, but Lucy bared down and refused to budge, a sack of cement in Lauren's arms.

"Daddy, you *have* to believe in God!" she yelled. "Otherwise you're a bad, bad man." Lauren squeezed Lucy tenderly who finally let Lauren lift her up onto her lap as Lauren sat back on her chair.

"Of *course* daddy believes in God." Lauren kissed Lucy's temple and gently wiped away the tears on her soft cheeks, *still so much a little girl,* Lauren thought gratefully. Lucy nestled into Lauren and leaned her head onto Lauren's chest. Lauren put both her arms all the way around Lucy. She felt as if she were erecting with her arms a living protective force field. She would do that forever, she knew. She would do that when Lucy was forty, if she had to.

Calm again, sniffling, and back in her own chair, Lucy watched as Jim cleared the table and Lauren cut the pumpkin pie she had made that afternoon, anticipating Lucy's happiness. Pumpkin pie was Lucy's favorite dessert, but Lucy insisted it *had* to be Lauren's *homemade* pie, which was none other than the recipe on the can of pumpkin, but still Lauren was proud of it and secretly thought she perhaps had a superior way of mixing the ingredients together that accounted for the exceptional taste. She spooned a generous dollop of whipped cream on each piece, giving Lucy hers first.

"Daddy, you *do* believe in God, right?" Lucy looked at Jim as they ate their pie. The coursings of her tears had left behind dried streaks on her cheeks, which had gone from the redness of her tantrum to an almost sickly pale.

"Of course, honey," Jim said, instantly wondering for how long and how much he would have to fake in his coming life with Lucy.

"Good." Lucy was using her fork to loudly scrape her dessert plate. She put the fork into her mouth and worked her tongue around it.

They sat in silence, the tips of their elbows edging out into the deep darkness outside the lamp's dim halo. Lauren was grateful for Lucy's return to happiness and peace; grateful that there would be no more tears at the dinner table, which was the mark of such dysfunctional family behavior and shouldn't ever happen again.

The pie tasted delicious. She was happy for Jim's response. They were a lovely family again; her daughter free to be her true, strong-minded self. She was simply *thinking* about things; she was exploring her universe! And Lauren and Jim had allowed for that; nurtured it. They were good parents.

"Otherwise. You. Will. Go. To. Hellllll." Lucy's quiet, resolute words punctured the silence. Lauren startled. The piece of pie fell from her fork and landed on her plate. "*You should really consider that.*" Lucy looked at Lauren and then Jim with serious, dark, condensed eyes, her little face splotchy with shadow and light.

Jim stifled a laugh. That had to have been one of the most hysterical and ridiculous things Lucy had ever said! But Lauren turned to him, her face a warning, and instead he shoveled in a piece of pie, not even saying anything about how much he loved it.

"I want her out," Jim quietly told the ceiling as he and Lauren lay in bed two nights later. He had wanted her out of the Tuttles last month, but Lucy liked dressing up in that ridiculous dress and bonnet like the other girls; liked brushing the goats and putzing around the Tuttle house and shop like it was the early fucking 20th century; liked the Bible stories. She seemed to like telling him and Lauren everything that they didn't know. Yet Mrs. Tuttle apparently only had good things to say about her; said that Lucy was a remarkably quick learner.

"What?" Lauren was almost asleep and wasn't sure she'd heard right. "Did you say something?"

Jim turned. "I want her out. No more Tuttle school. I think that's enough."

She turned to him and saw his wide-open eyes in the darkness. "What are you talking about?"

"Enough is enough." He would hold his ground. "I have a say too."

Lauren couldn't believe how insensitive Jim could be sometimes. For instance, like right now – why bother having this talk *now* of all times, right when she was about to go to sleep? And for her, sleep could be an issue, and he *knew* that. He also knew that this was what they had decided, sending Lucy to the Tuttles. That she had solved that very big problem *on her own*, without Jim's help, and that Lucy was thriving. *Thriving!* After all this time, hadn't she made the right decision? Hadn't he agreed?

She sighed loudly and clenched her jaw. "You'd pull her from the *one* place she loves and is succeeding in? You'd do that as her loving father? Don't you know we have a very special child, here? She's smarter than any other kid we know and things are going to be a bit different for us because of that? That we have an *obligation* to her? Don't you *get it*, Jim? She's our *daughter*."

When he kept staring at her, meanly, she thought, she pulled back. "I really need you to put in a little more effort. I can't be the only one who cares. It's tiresome."

They had agreed to never go to bed angry, yet here they were already in bed. Jim knew there was no winning with Lauren, especially regarding Lucy. *Was this impotence?* he wondered. They stared at each other and then Lauren turned onto her other side. Her heart was beating too fast and she debated getting up and getting herself some herbal tea, but did she really want to leave Jim at that moment? Even during the worst times, she felt physically and psychically tied to him. She started her meditative breathing, counting her breaths in and out up to ten and then back again. Maybe they'd simply forget about this conversation entirely. They'd feel better in the morning.

"I've decided to go home for Christmas. See my parents and sister again." Jim said into the quiet and turned again onto his back. He thought he would start crying, so he stopped and continued. "I think I'd like to go alone this time."

For a moment, Lauren couldn't breathe, yet she refused to act shocked or hurt. There was nothing to say, so she lay there and pretended to fall asleep. By the time Jim started snoring she had been through it all: hatred, sadness, fear, anger again, and, finally, a sense of knowing that, yes, people needed some time to themselves sometimes. That Jim going away was healthy and normal. Yet there she was, already feeling completely, utterly abandoned.

Jim would be back for the New Year, at least. This was good, Lauren told herself daily like a mantra to which she arose from bed from the time Jim left to now, two days before Christmas. Especially good for him. This break would give him some time and perspective so that he could come back and see just how good things were for Lucy and for them. Lucy was getting exactly what she wanted, after all; she was surrounded by honest, hard-working, happy, strong, smart people who just happened to be a bit religious. They also just happened to let Lucy be the best she could be; they challenged her and let her do things. They didn't expect her to be part of the inane masses of normal people out there who only wanted Lucy one way and one way only: demure, kind, gentle, mentally dull.

Lying on her bed in the shadows, Lauren knew she was right, yet she had begun to feel an uncomfortable nagging inside that had started when Jim left. And supposing she wasn't right? What then? Well, then why not open that bottle of whiskey! Why not just go ahead and tear down what she had so carefully, meticulously constructed! That's "what then." So, yeah, *fuck* "what then."

"Mommy," Lucy stood in the doorway, staring at Lauren collapsed on the bed. "When daddy's here, sometimes I hear you guys watching movies after I'm in bed." Her big blue eyes, shaded under her bonnet, stayed on Lauren who was now sitting, watching her daughter from the distance of her bed. For the first time, she didn't want Lucy near her; had no impulse to go to her and lift her or pat the spot next to her so Lucy would come and be with her. "You shouldn't watch such bad stuff." Lucy held Lauren's gaze like an expert power-monger, like the CEO or president or surgeon or lawyer Lauren knew she would be someday, and then turned and walked away, her long dress swishing across her covered ankles. The mid-winter sun was casting an orange beam down the hallway from through the windows in the living room. Soon it would be dark, dark as the middle of the night, and wasn't it something how it did that around here during the winter months—light and then, bam, pure darkness for hours and hours. And hours.

As Lauren sat on the bed in the growing darkness, she watched the beam of orange light slowly move up the wall and narrow. She knew the sun would now be setting in such marvelous beauty over the ocean, which they could view mere feet from their condo. Yet she wasn't eager to get up. The condo was quiet. She didn't know what she'd find Lucy doing.

Finally, she arose and left the bedroom. She turned and walked down the short hallway, following the withdrawal of the orange light, feeling as if life itself were being sucked out along with the setting sun.

Lucy was standing on the back of the couch with her enormous box of pastels open on one of the cushions. The Christmas tree they had just bought that afternoon at Hope Grocers stood empty and lightless in its stand by the window. They would decorate as soon as Lauren found the energy to pull out the Christmas boxes from their storage unit downstairs. Lauren watched Lucy throw her body side-to-side as a dark blue pastel crayon pinched between her fingers made a soft buzzing noise across the white wall above. She was turning an entire section of the wall into a blue, blue night. And below that she had drawn an enormous cross topped with a large silver star.

Her little body was jerking so energetically that Lauren thought she would at any moment lose her balance and fall. And surely that dark blue almost black pastel would leave an impossible smudge on Lucy's fingers. But as Lauren watched and the condo turned, just like that, dark and cold, she decided to just let her be. And for one quick, rampant moment, she could only hope that if Lucy fell, she wouldn't get back up.

-8-

Vinny's Glass Sculptures

Vinny came to Hope with the Coast Guard, eighteen-years-old, recently graduated from high school in Seattle, and itching to be free. His parents had divorced when he was ten and his dad, whom he hadn't seen since, had fled to Florida, his mom had said, and he could go see him if he ever found the airplane fare because she sure as hell didn't have that kind of money. Well, the Coast Guard might eventually get him there, but better yet, it would get him around; he'd finally *see* things. He might even make something of himself. He'd barely made it out of senior year. He had no talents or impressive interests. He had precisely one close friend, Stanley, whom he spent the weekends playing video games with while Vinny's mom worked the counter at the Starbucks on 5th Avenue. So, he was going to Alaska. It was wild and adventurous up there. He'd probably have to do intense ocean rescues. Maybe he'd learn to fly a helicopter. He might get into shooting bears if that was something a person could do.

When none of that had happened, and he had tired of the Coast Guard and all the boring tasks he was made to do, he got a job as waiter at La Iguana Mexican restaurant and at 23 married a local girl, Cheryl, whom he had met at Hope Baptist Church, and together they bought a three-bedroom ranch-style house in the new development, Big Woods, some local developers had hacked out of the old growth spruce forest on the north slopes of the mountain range that ran down the middle of the island. At $250,000, it was more than Vinny could imagine. He couldn't believe it would be his, thanks to a very generous gift (well, basically the whole thing) from Cheryl's father who owned two fishing charter companies in town and was, Vinny surmised, the only wealthy person he'd ever met in his life. Within a year, however, and typical of much in Hope, the house's foundation had cracked in several places and was causing the whole house to unevenly sink into the muskeg the development had hastily been built upon. The roof hadn't been laid correctly and needed to be patched. The pipes had burst below the master bathroom, leaking water into the surrounding walls; several of the cabinets had fallen off their hinges; the tub faucet had fallen out; there was mold growing recklessly around the panes of most of the windows. But it was theirs, together, and they were so very, very happy.

Cheryl made one of the bedrooms her office, for she had recently quit her job as 2nd-grade teacher and was starting her own on-line business supplying her own Christ-based curriculum materials to Christian homeschoolers nation-wide. They talked about eventually having children and filling up the bedrooms with cribs, though children had never exactly been a specific *desire* of Vinny's like owning a four-wheeler was. Still, for the first time in his life he was ridiculously, sometimes shockingly (as if such a destiny shouldn't have been in his cards) happy, and if that meant, in the future, children and going bald and a slight potbelly, well, that would be just all right because it also meant daily meals with Cheryl and nightly lovemaking and, even, their occasional, harmless spats that, he would only acknowledge to himself, usually came and went with the moods that Cheryl's period spurred on.

They were happy and in love in an aged, decades-old way, as if they had in fact been married for 50 years instead of going on two; as if they had known each other in some other life and were just picking back up again. She prepared chamomile tea for them every evening and made oatmeal with raisins and cinnamon weekday mornings, though she had a penchant for donuts that Vinny, occasionally, got up early to retrieve from Hope Grocers, placing the box of donuts nearest her place at the dining table so she would get first pick. He usually bought flowers then, too, and already had them in a vase on the table for her to see in the morning. He made pancakes Sunday morning before church, and after church they came home to pot roast, potatoes, and carrots slow cooking in the oven. Occasionally, they'd have lunch with Cheryl's parents who lived in a mansion by the ocean, and sometimes they'd invite other young married church friends over, followed by boisterous games of Nerts and Pictionary while snacking on popcorn and Cheryl's homemade chocolate chip cookies.

Vinny could barely remember his old, pre-pubescent life in Seattle. Whenever he did, it would come to him more as an anorexic fantasy rather than what had been at one point his absolute reality. He would shake his head, smile pitifully at who he used to be, and think about how lucky he was now, finally, a man with a wife and a religion and a house and an old Ford pickup he hauled firewood and just-shot deer in. What was most surprising to him was that for the first time since his dad had left those many years ago, he had no desire to see him. Several months into his and Cheryl's marriage, it occurred to him rather quietly, belying the incredibleness of the fact, that there was absolutely nothing else he desired.

Cheryl loved everything about Vinny. His plainness and gentleness; his lack of pride; his, to her, hilarious jokes; his down-to-earthness; his unruly straight brown hair that he let her cut because he refused to pay money to go to a barber. Cheryl was, frankly, quite fat in a way that had always embarrassed her parents (who viewed her obesity as somehow un-Christ-like), and she liked how that had never repulsed Vinny. It turned him on in the best ways. During lovemaking he'd tenderly grab her large breasts and gently squeeze them, put his entire mouth over her large brown nipples and suck, which always made her squeal, feeling the sensation all the way in the tips of her toes. He loved hugging her stomach and planting his face into her fat rolls; loved licking their softness and making her laugh. Unlike her breasts, he grabbed her bottom and all its massiveness as if it were a person he was rescuing from the ocean in one of his old Coast Guard exercises – thrillingly domineeringly, which made Cheryl ecstatic with a physical abandon she had never experienced before.

But she came to love his "gift," as she called it, most of all.

Their new house came with a detached garage. Vinny had never had a garage in his life, having spent his upbringing in various levels of run-down Seattle apartments. To Vinny, a garage was pure luxury, a sure sign of having "made it." Just one more dimension of what was turning into his perfect life. It was in the garage where his gift first came into being so that even in the winter when the snow and ice came, Cheryl parked her teal Taurus and Vinny his pickup in the gravel driveway, leaving the garage open for him. It had been only an idea, at first, that came to him after leaving an empty bottle of beer too close to one of the many campfires he and Cheryl had sat by on their camping honeymoon on the island. The brown bottle had cracked and shattered into a hundred pieces. On the ground each piece looked like a priceless jewel. He didn't see them individually, though. Among the charcoal dustings and spruce needles, he saw a bounding cat or was it a leopard? To think that the shattering of mere glass could make a recognizable creature, and that the creature could look more startling and beautiful as figments of glass than even the real thing!

Several weeks later, he visited the recycling center, inserting his entire upper body into the enormous bins and pulling out hundreds of glass bottles and containers and loading them into a large plastic bin he had bought at Seaside Hardware just for that purpose. He wore leather gardening gloves so he wouldn't get cut. What amazed him then, and would continue to, was that the glass came in so many unexpected colors. He found reds and yellows; blues and greens; shades of brown and black and white. Some had unusual textures; some were beautifully beveled. Of course, the colored ones were harder to find, and in the future when he stumbled across something vibrant and unusual, like pink or purple or magenta or sky blue, he received a zing of pure almost sexual joy. After that first trip, he had collected more than one hundred glass containers that bounced and clattered in the bin in the back of his pickup.

When he drove onto the gravel driveway before their detached garage and unloaded the heaving bin of glass, Cheryl came out in her apron (she was baking chocolate chip cookies, knowing Vinny loved them) and took it all in: his leather gloves, his straight hair hanging into his beautiful brown eyes, his thin arms under his sturdy Carhart jacket, his thin gorgeous bottom, his Xtratufs, his damp face despite the chilly pre-winter afternoon, an enormous bin full of glass that he sexily carried before him. She could turn off the oven, she supposed. She could finish the cookies after pulling him into their bedroom and tearing off his clothes. But why the bedroom? Why not the couch or the living room floor? After that one night, she would never look at their stuffed recliner the same way. When guests sat on it she would turn to keep from showing her blush; to tamp down the breathless giggle that wanted out like some crazy sprite.

"I have to install an oven in the garage." He looked at Cheryl out of the corner of his eyes as he struggled with the bin and dropped it with a loud glassy clamor near the side door of the garage.

"Oh." She couldn't help but admire his effort and his sweaty face and his long bangs; couldn't help but imagine him stark naked.

"For a project," he said.

And because she loved him, despite the worries she had that he would hurt himself somehow with that oven and all that glass and whatever he was up to, she agreed. And when two weeks later they installed the industrial oven, she also insisted they install a heater so he could work in comfort at night and during the winter months.

He went to the library and checked out books: *Glass Making*, *Working with Glass*, and simply, *Glass*. Cheryl had laughed when she saw the stack on his bedside table. He read them at night in bed before sleep while next to him Cheryl watched episodes of The Bachelor and Survivor on the small TV they had in a fancy entertainment cabinet they had bought and shipped up from Sears after buying the house. At La Iguana, he thought about glass; he went over lines he had memorized in the books. He thought about animals and plants of glass. Iguanas and slugs; eagles and otters. Vines. Sprawling oaks. Towering redwoods, spruces. Red-capped mushrooms.

Then, one month later, after his trip to the recycling center and getting his garage studio all set (Cheryl had snapped a photo of him when it was finished; him standing somewhat self-consciously in the middle of the smooth cement-floored garage; the large heater affixed in one corner, there, just above his left shoulder; a large sink just below that with only a tip of the oven showing; and Cheryl had said triumphantly as she pressed the button, "The artist in his studio!"), he began.

First, there was the outfit of his own design: heavy-duty Carhart pants; plastic goggles to protect his eyes (that Cheryl had excitedly picked up at the kitchen store–they were in fact goggles to wear while cutting onions); thick leather gloves that approached his elbows; a canvas apron; a red bandana to keep his hair back, for one of Cheryl's greatest fears was that his overhanging hair would somehow catch fire. Then, with the oven cranked up to 500 degrees, so hot that opening the oven door meant being hit by a wall of heat so intense that the first time he had instinctively fallen back because it had felt like a violent punch square in his face, he carefully inserted a glass bottle pinched within the grasp of long cast iron tongs. He held it there and waited for 8 seconds. At the beginning, he set a timer, but over time he just came to know, for some bottles needed more time and others less. If they had labels, he simply let them burn off, leaving ash on the bottom of the oven that he cleaned out daily. When the bottle was hot enough, he pulled it back out and quickly plunged it into the sink he had already filled with cold water and ice cubes. And this is when the miracle happened, which, he knew, was nothing other than pure science but still seemed, and would continue to seem, like a religious experience, for inserting the hot, hot glass into the icy water instantaneously transformed the previously smooth glass into a many-thousand-pieced object—one crazy complex 3D puzzle. Then, with the cooled, cracked glass bottle in his gloved hands, he would roll over in his padded office chair to the counter by the sink, turn on the table light there so that a section of the counter was suddenly cast in a circle of bright white light, place the bottle on the silicon cutting board below the light, and with his glass knife cut the bottle along one side, peeling it open like the cover of an ancient text. If he had done it right, the bottle would miraculously open without shattering, its glass edges smooth, and before him he'd have a pane of slightly flexible, veined, and, what felt like to him, living glass. And with this and a bit of caulk, he surmised he could form any creature, any plant, any object he imagined. He had never been a drawer or the slightest bit artistic, but now he had a sketchpad full of everything he wanted to make, from tropical fish to big-eyed chameleons, hummingbirds, mosquitos, bugs, spiders. As he got better, his ideas grew; he wanted to connect figures to make entire scenes: dinosaurs in a prehistoric jungle; colorful fish amid corals; long-tailed lemurs perched in trees.

He needed molds. The idea of wire had occurred to him, for couldn't wire be bent and shaped? Downtown at Ben Franklin he found a big ball of soft pliable wire sheathed in plastic. That Monday afternoon, his day off, Cheryl found him in the living room sitting on the floor, the ball of wire unraveled around him, odd wired shapes scattered about.

He had to go bigger, he discovered. So back to Ben Franklin he went, and soon there were wired animals and plants across their house. Sometimes he'd quiz Cheryl. "Can you tell what that one is?" he pointed to one, balancing near the edge of the dining room table. And she looked carefully and took her best guess. "It's a rat, love." She could tell by its long tail and long nose. "It's a cat, Cheryl. *A cat!*"

Wire was harder to shape than he imagined, and when he first draped a sheet of glass over one of them (it was the "little midget" Cheryl had laughingly called it when first seeing it standing on the floor to the left of the fireplace as if a senseless sentry standing guard; and Vinny had at first been offended, insisting it was a *gnome!*, a cute little gnome that they could eventually put in the garden they were planning for the ¼ acre of gravel and muskeg out back of the house), the hot glass fell into the empty spaces between the wire leaving behind a sadly warped and misshapen gnome that would, alas, never stand in their future garden.

It was at La Iguana one night as he was scraping out layers of ice that were accumulating in the deep freezer, that he thought of something better. Foam blocks could easily be carved. And so that very night after closing the restaurant, he drove home and destroyed every wire figure, smooshing them all into one big wire ball. The next day he returned to Ben Franklin, bought a small cube of foam, and used a knife to cut away the excess. That night Cheryl cried when she found a foam heart on her pillow that Vinny had put there before work, smooth-edged and the size of her hand. The next morning, she kissed him, though he was still asleep, and felt for his penis and gently squeezed it the way she liked until it grew in her hot hand and he was no longer asleep.

Afterwards, she asked him to make her heart his first glass sculpture, which he did right then and there, pulling on his sweatpants and old Metallica t-shirt; his socks and boots and walking out to the garage in the early morning and tying on his apron and bandana and goggles. He had a small red glass bottle he had found last week and was saving just for this. He heated and dunked it; carefully cut it open and molded it over the foam heart, caulking it together. Not quite as he had imagined; a bit more angular than he would have liked, for anyone knew a heart didn't have angles, was all curves and slopes and gentleness. He carefully wiped away the excess caulk and set it on the counter to cool and harden. It felt oddly holy to him ("oddly" because the only spirituality he had ever known was through Cheryl, and even then, it was only for her and not something he really believed in), all of it: the ideas, the compulsions, the fact that his first sculpture would be Cheryl's and that it would be what felt like was his actual heart pulled out for her to see and hold.

Sure, he had cut himself countless times since beginning, and he had had to get used to all the sounds that had initially kept his entire body on edge: the poppings and crackings and hissings and snappings. Once at the beginning, Cheryl had stood there looking over his shoulder as he stuck a glass container into the oven, her forearm up against her eyes to shield her from the waves of heat, and when the sounds started and the heat just kept on coming, she couldn't help it. "Turn it off, Vinny!" she screamed. "Off! Now!"

He couldn't understand what she was getting on about behind him, and when he initially didn't respond, she started wailing, tugging at his arm that held the glass, making him drop it in the oven where the whole thing exploded, splaying glass shards around the oven, a few miraculously missing him and embedding like jewels into the sheetrock of the unfinished wall behind them.

He'd gotten so mad at her then, couldn't understand what her problem was, yelled at her to get out, now!, and leave him the hell alone. It had shocked her into silence. She had immediately left, the tears starting.

Oh, how he had instantly regretted it. After turning off the oven, he had run after her into the house, held her, and they had worked it out, him letting her sobs soak the shoulder of his shirt because he could understand her fear and hated himself for having been so short-tempered, so hateful, with her.

Another time Cheryl had screamed when Vinny had come into the kitchen hugging his hand to his chest, a chunk of glass embedded into the palm of his hand (he had been so stupid, he would admit; had pulled his gloves off just for a moment so he could feel the glass like a living thing against his hands). She immediately stopped forming the crust for the bacon and cheddar cheese quiche she was making for dinner. She sped him to the ER down the hill, blood dripping onto her oven mitt, which was the only thing she could think to grab as they rushed out of the kitchen. In the end, it had only been two stitches, but it would never happen again, and over time they both grew glowingly full of their pride of what Cheryl believed was obviously Vinny's God-given talent.

Every day Vinny worked in his studio. After oatmeal in the morning and washing dishes afterwards, Cheryl went into her office and Vinny out to the garage. They worked the hours until lunch, usually followed by lovemaking before Vinny showered and put on his white shirt and black pants and headed over to La Iguana. If the neighbors wondered why Cheryl's car and Vinny's truck were always parked outside their garage, even when the rain fell for weeks on end and the snow started in October, it occurred to them only as a minor afterthought, for if Vinny and Cheryl were anything like them, their garage was already full of all the stuff that couldn't fit in their house, and weren't they lucky to have what most people in Hope only dreamed of instead having to pack their carports with the stuff everyone in town had grown accustomed to not hiding. The fact that Vinny and Cheryl had an art studio tucked away inside their detached cream-colored garage with its already molding siding and uneven foundation riding the slope of the clear-cut mountain, wasn't even a spark in anyone's imagination. And so Vinny could work away in there in complete silence and freedom, a few hundred-year-old spruce trees left standing sparsely around outside, the occasional staccato cry of a bald eagle piercing the wilderness just behind, feeling more alive than he ever had in his life.

He had two lives, the thought suddenly hit him once during one of those pauses his glass work gifted him, into which he often fell like into some kind of drug-induced bliss. His life in the garage and his life everywhere else. It was his life in the garage, among his gleaming organized piles of glass and wild sparkling creatures, that became what he would ever know of what could possibly be construed as some kind of "transcendence," even beyond lovemaking; beyond hunting and camping with the guys; beyond Cheryl's chocolate chip cookies and her enormously luscious thighs.

Over the first several months, there were many duds, and even though Vinny came into his studio as if he were re-entering the womb, into the safest, warmest, most truthful place in the world, he had thrown a piece or two in frustrated anger, exploding the disfigured thing against the cement floor of the garage and cracking the foam mold underneath. And then he would leave the garage without even removing his apron or glasses or gloves; without turning the light off or cleaning up the pieces of the ruined sculpture shattered across the floor. During such moments, early on, he thought about giving it all up; wanted nothing more than to torch everything inside and return Cheryl's car and his truck to their rightful places. But Cheryl would understand. "Just take a break, babe," she'd say, and she'd untie his apron and remove his goggles; she'd slide off his bandana and smooth back his sweaty hair; she'd kiss his cheeks and neck. And when he'd growl, "It can't always be handled with a kiss, Cheryl," she'd simply hold him until she felt his muscles loosen; until he took a big, deep sigh and told her he was a complete failure; how nothing was coming together at all and, as he had always suspected, he was a big fat loser. In fact, why had she married him? Why?

Cheryl didn't know any artists at all; only knew peripherally of Picasso and Monet and were there others? She had always known artists were Godless and druggies and, well, weren't they *unstable*? But it was different with Vinny. She had yet to see anything he was working on, but she knew for a fact that he wasn't an *artist* artist; he was so much more. What he had was obviously a gift from God. It was the same kind of passion she experienced from him during lovemaking; the kind of wholesome passion God approved of. Eventually, in Cheryl's fleshy embrace, Vinny would calm down enough to head back into the garage, momentarily wincing from the view: the light on, the sculpture aborted in pieces across the floor. Once, he had left the oven on full-blast and upon seeing this he pinched his eyes together tightly, as if in the throes of a massive migraine, feeling moronic for being reduced so easily to pure, stupid emotion. Thank God for Cheryl, he knew. She had never once, in all this, grown frustrated with him even though at night sometimes he lay awake next to her, wondering if she had bargained for this, his crazy artsy hobby. At times it made him feel gay, like *homosexual* gay. A complete fruit cake. Making glass sculptures, in his garage? Did Alaskan men do this? But before too long he was asleep, and in the morning felt free and normal again. Funny how the night could at times render him pathetic and neurotic; not himself at all.

After much prayer at Cheryl's insistence, and many sleepless nights, more than half a year later Vinny decided to go public. Their Bible study friends and Cheryl's parents saw Cheryl's glass heart every time they came over, but it was one thing having them see one of his sculptures, and another thing having complete strangers see. Cheryl had propped the heart up in a plastic stand in the middle of the mantle above the fireplace, and there it glowed a remarkable red from reflecting the lights in the living room, though at just the right angle it at times looked as if it were the sole source of a vaguely pulsing glow.

"Whatever is that?" her mother had said upon first seeing it, stretching out tentative fingers to it, unsure, as if it held some power.

"We are created in the image of God, after all," Cheryl had told her parents who were first a bit unsure. "God, the ultimate sculptor!" she had smiled.

"As long as it doesn't get in the way of . . . anything," her father had mumbled, looking at the gleaming heart suspiciously.

Their friends thought it was cute, very sweet. The men didn't talk about it with Vinny, thinking it just a bit too awkward, and thankfully he wasn't much for talking about it either. No one had ever thought that Vinny was "a catch" for Cheryl, but together they seemed so happy and they had a house and he had been baptized Christian before the wedding, after all (for even though he had been baptized as a baby, Catholics weren't really Christians, everyone knew, believing in Mary and the Pope and holy water and other pagan-like mysticisms). They could put up with a little eccentricity, they assumed.

Vinny knew as soon as it was done that the first sculpture would go to La Iguana. It was a life-sized iguana made entirely of gleaming emerald glass with eyes so realistic customers would stop to stare deep into its reptilian pupil and speckled iris, waiting for it to blink, perhaps, or show some signs of the magic suspected to reside inside it like a beating heart. He had spent nine weeks on it, perfecting its scales and finding and placing the right colors, browns bleeding into shades of green; the dirty white of the underbelly; the claws of the foot; the vague blooming of pinks and blues here and there. And then the eyes, which had consumed him, which he had dreamed about fitfully for weeks. What was it about the eyes that had to be beyond glass; that had to be as if receiving the heart's blood and seeing the world? Vinny would eventually realize that it was the eyes in each and every one that gave life to the thing. And he would be right, for people would talk incessantly about each sculpture's eyes. Vinny would watch them approach a creature and then be drawn forward, as if by a magical force, to the centimeters of space directly in front of the eyes, angling their heads, getting closer, mesmerized.

He carved out a space for the eyes on the sides of the iguana's foam head; carving out the sockets as he imagined God doing with Adam and Eve. He had a kid's book, *Iguanas!*, he was following, but eventually he went on intuition; he let his mind guide his hands, piecing, cutting, training the bright light of the lamp on his sheets of glass in order to find just the right shade of lime or light brown or orange or the creamy blue-tinge of the eye whites, until there came that moment when he looked eye-to-eye with the iguana and it looked back at him. It followed him with its eyes as Vinny puttered around the garage at the end of his work, sweeping the floor of glass bits; wiping down the counters and cleaning out the sink; scrubbing the bottom of the oven. Occasionally Vinny would turn, quickly, having suddenly felt the presence of something up against his back, a breath, and he'd take a good long look at the iguana frozen on the counter, its beautiful crest riding the precipice of its scalp and down its back, crouching above its scaly feet, its tail slightly wrapped and rounded behind. "You!" Vinny had laughed once into the garage. "You sneaky bastard!" Then had turned and continued sweeping out the corners of the immaculate garage.

At dinner that night, Cheryl couldn't hide a smile that kept inflating her mouth, though she kept her face down toward her plate, busy with her rib eye and mashed potatoes. Vinny noticed and eventually pointed his fork, at the end of which sat a hunk of steak, at her, "What's going on with you?" Cheryl couldn't control it anymore and burst into a laugh that splayed bits of steak and mashed potatoes across the table and onto Vinny's face.

"You're like an old man, Vinny," she said in between tears. "Talkin' to your creatures."

Vinny at first just sat there, wiping her food from his face, but Cheryl's laugh was more contagious than the flu.

"Don't choke, Vinny!" Cheryl sputtered.

"I'm not!" He was laughing in between coughing.

The next day, Vinny carefully wrapped the iguana in bubble wrap and placed it in a box on the seat next to him. He drove down to La Iguana and used his body to shelter the wrapped iguana from the pouring rain as he carried it from his truck.

"Oh my God!" Mrs. Alvirez, the owner, exclaimed, deep dimples popping out on each of her voluminous liver-spotted cheeks.

"Oh my *God*, Vinny! *Es bella*! *Eres algo más!*" And she placed it next to the host's podium at the entrance, pushing aside plastic cacti and long-flowing ferns and wide-brimmed Mexican hats balancing along the ledge that divided the entrance from the tables and booths.

Over the weeks, people wanted to know all about it. Who had made it and how? Were those *real* eyeballs in there? Mrs. Alvirez said that Vinny should make a little placard to put before the sculpture. And so he did, very carefully cutting a firm piece of heavy construction paper he had bought specially from the art store (spending way more than he ever had on paper). He used the back of some scissors to crease the piece of paper so that it would stand up-right, and then wrote in his finest cursive using a fine-point black gel pen after practicing several times on a piece of scratch paper: *Artist: Vincent Albini.* He put the placard, expensive looking and professional, he thought, below the iguana's chin several inches from its feet so that when people wandered up to get a closer look at it they couldn't miss seeing his name, *Vincent Albini*, and then how wonderful for Vinny to get the chance to say matter-of-factly, "oh, that's me," when the topic came up over a conversation at a table he was at that moment serving beers, tacos and burritos to. Occasionally, people would mistake the iguana for a live one. Upon opening the door and seeing it, crouching expectantly, they would startle just a bit, which usually entailed an instantaneous widening of their eyes that Vinny always found hilarious.

Over the next year-and-a-half, Vinny's sculptures began showing up around town. Larry of Larry's Radio Emporium wanted an enormous fictional movie character suspended from the ceiling in the DVD section of the store. "Make it Harry Potter on his broom," Larry had decided. "You can do that, right?" Vinny thought he could do that, and did. The public library wanted a life-size Cat-in-the-Hat in the children's room. The public radio station, KROAR, wanted a 5-foot brown bear to put in their entryway. The Native hospital wanted a raven and eagle together on a branch to hang in the brand new lobby with its 12-foot ceiling and wall of windows. Members of the General Assembly wanted something in the community center that the tourists would be impressed by. "A giant humpback whale," one had suggested. Mayor Marc Randal had been the sole vote against such a thing.

"We have enough art galleries in this town," he had said at their meeting one Tuesday night. "This isn't Aspen, people. This isn't Park City. We're not here to cater to the yuppies and millionaires. You wanna see art, go to New York City."

A few sculptures Vinny had placed around town with no permission at all. He felt it was one way for him to give back to a town that had welcomed and kept him; was nurturing of him, even. For the first time in his life, he felt truly at home. So, he placed one in the entryway of Hope First Bank—a four-foot totem pole that welcomed people as they stood in line to use the ATM machine in the lobby. To Laura's Flowers and Gifts, he gave a large glass vase full of glass flowers, which Laura proudly put in the window. To Joe's Chocolates, he gave a giant glass candy bar that perfectly mimicked the dark chocolate bar Joe had invented called Hope Hour, his biggest seller. Vinny had even decided to leave some outside, chancing people's goodness to leave them be. He tucked a life-sized raven into a spruce tree near the trailhead in Totem Park. He hid it just enough so that people wouldn't notice it immediately, but out enough so that they'd see it if they happened to be looking up a bit, tilting their heads back to take in the smells of the ocean and the tops of the glorious spruces as he liked to do there. A giant king salmon, its back arched as if in the middle of a massive leap upstream, he left suspended from wires in the harbor shelter at Town Harbor past which the tourists walked in the thousands during the summer, and under which the town hosted the crab feed, the salmon derby, the annual Blessing of the Fleet, and the firemen's band on the Fourth of July.

One Saturday morning Vinny was in the garage working on his latest, which was something he was feeling particularly serious about. It was something he had only dreamed about and never would have tried if, now almost two years in, he hadn't begun to feel more confident. He was creating *more* than a single creature, an entire scene of bright-colored fish among coral. He'd always wanted to go snorkeling in some warm, exotic waters somewhere. Cheryl hated swimming, but he'd convince her when this was done to go with him to do just that. Mexico? Hawaii? Maybe that would be the time to go to Florida to see his dad, once and for all. The varieties of the coral were turning out to be harder than he had imagined, which was rejuvenating in its way, and he was already on his third try when Cheryl entered with the cordless.

"The mayor," Cheryl whispered.

Vinny knew the mayor wasn't into niceties, and this had never bothered him. Marc was from an established Hope family and seemed to Vinny a true Alaskan man. In retrospect, though, Vinny would wonder about Marc. Why was it that the mayor couldn't at least say "hi" to him?

Vinny took off his goggles and gloves. He had to admit, there was something exciting about getting a personal call from the mayor.

"Hi, Marc!" he smiled at Cheryl who was leaning in the doorway through which the gray light from outside made visible the roundness of her thighs and hips under her white nightgown.

"You can't leave your things just willy-nilly across the town, Vinny. There are city rules for this sort of thing," Marc said.

"Oh, I see," Vinny's mouth went suddenly dry, though he kept his smile for Cheryl whose mouth was open in expectation, as it tended to do during sex, though her eyes were more pointed as if she were a teacher again, waiting for the right answer.

"If I let *you* break the rules, then everyone will."

Vinny had nothing to say, but Marc seemed to be waiting. Vinny heard the rain hitting the garage roof, which normally was a sound he loved almost as much as Cheryl's sighs.

"You know, Vinny," Marc's voice was louder, as if he were compensating for the strange silence. "Ya'ever think about getting a diff'rent hobby? Ya'ever think it might just be a little bit . . . odd? For a grown man?"

"Yeah, I'll think about it," Vinny said while looking at Cheryl, the rain falling on the gravel behind her. "A commission," he turned off the phone. He couldn't lie directly to her face, so he turned away, as if busy with something on the counter. He pulled back on his gloves and goggles.

"A commission!" Cheryl jumped and squealed, clapping her hands once. She let the door close behind her and the rain pummeled the small glass window in it. She ran to him and hugged him. "The pay doesn't matter, of course. But, still, it will be nice, right? Like, you'll be a *professional*. Oh!" She clapped once.

Vinny had met one or two bullies in his life. Justin in high school had made it his mission to prove Vinny was gay, and there had been some girl (he'd almost entirely forgotten her) in one of his elementary schools who used to steal his after-school snack money his mom gave him most days so he could stop by the 7-Eleven on his way home. Sure, he'd met men who were rough; liked to swear and get drunk; paid for hookers; sampled a drug or two. Those men seemed to him harmless and forgettable. They could be astoundingly funny and were usually stupid. But the mayor lodged in his brain and visited him at night. Vinny ran from him in his dreams and once hit him square in the nose, upon waking feeling the resonance of the punch so painfully in his knuckles that he quickly turned to Cheryl to make sure he hadn't accidentally punched her instead. Well, enough was enough, he finally determined, exhausted and fed up with his own weakness. He would, for once, be strong; be a man. No one would stop him.

And so the sculptures continued. A totem for the Hope Hotel lobby appeared. A sailboat he hung from under the roof of the ramp leading down to Eastern Harbor. Finally, he had no qualms lying to Cheryl, telling her that the commission was in fact the 5-foot humpback whale he enlisted her father to help him carry into the community center one Friday afternoon, placing it majestically opposite the entrance along the wall hung with the framed portraits of all of Hope's mayors since the town became incorporated in 1951.

After placing each new sculpture, whether requested or not, *The Daily Storm* published letter after letter to the editor. "How wonderful finding the raven in the historical park," one gushed. "I was walking and just happened to look up, and there it was!" "How does Vinny do it?" another asked. "We appreciate it," many said.

Still, there were those who thought it was a bit pretentious, as if *everyone* in Hope wanted to see those things every time they turned around. Quite a few said that Hope was getting too artsy and touristy; Hope could do with just a little less of Vinny's sculptures. "How about a break, Vinny?" one letter pleaded.

The nasty ones bothered Vinny, so Cheryl got into the habit of scanning the paper every day before he read it to make sure there wasn't a mean one. He would pretend it didn't bother him; would read it and shrug his shoulder as if letting something putrid slide right off (his "zombie-hand-on-shoulder move" Cheryl laughingly called it). Cheryl knew, though – people's opinions about his sculptures mattered to Vinny, and it was no coincidence that after a rude letter, Vinny went to bed later than Cheryl because he simply couldn't settle down. Thankfully, though, the letters started coming less frequently over the year and into the second year of Vinny's going public. People simply grew accustomed to them, which was actually a type of forgetting that didn't bother Vinny at all.

There were times he wondered whether it had been smart to send his sculptures out there, into the world. All he really wanted was to continue to make them without any recognition at all. It took Cheryl to remind him of all the blessings his sculptures had incurred: all the letters of praise!, the beauty he was sharing with the people of Hope!, the fact that no stranger was interested in finding out where he worked and lived because that type of person wasn't the type to live in Hope. "Though can you imagine having your own private stalker?" she had joked.

So, Vinny decided to save only the kind letters; the letters of profuse praise; the ones that kept him going and sent him to bed with Cheryl on time. Those he cut out and kept in a folder labeled "Letters to Editor," and though he never read them again, he suspected he might want them for the future when and if he began to enter fully into that space he had previously only glimpsed, which was the room of his self-loathing; the space of his shattered pieces.

It was the 5-foot humpback whale that Vinny and his father-in-law had placed in the community center that, eventually, did it. Mayor Marc immediately brought it up at the next General Assembly meeting.

Vinny knew the whale was his way of fighting back, though he would never admit this to Cheryl or anyone; would continue to feign surprise and humility in the face of Marc's attacks, both men fully aware of their intentions. Marc had never been so publicly crossed before in his life, unaccustomed as he was to being stood up to or made a fool of.

"This is no laughing matter," Marc told the members of the Assembly the following Thursday night, fingering the gavel under his hand. "We have not come to a majority decision on this matter, and, look, there goes Vinny doing it anyway. Sorry to be rude, but *what the hell!*" And many of the members nodded their heads in agreement just because they enjoyed getting riled up and respected Marc's ability to take control.

Before this, though, came Vinny's own sickening regret that had set in a mere 24 hours after leaving the beautiful whale behind, surely one of his masterpieces. It set in stone his lie to Cheryl and also meant that now he was most assuredly Marc's bull's eye. *Why oh why did I do it?* he thought over and over again, until realizing that he would just have to eat it. He would face Cheryl immediately, who he knew would forgive him, and he would face Marc who would be another matter altogether, but so be it. He'd also have to face Cheryl's father, whom he had stupidly enlisted to help him, making him an unknowing accomplice. Cheryl's father, he knew, would be livid. Oh, life had a way of becoming complicated, and Vinny discovered that he hated that aspect of life. But he had his studio, and he had a thousand more creatures to bring to life.

Telling Cheryl had been harder than he'd imagined. For two days she wouldn't talk to him, her silence encompassing them for the first time in their marriage. But then she softened and insisted they talk about it all the time for what felt like to Vinny many endless days.

"Can't we just let it drop?" he looked at Cheryl over dinner a few days later, his stomach full-feeling though his peas and pork chop remain untouched.

"No," she scooped some peas into her spoon and put it into her mouth. "No, babe, we can't." She swallowed. "Because it was a *lie*, to *me. Your wife.* And it was also a lie to yourself. And *Dad.* Not good for your heart or soul." She pointed her spoon at his chest.

After they continued in silence, her scraping her plate with the last of her chop bone and sucking it clean, she said, "You won't lie to me again, right? You won't go so low again."

And with that, Vinny knew the talk was finally over; that he had borne the brunt of her working-it-through. She had finally forgiven him and that was that.

"I won't." He was so grateful that his eyes filled with tears. He pushed back his chair and rushed to her, and they immediately went to the bedroom where all their workings-through cemented themselves in the best way possible.

The General Assembly meeting, a week later, momentarily brought it all back. Cheryl's parents, who always watched the meeting live on the local TV station, called immediately, the meeting still in full-force before them. Her father's voice, low and shot through with bursts of anger, carried through the phone like muted thunder as Vinny held it to his ear. Cheryl eventually yanked the phone from Vinny and told her father to cool it. That she and Vinny had already dealt with it; that Vinny was forgiven. And as it turned out, one brave member of the Assembly suggested they just vote that night, once and for all, because the whale was already there and it would save Vinny having to remove it if everyone agreed to keep it there. The vote was 5 for and 3 against, and though there was nothing he could do about it, mayor Marc was visibly angry; kept sighing and twisting in his seat the entire meeting; was gruffer than usual with the other members, especially the one who suggested the vote. Even more infuriating was that the members had also agreed to let Vinny keep every single one of his sculptures exactly where they were; that they were doing no one any harm despite being placed "willy-nilly across our beautiful town," Marc had growled looking directly at the one member (who happened to be the director of the conservation society, which Marc had no respect for) who had initiated the whole vote.

"Marc's always been a sore loser," Cheryl said after she and Vinny turned the TV on to watch the meeting. "You should have seen him in high school." And Vinny was happy, then, that he had never gone to high school with Marc. Sure, his whale sculpture would remain in its prominent position but he felt uneasy about it all now; too much emotional baggage wrapped up in that gorgeous whale. He would just have to let it be, he concluded late that night in bed with Cheryl asleep next to him. And because he couldn't sleep, he quietly got up, tucked in the blankets around Cheryl's hot body, and went back to his studio, the smell and presence of which immediately wiped his anxiety clean.

Cheryl's parents urged Vinny to take the sculptures down anyway, seeing as they bothered the mayor so much. No harm in doing that, they said. But taking away the sculptures seemed to him a violation of the sculptures' lives, for he did think of them as living, in their own way. Taking them away from the beautiful spots he had found for them, out there in nature and in the town, would mean storing them in the garage until someone wanted one, and he was sure the sculptures wouldn't like it, as crazy as he knew it sounded.

Cheryl told him to ignore her parents. The sculptures were little miracles, she said.

Daily he waffled between boiling anger toward Marc who had set such meanness in motion, peaceful relief for knowing that he didn't have to do a thing if he didn't want to, and despair for having been so reckless with his creations. He decided. His sculptures would live happily after all.

It was late evening and Vinny was walking back in the pouring rain from the pick-up basketball game he played every Sunday at the middle school. He had his shoes in a plastic bag and gripped in his waterproof-gloved hand. The rain pummeled the hood and shoulders of his raincoat and his lashes were heavy with raindrops. He had always liked walking in the rain, though. Liked the way it sounded, the feel of it against his body. Liked how his Xtratufs kept his feet warm and snug. There was something rejuvenating about life in Hope; it meant hundreds of walks just like the one he was taking now. As he headed up the road to his house, he heard the low, easy rumble of a slow-moving car behind him and moved to the side to let it pass. It stayed there, though, following him at his elbow. Vinny stopped and turned. The car's headlights were on, hitting him painfully in the eyes. He squinted to make out who it was, though the rain kept blurring his vision like in countless nightmares he'd had. The car eased forward, a new Mustang, and idled next to Vinny who was still squinting, could only make out a shadow inside.

"You're kind of a nasty little prick," Marc said from the open window, his elbow leaning on the frame, the pouring rain wetting his sleeve.

Vinny turned and kept walking, though he was feeling jumpy, suddenly; knew he could take off running if he had to, through the woods where the Mustang couldn't go.

"You take 'em or someone else will." Marc gunned the car and it heaved forward enough so that Vinny, though walking faster now, was forced to remain by its rumbling side, trapped between it and the forest. "Not everyone agrees with the Assembly, Vinny. There's lots don't."

Vinny stopped then, the rain coming harder than before, his face a wash of water. His head was buzzing and he felt a growing heat in his chest, as if his inner core were being melted and reshaped from within. He turned to Marc and, like he never had before in his life, roared into the rainfall, his arm extended like a source of coursing power in front of him, pointing a finger from the hand that was also holding the bag of his shoes.

"Get awaaaaaaay!" he bellowed, his heart there in the sound of his voice, his body feeling electrified, invincible. But beneath all that he was also scared of himself. He didn't know himself, then. Had never known such anger. With his arm rigid before him and his whole upper body unmoving like a single block of hardened glass, and the plastic bag suddenly swinging side-to-side and rustling in the air from the clasp of his fingers bent like claws, he lifted his foot and kicked the side of the Mustang again and again. He felt nothing except the impact of the car against his boot, and each time it left him feeling oddly comforted, invigorated. He could do this forever! The sound of it he would only vaguely remember later, how the bang, bang of it usurped the loud shushing of the rain and the sound of his heart in his ears and the roaring of the demon inside.

"That's it, Vinny!" Marc was so surprised he couldn't think of anything else to say. He was so worried about his car that he gunned it and peeled out into the rain, but then thought better of it and reversed to where Vinny was still standing facing the road, clenched up, shaking and still pointing his finger into the dark night of the lightless road. *The fucking nerve*, he thought. He couldn't fucking believe it! "You. Vinny. You're a fucking dead man." His hands on the steering wheel were shaking, a drop of saliva down one corner of his mouth.

Vinny stood there after Marc sped off, still facing the dark road and feeling the rain now against his neck and chest. His foot was still buzzing inside his boot, as if still in the process of kicking. He stood there until he couldn't stand anymore and walked home.

When he opened the door and walked into the living room, Cheryl was watching The Bachelor. He stood in the entryway, dripping onto the linoleum, the bag clutched in his hanging arm. Soon, a growing puddle was making an island of his boots. When Cheryl turned to him with a smile, her legs tucked under and a blanket wrapped around, she only had to see his face, his black bangs plastered against his white forehead, to throw off her blanket and run to him.

"Vinny! What is it? What happened? Vinny!" She started unzipping his raincoat and pulling it off. She ran her eyes across his face and down his chest and hands to make sure he wasn't bleeding anywhere.

When Vinny simply looked at her without talking, his eyes a single dark color, she thought he looked confused and disoriented. She ran her hands over his head to feel out a bump or blood hiding beneath his hair.

"Vinny!" she shrieked. "Vinny, what is it? Damn it!"

Her swearing was what did it; he had never heard her swear before. The time she had been in his studio and caught him muttering "Jesus Christ!" into one of his more difficult sculptures, she had rushed to him and yanked him off his stool by his arm, causing him to lose the part of the sculpture he was trying to affix; told him she never wanted to hear him swear like that again in their house ever, *ever*. And because he had never seen her so angry before, he hadn't minded the botched sculpture. He had promised to never swear in their house again.

He simply hugged her, now, deeply. He crushed her into his ribs and felt the soft spongey-ness of her large breasts and stomach, hot and beautiful against his cold and damp and hard body. He kissed her and breathed and kissed her again. And she returned his kisses; felt his lips warming.

"Just cold," he said.

"You're hungry," she said. "Will you ease off on the basketball, babe? Just a bit, huh."

She went to the kitchen and pulled out the plate of leftover ribs from last night's dinner. She ripped off the plastic wrap and stuck it in the microwave, and before Vinny knew it he was sitting at the table eating hot ribs, the sauce sweet and sticky on his fingers and collecting in the corners of his mouth. He was drinking a tall glass of 2% milk Cheryl had warmed in the micro.

It happened so fast that Vinny would wonder how it was even remotely possible; how someone so healthy could become so sick so suddenly. And after the wondering there was the railing. *Why? Why?* he would ask no one again and again, sometimes shouting it into the walls of their master bathroom where he could rest assured that the walls couldn't answer back inanely and sympathetically, *There are no answers to this, Vinny. There is no human reason to God's plan.*

He needed no goddamn sympathy. Didn't want anymore goddamn soft words from pastor Barry. For when Cheryl was diagnosed with a rare breast cancer three long weeks later and only three short years into their marriage, and the cancer wasn't the going away kind but the staying-and-settling-until-dead kind, Vinny spent the six months between her diagnosis and her death in a sleepless world of his own creation. He fueled up on Red Bulls and coffee and donuts, though continued making their oatmeal in the mornings until Cheryl lost her appetite entirely. For a few months, though, there were many mornings of oatmeal and evenings of their usual chamomile tea. In retrospect, he would have to concur that, yes, there had been much normalcy even after finding out; that it hadn't gotten bad until the very, very end.

Before each round of chemo, he spent his hours in the garage, working late into the day, then taking her to the hospital, heading to La Iguana for work, and then heading back over on his break to pick her up and take her home. In the past, he loved bringing her favorites from the restaurant: steak burrito with extra guacamole; tortilla soup, extra spicy. He brought them to the hospital, again and again, hoping she'd eat in the car on the way home until understanding that the chemo made her feel full and sick; that she wouldn't be holding on to anymore of her weight. When he drew her close he could feel bones on her he never knew she had, and suddenly, she had cheekbones that edged through the puffiness of her face. She would get through this, he told her. They would tell this story to their children and, yes, find things to laugh about!

Eventually, when the doctor said she would be most comfortable "riding it out" at home, Vinny took a leave from work. He carried the new sofa sectional out to the driveway where someone out garage-saleing picked it up on Saturday morning despite its dampness from the rain, and moved their bed into the living room because then Cheryl could still be there in the heart of the house while Vinny putzed around. He started baking because he hoped Cheryl would love the smells of the brownies and pies and cakes she wouldn't eat; the kinds of smells that filled a house with happiness and the promise of a future filled with abundance. "Oh, that's good," sometimes she'd say. "What is that, Vinny?" And he'd say apple pie or coffee cake or lemon bars.

When she grew more silent over the weeks, he just wanted to be there in bed with her. Even though she spent almost all her time asleep, the morphine drip the one constant subtlety in the room like the soundless clicking of a clock, he still watched night-time TV with her tucked up under his armpit and held her against his chest while he tried to sleep. At such times, all he wanted to do was smell her, and he did. He ran his nose through her hair and across her face and into the folds of her neck. There were smells new to him, though, as if her inside had been taken over by an alien creature. He decided he would continue to smell her, to take her all in regardless, because these new smells, however sour and foreign, were also *her* now. He hated those smells, but he also embraced them, like a mother still embraces her ugly, ugly child. Once, as his hands ran over her body, she smiled though her eyes remained closed. His hands searched out the former fleshiness of her hips and bottom. They ran down her legs and cupped her calves.

When the "dying nurse" (Vinny secretly called her, he hated her so) began coming every morning, she found Vinny and Cheryl in bed. The nurse began to wonder whether Vinny didn't want to get some time in the garage; that she could take care of things for a while. But that's the last thing he wanted. How could she have suggested such a thing! He hadn't been in his garage in weeks! Why in hell would he ever do that? He yelled at her, finally, to *get out*, out of the house, *now*! And she had, silently, understanding. She called, after that, to check on the morphine; did they need more? She would be by, and when she arrived, he would cry and cry, not understanding where it came from

It was shortly before this that Vinny's sculptures began to vanish. The raven in the woods; the salmon in the harbor shelter; the totem in the bank; the sailboat; the humpback whale; even all the commissioned ones though people couldn't remember seeing anyone come and go; no one with a sculpture conspicuously bulging under jacket. Gone.

About this time, Mayor Marc had also just decided to take a bat to the stupid things once and for all, having grown tired of seeing them week after week, even after his meeting with Vinny that night. He thought he had been menacing enough. He couldn't understand the belligerence of such a man. He had obviously given him way too much time. If people would only do what he wanted them to do! He was the mayor, after all. But before Marc could do anything, they were gone, as if someone had managed to get to all of them at once and simply haul them away. Ok, well that was good, he thought. But it would be nice to know who, he decided. At least so he could thank the man; maybe destroy one or two just to get them out of his system once and for all.

People began writing letters to the editor again. "I, for one, enjoyed seeing Vinny's sculptures around town. I especially liked being surprised by them." "Put them back! Whoever is doing this, just put them back!" "Has anyone checked Mayor Marc's house?" an anonymous writer said. "They're just sculptures, folks. Take a chill pill."

The few times Cheryl opened her eyes, then, at the end, in between morphine hazes and the great pauses between breaths, her eyes slits in the awful deflated puffiness of her face, semi-propped up in the hospital-issued bed in the middle of the living room, she saw it all. The way the daylight coming in through the large living room window ricocheted off all the glass pieces of every single one of Vinny's sculptures crowded into the living room atop furniture and hanging from the ceiling and blocking the TV. The iguana was smiling at her; it blinked at her, the action of which seemed to emanate a chain reaction of the love that is held within every single atom of every particle of oxygen, which reached her instantaneously there on her bed like shock waves of pure love. Like God's love. The humpback whale assumed the whole room at the foot of her bed. Vinny had angled its head toward Cheryl's elbow so that she would see its mellow half-open eye when she awoke. Above, she watched the bald eagle with its six-foot wingspan slowly sway in silent house breezes, its massive talons outstretched. It would alight on her gently, as if the world's largest butterfly. In fact, it was coming to her! She lifted her arm as much as she could to allow it to land. She had never felt a bald eagle on her arm before. How amazing it was; how surprisingly light!

On her right was Vinny's latest. Such magnificence. The fish were tropical and more colorful than anything she had ever seen in her life; one striped like a zebra, another hot pink with velvety black spots; a school of lime green ones with long blue noses were swimming luxuriously in between blue and green sea anemones and pink corals anchoring strands of plants bent from the lazy current of the warm ocean. She could feel the warm water. She was completely submersed. It felt like the sculptures' refracted light: warm and light and pure and full of joy. When the sun, on its rare appearance, filled the room, it ignited every single animal into a sparkling creature from her wildest, most wonderful dreams. There were crystal lights everywhere in the room, colored like the flavors of the jellybeans she had loved, previously, in the life that was becoming a very distant and mind-blowing dream.

Suddenly, it came to her. Heaven would be like that. It would be as her life had been, full of love and light. For the dying *do* dream at the end, even when the morphine gives permission to breath and heart to relax. To stop. Everyone, at the end, dreams of love.

-9-

Leaving Hope

When I returned, I hadn't been to my hometown in five years. My son Samuel had already been dead for three, and I hadn't been anywhere since. "Come up," Mom called months before, eagerness in her voice. "I love you," my husband encouraged me to go. They seemed to think anything could be reclaimed.

I walked the same trails into the woods by the ocean. There was snow in the fields of the estuary and the boardwalk was laced with ice. I had been on this trail when Samuel was one, and again during visits when he was three and five and seven, and despite all that passing time, the smells were the same. The salt from the estuary and the pure cold air coursing down the canyons of the mountains, and the dense plants of the forest, not yet completely frozen, reanimated a spot on my brain that bleeped with recognition like an alarm light soundlessly pulsing. My body knew these smells like those of my son, only more primordial, as these smells were also those of my own youth long gone.

Mom and Dad, as usual, had a place for me in their house, though it was one they had bought, after a string of rentals, when I was in college, and thus I had never come to it as those do to a house that they have been born and raised in. Still, there was some comfort there. I had the room with the double bed, downstairs.

One night, I awoke in the middle of the night thinking I had heard Samuel's long-ago baby cry, but instead heard the silence of the wilderness.

Dad was in the throes of a forced and early retirement, his position as head curator at the State Historical Museum of Tlingit & Haida Arts having been eliminated due to budget cuts five months ago. The City Assembly had also voted to close the public library three days out of the week and had frozen all the city employees' salaries. As Mom and I drove from the airport, stuffed into her gray '91 Honda Accord, the heat inside creating a world opposite from the crystal snowy one outside, I saw the library by the sea closed and dark. Also that the brown paint was peeling on town hall, leaving blips of piercing dirty white here and there like raised scratches on an arm. "Oh that," Mom said. "They have plans to repaint it soon, before the tourist season begins." Otherwise, things were as I remembered it: the downtown rooflines like a tracing of some fake early 20th-century western town against the ice-gray sky; St. Ignatius Russian Orthodox church at the downtown helm, its onion domes satisfyingly contiguous in their sloping, rounded lines; the two banks like point-blank shots of reality; the town's second traffic lights at the intersection. "One of the big cruise liners bought up the hotel last year," Mom said as we passed the Hope Hotel on the corner. It looked almost the same, perched on the hill with views of the ocean, except it had been repainted dark green like the wilderness across the span of the island, and another trinket shop and spa had been added to the shops underneath. The sign, "Hope Hotel," had also been enlarged and done in a style to make the place seem like an upscale wilderness lodge, though the old Nazarene minister had murdered his mistress and then stuck the gun in his own mouth there three years ago and there was no way the locals would ever not associate the place with that. "We'll go there for breakfast," Mom smiled.

"Even though their service gets worse and worse. Your father won't eat there anymore."

As we passed Larry's Radio Emporium on the corner by the traffic lights, Mom said how Larry was in jail on the mainland. No one could prove that he had killed Mayor Marc Randal last year, but the police finally got him once and for all on drug charges. His parents were running the store and it was doing better than ever. It looked the same to me: glossy, overlarge, pretentious. But I had to give it to Larry for going against the obnoxious Western Frontier theme the rest of the town had adhered to. The square stone and glass of it didn't easily retain the constant moisture of the seaside weather, and so it seemed to glow among the peeling, moldy downtown buildings that were currently covered in patchworks of dirty brown snow. Everywhere I looked were shades of brown, gray, and black. It suddenly occurred to me that Hope would remain one of the most monotone places I had ever seen, but the question was whether that itself accounted for the annoying pressure, just this side of pain, that I felt behind my eyes.

"You'll never believe it," Mom's voice piqued with excitement. "Blake, you remember him?, fell off the cliff by his cabin and died this past winter. Can you believe it?"

"Wow." I couldn't believe it, not mountain man Blake.

"I know," Mom shook her head. "But Anna and Sasha are staying put, and Anna just had another baby. What a tragedy."

Loon Lake wasn't completely frozen, and there were three swans floating in a patch of water in the middle. Obviously the shot and killed one last year hadn't dissuaded the others. There they were. The Hope Police still hadn't discovered who had killed the bird. The prefab houses across the lake were covered in dustings of mold. They had crowded lawns full of statuary, used boat parts, tires, crab cages, four-wheelers, and broken-down cars with flat tires. The double-wide on the corner of the street leading up to

Mom and Dad's house still startled me with its pristineness: its carport spotless, its gravel driveway shoveled, its shutters lusciously cream colored as if recently painted despite the continuous rain and snow. It popped out like a beacon.

Mom and Dad's place was strung with tiny white lights. Mom's garden was in repose. Dad's old Toyota pick-up was accumulating snow parked by the side of the road, a short snow berm hedging it in. On closer inspection, I saw how their house was slowly being covered in mold, just as Hope cars grow moss and licheny strands in their rust.

Mom was keeping her job as school secretary for as long as she could. The pay wasn't great but it wasn't bad, and her retirement fund would be decent. She had told me over the phone that Dad needed to stay busy or he was just going to sleep on the recliner all day. That people had choices in life, and anyone could choose to be depressed and lazy, while others could make an effort and find happiness and work.

"One could even choose to move on, if one had to," she told me.

Immediately upon entering the hallway from the downstairs door, I had noticed something different, but didn't know what. *It's that I'm older,* I thought. *It's that I have no young child around my knees.* The thoughts came to me before I could stop them. Now that they were there, I couldn't move past the threshold of the doorway. I could feel the blood drain from my head. The dark hallway began to flash with bursts of mysterious light. My toes felt heavy and solid, as if I were turning into a statue and that's where my metamorphosis would begin, though I suspect it had already started elsewhere.

But I could go back even farther. It seemed like just recently I had stepped into this hallway for the very first time, twenty and home on college break. I had been worried that they hadn't bothered to move the ancient twin bed great-grandmother had given me when I was twelve and had used since. In my new bedroom, with windows overlooking the forest and muskeg in the back, I saw that in fact they had moved it. Sleeping on it in my new bedroom in Mom and Dad's first bought house, with the silence of the great wilderness all around, was, even at twenty, the most perfect thing on earth. There were old school friends to see and gatherings to go to: bonfires on the beach, coffee at Lucy's Cafe, hiking up Bear Bread mountain, kayaking into the bay, movies at the theater. Young, happy and carefree. The playground at the elementary school had been almost completely redone, but still there was the old rusty swing set I had swung on as an eight-year-old. *I can go back farther,* I reassured myself. *I am not stuck,* and lifted my booted feet into the hallway.

Last year, Mom said, she had pulled up the old blue carpet and put down cream-colored wool carpet. So that was it. It lightened up the whole downstairs, which was only a hallway, a bathroom, and three small bedrooms. The stairway, too, was lighter with the new carpet, and when I switched on the light on my way up, I noticed in greater clarity the framed art, originals of ravens, herons, and Tlingit totems painted by locals that Mom had hung in the stairwell, and the magnificent metal star light she had somehow managed to suspend from a hook eight feet above the mid-way stairs. Upstairs, I smelled something cooking; a fire was crackling in the wood burning stove. I placed myself between living room and dining room. I watched the big snowflakes slowly falling outside the large front window, then turned and watched the ones falling out the large window behind. It was late afternoon, but Mom had already set the table. There were plates and beautiful glass goblets; a lace tablecloth that I remembered from my childhood; pastel yellow butter dish; pale blue glass pitcher full of ice cubes and water; stainless steel silverware, gracefully globular at their ends. Two stained glass pieces hung suspended from chains suction cupped to the dining room window. One glowed pink and silver, its lines and shapes long and geometrical like a Frank Lloyd Wright; the other buzzed with chaos and accumulated blue, a re-representation of a Munch that I had bought, long ago, at the Chicago Art Museum when I was a young adult and could spend hours wandering museums.

Sure enough, there was Dad in the recliner, legs out-stretched, a blanket over his body and tucked up under his armpits, looking like a full-sized toddler tucked in for a nap. I couldn't believe how his hair had changed since the last time I'd seen him four years ago when he and Mom had made a visit to see us. He'd lost most of it on top. What remained was a motley mix of grays. Jerry the cat was asleep on his chest, his white-tipped paws tucked under his body and his eyes sealed blissfully shut like a genuine Egyptian cat god. Dad opened his eyes when I stood there in the middle of the large room between the windows. "You made it," he said. "Here I am," I answered.

Dinner was a warm affair. What I had smelled was turkey roasting in the oven, and stuffing. Mom's homemade rolls pulled apart easily and immediately melted the butter. There was mashed potatoes and steamed broccoli; pumpkin and apple pies afterward with whipped cream. There was an extra spot set for my only sibling, Amy, but she had yet to show. The snow was falling faster outside. Its complete silence is one of its most beautiful and surprising aspects. Momentarily, I closed my eyes, and heard only the snapping of the burning logs in the stove; the gentle clinking of silverware against plates. "Where's Amy?" Dad said. Mom had carefully sliced the turkey and placed the brown and white meat next to each other on the ruddy stainless-steel platter. The rolls were in a towel-lined basket, covered. There was the little glass bowl of jam with the tiny jam spoon buried inside. "She's coming," Mom said. "And Jack?" I asked. "Oh, I doubt it," Dad said. Her boyfriend had never met the family. Preferred, Amy said, to stay away from such gatherings. He lived in a cabin he had built by hand on a nearby island, and for money helped friends on their seiner. "He's shy," Mom had said. "He prefers not getting the attention."

When Amy arrived, we at first heard the thumping of her boots on the stairs outside as she climbed up. We were already eating pie, and Mom was brewing decaf. The gray light outside had turned into the purple darkness of the just-post dusk, though with startling clarity I could still see the pure white flakes falling, the size of dimes. She came in with a large basket of dirty laundry. "Hi," she smiled from the entryway, before turning and, one-by-one, putting her clothes into the washing machine in the alcove in the hallway.

I hadn't seen Amy in nine years; she had been traveling the last time we were in Hope. Nine years ago she had stopped for a one-day layover in Seattle on her way to Panama for a vacation with a boyfriend from Mexico, another one none of us had met and never would. She had spent one night with us to say hi, though I knew that there were old friends in Seattle she wanted to see, and she could, after all, spend a free night with us. Samuel had turned three the week before. I hadn't slept for longer than three simultaneous hours in years. My hives started around then and have been a constant companion since.

Samuel was then still deep in the throes of tremendous tantrums that would continue for another few years. When he fell to the floor in a fit of screams, Amy sat on the couch and watched. "Sarah's son, Abe, you remember him? He doesn't have tantrums." Her long brown hair she liked to twist into a rope over one shoulder. Two hours later, I was in the kitchen preparing a dinner as if in last night's distant dream. Amy came in and said she was going to see a movie. "I don't need any food," she said. She had those friends to see; she hadn't seen them in years. "But I've made enough for you too," I was frustrated but tried not to show it. "Oh," she stroked her long brown hair, pulling out the loose ones and leaving them on the floor. "Don't you have any friends you can take a night off with?" she asked.

"Hi, Michelle," she now looked at me. She wore loose black pants and a brown sweater; heavy socks. Her hair had gotten longer. It was in one long braid almost to her bottom. Her cheeks were rosy from the cold, which made the brown freckles across her nose pop. She took her place next to me. She smelled like wet wool and log fire smoke and pot. Mom got up to get the tray of turkey in the kitchen. "I've already eaten," Amy said. She had spread her forearms on the table and was leaning on them. "Are you sure?" Mom asked. "Yeah," Amy said. "Mom made this food for us," Dad looked at her. "I've already eaten. With Jack," she said, and began pulling off her thick wool sweater, a thin silk long-sleeved shirt underneath and no bra. She then leaned back and pulled her legs up onto the chair and crossed them like a yogi. "You know we don't eat that meat, anyway," she said. "Amy and Jack only eat what they hunt," Mom explained to me. "It's called 'subsistence'," Amy added.

"So, what's up with you?" she looked at me while winding a long colorful wool scarf two, three times around her neck. Without waiting for an answer she said, "For you," and pulled a book out of a Tibetan shoulder bag she had hooked on her chair. *Zen and the Practice of Now.* I could feel the hives on my neck. They appeared like that, instantaneously, without consciousness, though usually closer to bedtime when I was fatigued with the exhaustion of living. Itching them would make them worse, but I couldn't help it. I rubbed my fingertips across the soft ribbiness of my neck. In the past, years and years ago, I would have happily hugged her, grateful for a gift. Now, I took it and chocked it up to the others she'd given me: *Becoming You, The Infinite Earth Woman, Peace Within, A Grief Observed.*

I'm able to admit this now, so I will. When Samuel died, I hadn't wanted anything: no ceremonies, no services, no rituals. People disliked me for this, couldn't understand that past the mourning period and past the wailing and past the tears and the cremation, I would continue to want absolutely nothing. I hadn't called Mom and Dad; hadn't even thought to call Amy. "Why not?" Mom had cried into the phone a week later. "Why wouldn't you call us?" I hated her for putting that weight on me, which my body eventually sucked up through its skin, which has shown me that there are places inside for inorganic matter that don't ever bleed away.

Dad had moved back to the recliner, and Jerry with him. "*Survivor* is on," he excused himself quasi-bashfully and flipped on the TV. I had finished my second piece of pie, though suddenly I had lost my appetite and, for some reason, wanted to bring it all back up for enjoying it so. "Dad and his TV," Amy said as she walked to the kitchen and cut herself a slice of pumpkin pie. "Why isn't Jack here?" Dad said, as if in rebuttal. But Amy must not have heard. She carried her pie with whipped cream back to the table, pulled her legs up, and began eating. "Mmmmmm," she moaned. "Soooo good, mom!" Mom smiled widely.

The spot where Samuel would have eaten seemed very obvious to me: next to Mom directly across from me. He was a beautiful boy who had chosen to grow his hair long before it all fell out. Long and wavy and thick. *I want his hair!* my girlfriends had joked. He brushed his own hair, but occasionally I would brush it to make sure he had gotten out all the tangles. During such times, I brushed slowly because I was aware of the moment already turning into a memory; that soon he would be a teenager and not want me so near. I'd have to learn how to connive my hugs from him, and, as I kneeled brushing, was coming to a prideful peace with that approaching future. Now, before me, holographically, the perfect age he was during our last visit, he took each bite slowly and purposefully like he did with everything he enjoyed. He could let a piece of dessert sit in front of him for an hour, if he had to, just so that he wouldn't have to sit with nothing while others enjoyed theirs.

With Dad at the TV, the three of us could play Scrabble, our old stand-by. We helped Mom clear the table and stack the dishwasher. "Leave the rest," she instructed, and we did, across the counters and in the sink. We were neck-and-neck until Mom strode ahead with the word "quiz" and Amy played off that with "quaff." When I knew that I would lose, as I usually did, Amy said, "Come on. Don't give up so easily." "I'm not!" The laugh I had tried for came out instead like a tired sigh. I had actually been trying really, really hard.

*

The days went by.

At last, I was leaving in two, and perhaps because of this Amy had invited me along with some of her friends to the Sea Farers bar in the Indian Village just past downtown by the string of fish processing plants. Why had she invited me? I couldn't even imagine. During our visit, she had been busy at her job at the bookstore, sleeping in late in her and Jack's cabin on the island, and going on a four-day kayaking trip with Jack to the Outer Islands northwest of Hope. She carried the smell of pot on her as if it were some holy leftover from an incense-clouded temple.

The place was full of fishermen back from the herring run. Some of them were already rich from the run and were buying drinks for everyone. It was noisy and hot; framed photos of boats and proud fishermen across the walls. The booths were tall and comfortable; the lighting not bright; the hanging lamps above did just the right amount of illuminating and hiding. All around me, people in the middle of hugs and laughs; smiles wide and eyes bursting with light. It was the happiest place in the world.

At first I couldn't find my way, people brushing against me like clouds of grasshoppers, the heat like a great big constricted fist, the orbs of light amplifying my bewilderment. But there she was with some others in a booth by the window. For once, I was relieved to see her and had intimations of a wild, happy welcome, though there had never really been anything like that between us in the past. I squeezed through the crowd and for a moment stood before the booth, watching her friends drink their beers, take off wool sweaters, touch bare shoulders, laugh.

One woman had long fabulous dreadlocks. A man with a dark beard wore a wool skull cap. I had to look at him again to see his long, dark lashes, like a woman's, but on him, unbelievably handsome. Another man was tracing a remarkably detailed face in the condensation on the window. I had never seen such beautiful, healthy people. But I had absolutely nothing to say and felt the burgeoning of panic. I stood there until a woman on the end with long hair like Amy's and big brown eyes looked up at me. "Oh!" Amy turned from laughing with the bearded man on her right. She was squeezed in between him and the dreadlocked woman. "My sister, everyone!" The long-haired woman made a space for me, and I slid in. I didn't like to drink and ordered nothing except a glass of water. Amy, at the booth with her friends who regarded me tentatively, couldn't stop laughing, and I was sure I had interrupted a joke. I sat there like a pole and managed a smile for the woman who sat next to me. "You must come here a lot," I said to her, and though I intended it only as a bit of small talk, it occurred to me instantly that it might have sounded pretentious, condescending. She looked at me and whispered to the man on her right. He had already finished his portrait on the window. *An illustrator, an artist,* I knew. I thought Jack would be there too. He was on the island,

Amy said, finishing the sauna he had started building last week. I was beginning to think that he just didn't want us to meet.

Amy, who I'd never seen drunk before, discounting those photos she'd e-mailed me years ago from one of her trips to Mexico, couldn't stop laughing. Everyone's carelessness began to affect me like too much yeast in a loaf of bread, and me, I was the one bit of hardness settling to the bottom of the pan; the pebble that had gotten mixed in with the flour. Finally, Amy looked at me. She was across from me staring, so I took a sip of my ice water and felt its coldness slip down my throat, getting dammed up, briefly, at my voice box. My shoulders were bunched up at my ears. So I released them and tried to take up space like the happy do. My neck was itchy, but I told myself that this time, in this place, I would let it go. If I didn't itch, would the hives just disappear?

"What's your problem?" she said. "What's yours?" I said immediately. My voice surprised me; it wavered like someone teetering in imbalance. "I think your sister doesn't like it here," the woman with the long hair stared at me with her large brown eyes. Beautiful. Incredible. She was pulling her long hair from behind her back over one shoulder. It looked strong and silky. The other friends snorted and the artist turned to look out the window with his hand over his mouth.

Outside there was rain bordering on sleet. It blurred the neon light of the reflecting beer signs. It pelted the windows and left behind a wavering sheet of falling water. It took some time getting out of there, past the happy drunk fishermen and locals crowding the floor and all spaces. When I burst out into the cold night, the darkness felt like a transition. But to where? The rain pelted my hot face like a jump into the ocean. I stopped and listened to the muted sounds behind me in the bar until they faded and I heard the sounds of the boats' masts tinging in the raucous wake of the ocean waves across the street beyond the fish processing plant.

Amy was behind me. "Hey." Her eyes were dilated from the alcohol and the dark night, and, perhaps, pure happiness. She touched my upper arm. I could feel the pressure of her bare hand even under the bulk of my t-shirt, sweater, and jacket. In coming after me, she hadn't bothered putting on her jacket or wool hat or mittens. "You don't seem happy," she said. Her one long braid fell down her back and the cold wind was moving her shorter side hairs up and into the air. She let them move around her freely, without pushing them back, as if she loved them and would let them be. Her eyes were beginning to water from the weather and her nose was running. Just like her hairs, she let the snot fall. It didn't bother her at all. "You need some help. So you can enjoy life again. And just, yeah, *enjoy*." She spoke matter-of-factly, as if giving me a grocery list, and I saw that even in this matter, even in the most emotional, most awful circumstance, she could remain peaceful and even tempered. She could be truthful and open, and free. She had never let anything bother her in her life. She was going through it like a spirit, hovering just above the ground, unattached to anything.

I knew then that this was the end of the past. That I would never return again. There was no help to be found there. I knew then that what life was, was one big long process of letting go. And how could anyone not know that! How could life not destroy a person, render her paralyzed and prostrate on the unclean ground? How dare one venture forth unscathed.

I was instantly sad; the tears were on my cheeks before I felt them in my eyes. I jerked my arm away from her touch. It made me nauseous. At some point, the rain had turned to snow. Amy's head was accumulating and melting the flakes. They were big, fat ones, though, that, because of the cold, stayed intact on our clothes for seconds before melting completely.

When Samuel had been born, Amy came down to spend a week on her way to Hawaii. The guest bedroom was ready for her. I had put fresh lilacs in a vase on her bed stand. Henry had laid a folded bath towel on her bed with a washcloth on top. She would laugh at it, the preciseness and preciousness of it all, but I would too. I watched as she threw her duffle bag on the bed. I welcomed her smell of incense and body odor, and her long brown strands of hair that I found afterwards scattered across the floors. She was taking photos, then, with an old Canon SLS. With her, Samuel opened his big, brown eyes to full capacity; she zoomed in on them so that they looked like deep caves leading into the very center of his baby soul. In that photo, even as he grew into boyhood, I would continuously smell his hot milky breath; feel the touch of his fingers; hear the contented mash of nonsense words of his remarkably low baby voice. In other photos, she zoomed in on his tiny fingers, bent in relaxation against my or Henry's hand. When his fingers were little, they never extended fully; they made hot little chubby fists next to his oversized cheeks. Even now, I could remember how much he cried; how he only attempted sleep swaddled and tucked into his car seat in the bathroom with the loud fan going, needing the perfect resemblance to what it had been like in my womb. I took some strange pride in that even now, I could still remember the awful parts; I could still be realistic in my memory of him.

There was a car coming down the narrow, empty road. Its headlights illuminated the crazy coming of the big, fat snowflakes. Amy was closest to the edge of the sidewalk, my back was to the bar. It would have been nothing to push her into the road just as the car was there. To see her body hit the car's lights and hood and grill; to be heaved upward to the dark sky, and to fall behind onto the road. I would do it. I would simply give her one quick easy shove. Her body, so relaxed and effervescent, would never expect it; would go easily.

The last walk I took in Hope I took alone. Not a five-hour hike up Bear Bread mountain; not a kayak trip across the bay to the Pyramids. I was ill prepared for life in Hope. One needed expensive gear and the time and gumption to put it on. One needed to have researched and bought the best dry sack and toughest wetsuit. To have the best kinds of friends to share information with and to buy the best used kayak from. One needed to have a boiling love for the wilderness. The people in Hope were like the barnacles who live atop humpback whales, having constructed a network of life and support in what appeared to be the most true and natural way. On the other hand, one could get away with a lot in Hope. One could do things without anyone's notice; could still persistently live even without much love or guidance or joy or care. But, at any rate, it would be that, simply. It would be whatever it could be and was, way off here, away from the rest of civilization and life.

I walked through the historical park by the ocean, several acres of preserved forest fringed by rocky beach, lapped by salty waves. Here Salmon River entered the ocean, creating an estuary frequented by mergansers, kingfishers, great blue herons, bobbing American dippers, bald eagles, and brown bear when the salmon ran every August to September. When I was a teenager, I liked to walk there to see what I could find, delighted, at times, by mommy mergansers carrying babies on their backs as they floated on the river, or a bald eagle partially hidden in the grasses in the tiny island in the middle of the river at low tide, or two river otters swimming loops around each other beneath the foot bridge. In retrospect, those otters must have been in love.

I entered the forest from the ocean-side, and immediately the whole park came back to me. Up ahead there would be the little, gnarled tree stump with notches and cavities that people liked to leave spare change in for good luck. *For the forest goddess,* I had told two-year old Samuel as I once gave him a penny to place on the stump. *She hides in the forest. She could be watching us now.*

The path wound in a mile loop to the other side of the visitor's center. Across the footbridge on the other side of Salmon River was another, more rugged path that looped for 3/4 of a mile. There was an outhouse and a Russian-Tlingit memorial. The park had been the site of a major battle, centuries ago, though no one talks about the blood and decayed bodies that the ground sucked up those centuries ago; that are still there, really, deep, deep below it all. The spruce trees towered and arched above; the forest was dark and smelled of the dried, brown spruce needles across the path making the ground buoyant beneath my weight, and the long, scraggly strands of blue-green lichen hanging from branches, and the banks of bull kelp pushed into long, brown lines along the rocky beach. I could see the kelp banks in between the gaps of the tree trunks, revealing and hiding the startling white rocks of the beach like flashes in a movie reel; the dark kelp, the icy looking waves of the green-tinged ocean, also there. My fingers were cold. I pulled them out of their spots in my gloves and tucked them into my palms.

Well, there he was. I saw him at the bend in the path, the tall trees all around, making him look like a happy forest sprite. He was definitely two, but had run expertly ahead and was waiting for me with humming body. Yes, he had been that age the time he had gone walking with Mom, Amy and me those many years ago. In fact, he had run the entire mile. We had had to speed walk to keep up with him, to make sure he wouldn't disappear entirely after rounding a tree-shrowded corner. I had had visions of him sliding into Salmon River. As I walked closer, he looked like he would start running again, so I began to run to catch up. It didn't take long. His breath was loud and coming quickly in little high-pitched bursts that sounded, to me, like the music of pure human life, which is a sound I had not really known until just then. When I looked down, he looked up. I couldn't believe how chubby his cheeks had been, how red from cold and exercise. Inside his smile I saw his four brand new teeth, tiny and white, and there too I saw the dimple in his left cheek and the tiny cleft in his chin. His nose was running, but he took no notice. He had always been most happy in motion.

He led me around the bend and then, at the fork, he took the way I had always taken, down the smaller side trail on the right that led to a view of the beach and ocean and eventually wound along the banks of Salmon River. At the sudden opening and small grassy space by the beach, I said, *Dad and I were married here. A raven perched on that tree there for the ceremony.* But he kept running, past the opening and down the narrowing trail, decaying skunk cabbage on the left, arched alders above, the ocean making sound though invisible from behind alders and salmonberry bushes on the right. His puffs of breath seemed to echo in the air, and each one made me happier than the last.

I ran to catch him before he took off further down the path, and in my arms his body seemed to want to stop, for the moment. To rest. Across the curve of the bay and the boats in the harbor, we could see downtown. *That's Hope,* I said. *There's the Russian Orthodox church and the bridge to the airport. There's the library and downtown. See! And over there, beyond where we can see so you just kind of have to imagine it, is Grandma and Grandpa's house.* I had kneeled down and felt the cold, wet ground creeping into my pants and onto my skin. But it didn't matter at all. I felt his hot weight against my breast and collar bone. I turned to him and took off my gloves. I put both my hands on each side of his face, his cheeks cool and soft underneath; buoyant with young life. *You are my lovey,* I said, and kissed his forehead and then each cheek. I moved to kiss his lips, but he had always hated kisses, and veered away at the last minute but leaned in to my body, to that warmest space between armpit and chest. *Hope used to be beautiful,* I told him.

It was getting cold and time to go. I was about to lift him and carry him back in my arms or, because of his weight, heave him up over my head and onto my shoulders.

I should have know it was coming, but still, it took me completely by surprise. Because even in the finality of the act, there was the love he had always showered on me without words. The love a very young child gives, even without knowing it, to his mom and dad, and, perhaps, in particular to his mom for subconsciously feeling the fact that he is the love of her life and that there is nothing she will not do for his happiness, for his growth, for his betterment. His short, chubby arms reached all the way around my neck. They cinched in so tightly that I felt his little strength against my throat. I knew he was right, it had been confirmed to me almost from the beginning, but I put my arms around his body and held on while I could anyway. He squeezed out from under my arms, and this time I just watched him as he disappeared into the shade of the forested trail.

Slowly, I began to see everything around me in extra clarity, as if my eyeballs themselves had just been doused and washed, but knowing fully that it was simply a peculiar trick of the brain, to see things so clearly. All things seemed to want to pop out and touch me: the lines of kelp on the beach, whose textured leaves I could see clearly; the millions of rocks hiding shy, clicking heart crabs underneath; the barnacles, striated, bleach-white, closed up tight in the low tide; the beacon heads of two bald eagles perched miraculously atop the very tips of two tall spruce trees farther up the beach; the burning white of Mt. Agnes's dome of newly accumulated snow, rising directly out of the water miles out of the bay. One million years ago it had been spurting lava and fire. Five thousand years ago the Tlingits witnessed its final eruption.

I left the park with no memory, as if it had been wiped clean by the sensations of the wilderness that continued to cling to me like priceless perfume long buried in an ancient tomb and suddenly, to great applause, uncovered.

*

Before leaving Hope for the last time, I took my parents' house all in: Dad on the recliner, the wood burning stove, the art hanging in the stairwell and on every wall, the framed childhood photos of Amy and me, those of my parents in their twenties (thin and smooth and hippies and self-assured by their happiness and a long life still ahead), the ones of Samuel as a baby and toddler and young boy, the small kitchen, Mom's African violets and blue bottle collection in the small bay window above the kitchen sink, the bedrooms, the colorful Lebanese rug in the living room, the muskeg out back, Mom's wind chimes hanging from below the rafters above the large deck upstairs. I left *Zen and the Practice of Now* on the bedside table beneath the beautiful table lamp fringed with long strands of beads. It was unusually sunny and clear and warm, the snow already beginning to get that sheen of melting ice. A typical Hope winter. Dad followed Mom and me in his pick-up, always looking for an excuse to drive it, though for a moment it appeared as if it would not start ever again.

In the airport, I turned to Mom and Dad and knew that as it was with most things, it was simply a matter of hoping not to cry. Amy had not come. We all knew she had things to do in Hope; a busy, full life to live in her wilderness paradise. I hugged them. Smelled them, felt them. Their bodies were dense and full and soft; they gave and resisted at the same time; they made no apologies, like bodies having lived a while and finally found their ease.

In the airplane, I found my seat by the window. I had kept the tears in my throat, and now that we were about to leave, I felt them almost completely disappear. I eased into the uncomfortable seat. Out the tiny window I watched the people loading suitcases onto the conveyor belt; the splashes of waves coming up against and over the rocks at the edge of the runway. There were ravens crossing the sky, and gulls circling a fishing boat slowly coming into the harbor from the sea. Clouds were beginning to come in from over the ocean, but they were white and harmless looking. The mountains all around were covered in snow, as if straight from a wintry fairy tale. When the plane took off, for the first time I really knew it.

"Goodbye," I said to the plastic window.

At this moment, I should have felt something like relief. Instead, I had the usual sense of a nugget of something hard and vaguely painful. It roamed around my body and could never be pinned down.

I had a perfect view of the town and scattering of islands below. I scanned the ocean waves for the shadows of whales, for rafts of sea otters.

Instead, I could see them. *There he is.* I grabbed the arm of the seat. *Jack.*

The airplane was passing their island quickly, gaining height, miniaturizing Hope's two-block strip of picturesque downtown and the historical site of the buried cabin; the dozen islands, tree-full, rising from the mercury silver surface of the ocean; the rocky outlines of the beaches riding the lines of the island like an ancient cursive message, brown and barnacle-white, a welcome shock against the dark greens of the forests. I could have tried to find the white heads of bald eagles, balancing unbelievably on the very tips of the spruce trees, or scanned the ocean for eruptions in its gentle wave patterns, signaling the release of air from some hidden whale's blow hole. Instead, I strained to see them better, my sister and her lover.

His hair was a ball of curly black, hers long and brown and flowing freely behind, the tips skimming the startling whiteness of her bottom. He was tall and muscular; his chest covered in black hair. His legs were short, but shapely; his thighs and calves protruding and edgy with muscles. They were walking hand-in-hand barefoot and naked across the island, taking the sharpness of the barnacle-covered rocks with apparent ease, the trees rising up around them like in the beginning of time.

Acknowledgements

Thank you thank you thank you, Unsolicited Press, for partnering with me again on this second book. Look at you, enriching our world with literature, truth, and beauty. Long may you continue to uplift and support writers around the world. You are singular in your fabulousness.

Thank you, *The Carolina Quarterly*, for first publishing "Leaving Hope," in Volume 67.1.

I am so grateful for my writing crew at The Forge—you are all so smart, so creative, so gifted. You inspire and ignite me all the time.

Thank you, B Team. You know who you are.

Thank you, Liyah, for the translation.

Finally, Felix, Beatrix, and Noam, words simply can't convey your magnificence. Rock on.

About the Author

Sommer Schafer is Senior Editor of *The Forge Literary Magazine* and widely published, including a Distinguished Story in *Best American Short Stories 2019*. Her first book, THE WOMEN, a collection of short stories, was released by Unsolicited Press in November 2023. She lives on Coast Miwok land with her family, a rescue dove, and a bearded dragon.

About the Press

Unsolicited Press is based out of Portland, Oregon and focuses on the works of the unsung and underrepresented. As a womxn–owned, all–volunteer small publisher that doesn't worry about profits as much as championing exceptional literature, we have the privilege of partnering with authors skirting the fringes of the lit world. We've worked with emerging and award–winning authors such as Savannah Cooper, Amy Shimshon–Santo, Brook Bhagat, Elisa Carlsen, and Rosalia Scalia.

Learn more at Unsolicitedpress.com. Find us on Twitter and Instagram at @UnsolicitedP.